The Absolute Best Little Book of Christmas Stories for Everyone

Candy Canes and Mistletoe,
Winter Wonderland, Stockings by the
Fireplace—and Christ,
The Reason for the Season

*All Selections Hand-picked with
Commentary and Notes by Linore Rose
Burkard*

Lilliput Press
OH, USA

Contents

A Note to the Reader

Stockings by the fire, winter wonderland, frosted noses, glittering trees... This book is brimming with the fun and joy of Christmas, the time of goodwill. It's a unique time when the very best in a person conquers what is not good in them. Why has Christmas such power? Because, above all else, it's a holy season.

That's why, nestled among the light-hearted fare (some of which you may never have seen before), you'll find stories and poems that give homage to the Savior. Jesus, after all, is "the reason for the season."

May this collection not only entertain, bring a few chuckles, and reinforce your love of Christmas, but I hope it does more. I dare to hope it may renew faith in your heart as to the reality of what the Savior brought to earth when God sent his Son to Bethlehem. Not just a Babe in a manger but the power of God revealed in Christ, the power of regeneration for men's hearts.

His birth enables our rebirth.

I wish you the very merriest of Christmases and warmest Yuletide blessings!

Linore Rose Burkard

Linore Rose Burkard

Special Feature

Going Further

A few selections in the book are followed by thought-provoking questions called "Going Further" for educators, parents, homeschoolers, or anyone wanting to dig deeper.

The Reason for Christmas

LUKE 2:1-20

The Book of Luke 2: 1-20

They say 'familiarity breeds contempt.' Don't let familiarity with this account anesthetize you to the meaning of its extraordinary, miraculous event!

> The Word became flesh and dwelt among us, and we beheld His glory, the glory as of the only begotten of the Father, full of grace and truth.
>
> I John 1:14

Luke 2: 1-20

In those days a decree went out from Caesar Augustus that all the world should be registered. [a] This was the first registration when Quirinius was governor of Syria. [b]

³And all went to be registered, each to his own town.

[4]And Joseph also went up from Galilee, from the town of Nazareth, to Judea, to the city of David, which is called Bethlehem, because he was of the house and lineage of David,[5] to be registered with Mary, his betrothed,[c] who was with child.[6]

And while they were there, the time came for her to give birth.[7]And she gave birth to her firstborn son and wrapped him in swaddling cloths and laid him in a manger, because there was no place for them in the inn.[d]

The Shepherds and the Angels

[8]And in the same region there were shepherds out in the field, keeping watch over their flock by night.[9]And an angel of the Lord appeared to them, and the glory of the Lord shone around them, and they were filled with great fear.

[10] And the angel said to them, "Fear not, for behold, I bring you good news of great joy that will be for all the people.[11] For unto you is born this day in the city of David a Savior, who is Christ the Lord.[12] And this will be a sign for you: you will find a baby wrapped in swaddling cloths and lying in a manger."

[13]And suddenly there was with the angel a multitude of the heavenly host praising God and saying, [14] "Glory to God in the highest,and on earth peace among those with whom he is pleased!"[e]

[15] When the angels went away from them into heaven, the shepherds said to one another, "Let us go over to Bethlehem and see this thing that has happened, which the Lord has made known to us." [16] And they went with haste and found Mary and Joseph, and the baby lying in a manger. [f]

[17] And when they saw it, they made known the saying that had been told them concerning this child. [18] And all who heard it wondered at what the shepherds told them.

[19] But Mary treasured up all these things, pondering them in her heart. [20] And the shepherds returned, glorifying and praising God for all they had heard and seen, as it had been told them.

[a] Some versions, "taxed."

[b] *Luke 2:2 Or, This was the registration before*

[c] *Luke 2:5* One legally pledged to be married

[d] *Luke 2:7 Or, guest room. Recent exegesis suggests that the "inn" was really a private home. Guests would normally be welcomed upstairs where the family slept, instead of the ground floor where animals were kept. Since the town was overflowing with relatives, the guest quarters had no more room, forcing Mary and Joseph to the" stable," or ground floor of the home. Also, it is possible that Joseph or Mary were distant relatives of the homeowner .See https://answersingenesis.org/christmas/christmas-no-room-for-an-inn/*

[e] *2:14* Some manuscripts, *peace, good will among men*

[f] *Luke 2:17. The fact that these lowly shepherds hurried to the place where the baby lay is further evidence, some suggest, that there was no "inn" involved, but a simple, typical home. Mary and Joseph, on the ground floor or stable level, would have posed no social threat of rejection for the peasant shepherds.*

[a] *Luke 2: 1-20 from The English Standard Version Bible. (2001). ESV Online. https: //esv.literalword.com/*

As long as I am in the world, I am the light of the world."

John 9:5

Adoration of the Child, Gerrit Van Honthorst, 1620

A Christmas Mistake, A Christmas Inspiration

L. M. MONTGOMERY

L.M. Montgomery

1874 - 1942

Canadian Author of the Anne of Green Gables Books

While best known for creating the much-loved character Anne Shirley, (Anne of Green Gables) Lucy Maud Montgomery published a whopping 530 short stories, as well as 500 poems and essays. It is hardly surprising, then, that two of her stories—Christmas themed morality tales, you might say—appear here.

A CHRISTMAS MISTAKE

"Tomorrow is Christmas," announced Teddy Grant exultantly, as he sat on the floor struggling manfully with a refractory bootlace that was knotted and tagless and stubbornly refused to go into the eyelets of Teddy's patched boots. "Ain't I glad, though. Hurrah!"

His mother was washing the breakfast dishes in a dreary, listless sort of way. She looked tired and broken-spirited. Ted's enthusiasm seemed to grate on her, for she answered sharply:

"Christmas, indeed. I can't see that it is anything for us to rejoice over. Other people may be glad enough, but what with winter coming on I'd sooner it was spring than Christmas. Mary Alice, do lift that child out of the ashes and put its shoes and stockings on. Everything seems to be at sixes and sevens here this morning."

Keith, the oldest boy, was coiled up on the sofa calmly working out some algebra problems, quite oblivious to the noise around him. But he looked up from his slate, with his pencil suspended above an obstinate equation, to declaim with a flourish:

"Christmas comes but once a year, And then Mother wishes it wasn't here."

"I don't, then," said Gordon, son number two, who was preparing his own noon lunch of bread and molasses at the table, and making an atrocious mess of crumbs and sugary syrup over everything. "I know one thing to be thankful for, and that is that there'll be no school. We'll have a whole week of holidays."

Gordon was noted for his aversion to school and his affection for holidays.

"And we're going to have turkey for dinner," declared Teddy, getting up off the floor and rushing to secure his share of bread and molasses, "and cranb'ry sauce and—and—pound cake! Ain't we, Ma?"

"No, you are not," said Mrs. Grant desperately, dropping the dishcloth and snatching the baby on her knee to wipe the crust of cinders and molasses from the chubby pink-and-white face. "You may as well know it now, children, I've kept it from you so far in hopes that something would turn up, but nothing has. We can't have any Christmas dinner tomorrow—we can't afford it. I've pinched and saved every way I could for the last month, hoping that I'd be able to get a turkey for you anyhow, but you'll have to do without it. There's that doctor's bill to pay and a dozen other bills coming in—and people say they can't wait. I suppose they can't, but it's kind of hard, I must say."

The little Grants stood with open mouths and horrified eyes. No turkey for Christmas! Was the world coming to an end? Wouldn't the government interfere if anyone ventured to dispense with a Christmas celebration?

The gluttonous Teddy stuffed his fists into his eyes and lifted up his voice. Keith, who understood better than the others the look on his mother's face, took his blubbering young brother by the collar and marched him into the porch. The twins, seeing the summary proceeding, swallowed the outcries they had intended to make, although they couldn't keep a few big tears from running down their fat cheeks.

Mrs. Grant looked pityingly at the disappointed faces about her.

"Don't cry, children, you make me feel worse. We are not the only ones who will have to do without a Christmas turkey. We ought to be very thankful that we have anything to eat at all. I hate to disappoint you, but it can't be helped."

"Never mind, Mother," said Keith, comfortingly, relaxing his hold upon the porch door, whereupon it suddenly flew open and precipitated Teddy, who had been tugging at the handle, heels over head backwards. "We know you've done your best. It's been a hard year for you. Just wait, though. I'll soon be grown up, and then you and these greedy youngsters shall feast on turkey every day of the year. Hello, Teddy, have you got on your feet again? Mind, sir, no more blubbering!"

"When I'm a man," announced Teddy with dignity, "I'd just like to see you put me in the porch. And I mean to have turkey all the time and I won't give you any, either."

"All right, you greedy small boy. Only take yourself off to school now, and let us hear no more squeaks out of you. Tramp, all of you, and give Mother a chance to get her work done."

Mrs. Grant got up and fell to work at her dishes with a brighter face.

"Well, we mustn't give in; perhaps things will be better after a while. I'll make a famous bread pudding, and you can boil some molasses taffy and ask those little Smithsons next door to help you pull it. They won't whine for turkey, I'll be bound. I don't suppose they ever tasted such a thing in all their lives. If I could afford it, I'd have had them all in to dinner with us. That sermon Mr. Evans preached last Sunday kind of stirred me up. He said we ought always to try and share our Christmas joy with some poor souls who had never learned the meaning of the word. I can't do as much as I'd like to. It was different when your father was alive."

The noisy group grew silent as they always did when their father was spoken of. He had died the year before, and since his death the little family had had a hard time. Keith, to hide his feelings, began to hector the rest.

"Mary Alice, do hurry up. Here, you twin nuisances, get off to school. If you don't you'll be late and then the master will give you a whipping."

"He won't," answered the irrepressible Teddy. "He never whips us, he doesn't. He stands us on the floor sometimes, though," he added, remembering the many times his own chubby legs had been seen to better advantage on the school platform.

"That man," said Mrs. Grant, alluding to the teacher, "makes me nervous. He is the most abstracted creature I ever saw in my life. It is a wonder to me he doesn't walk straight into the river some day. You'll meet him meandering along the street, gazing into vacancy, and he'll never see you nor hear a word you say half the time."

"Yesterday," said Gordon, chuckling over the remembrance, "he came in with a big piece of paper he'd picked up on the entry floor in one hand and his hat in the other—and he stuffed his hat into the coal-scuttle and hung up the paper on a nail as grave as you please. Never knew the difference till Ned Slocum went and told him. He's always doing things like that."

Keith had collected his books and now marched his brothers and sisters off to school. Left alone with the baby, Mrs. Grant betook herself to her work with a heavy heart. But a second interruption broke the progress of her dish-washing.

"I declare," she said, with a surprised glance through the window, "if there isn't that absent-minded schoolteacher coming through the yard! What can he want? Dear me, I do hope Teddy hasn't been cutting capers in school again."

For the teacher's last call had been in October and had been occasioned by the fact that the irrepressible Teddy would persist in going to school with his pockets filled with live crickets and in driving them harnessed to strings up and down the aisle when the teacher's back was turned. All mild methods of punishment having failed, the teacher had called to talk it over with Mrs. Grant, with the happy result that Teddy's behaviour had improved—in the matter of crickets at least.

But it was about time for another outbreak. Teddy had been unnaturally good for too long a time. Poor Mrs. Grant feared that it was the calm before a storm, and it was with nervous haste that she went to the door and greeted the young teacher.

He was a slight, pale, boyish-looking fellow, with an abstracted, musing look in his large dark eyes. Mrs. Grant noticed with amusement that he wore a white straw hat in spite of the season. His eyes were directed to her face with his usual unseeing gaze.

"Just as though he was looking through me at something a thousand miles away," said Mrs. Grant afterwards. "I believe he was, too. His body was right there on the step before me, but where his soul was is more than you or I or anybody can tell."

"Good morning," he said absently. "I have just called on my way to school with a message from Miss Millar. She wants you all to come up and have Christmas dinner with her tomorrow."

"For the land's sake!" said Mrs. Grant blankly. "I don't understand." To herself she thought, "I wish I dared take him and shake him to find if he's walking in his sleep or not."

"You and all the children—every one," went on the teacher dreamily, as if he were reciting a lesson learned beforehand. "She told me to tell you to be sure and come. Shall I say that you will?"

"Oh, yes, that is—I suppose—I don't know," said Mrs. Grant incoherently. "I never expected—yes, you may tell her we'll come," she concluded abruptly.

"Thank you," said the abstracted messenger, gravely lifting his hat and looking squarely through Mrs. Grant into unknown regions. When he had gone Mrs. Grant went in and sat down, laughing in a sort of hysterical way.

"I wonder if it is all right. Could Cornelia really have told him? She must, I suppose, but it is enough to take one's breath."

Mrs. Grant and Cornelia Millar were cousins, and had once been the closest of friends, but that was years ago, before some spiteful reports and ill-natured gossip had come between them, making only a little rift at first that soon widened into a chasm of coldness and alienation. Therefore this invitation surprised Mrs. Grant greatly.

Miss Cornelia was a maiden lady of certain years, with a comfortable bank account and a handsome, old-fashioned house on the hill behind the village. She always boarded the schoolteachers and looked after them maternally; she was an active church worker and a tower of strength to struggling ministers and their families.

"If Cornelia has seen fit at last to hold out the hand of reconciliation I'm glad enough to take it. Dear knows, I've wanted to make up often enough, but I didn't think she ever would. We've both of us got too much pride and stubbornness. It's the Turner blood in us that does it. The Turners were all so set. But I mean to do my part now she has done hers."

And Mrs. Grant made a final attack on the dishes with a beaming face.

When the little Grants came home and heard the news, Teddy stood on his head to express his delight, the twins kissed each other, and Mary Alice and Gordon danced around the kitchen.

Keith thought himself too big to betray any joy over a Christmas dinner, but he whistled while doing the chores until the bare welkin in the yard rang, and Teddy, in spite of unheard of misdemeanours, was not collared off into the porch once.

When the young teacher got home from school that evening he found the yellow house full of all sorts of delectable odours. Miss Cornelia herself was concocting mince pies after the famous family recipe, while her ancient and faithful handmaiden, Hannah, was straining into moulds the cranberry jelly. The open pantry door revealed a tempting array of Christmas delicacies.

"Did you call and invite the Smithsons up to dinner as I told you?" asked Miss Cornelia anxiously.

"Yes," was the dreamy response as he glided through the kitchen and vanished into the hall.

Miss Cornelia crimped the edges of her pies delicately with a relieved air. "I made certain he'd forget it," she said. "You just have to watch him as if he were a mere child. Didn't I catch him yesterday starting off to school in his carpet slippers? And in spite of me he got away today in that ridiculous summer hat. You'd better set that jelly in the out-pantry to cool, Hannah; it looks good. We'll give those poor little Smithsons a feast for once in their lives if they never get another."

At this juncture the hall door flew open and Mr. Palmer appeared on the threshold. He seemed considerably agitated and for once his eyes had lost their look of space-searching.

"Miss Millar, I am afraid I did make a mistake this morning—it has just dawned on me. I am almost sure that I called at Mrs. Grant's and invited her and her family instead of the Smithsons. And she said they would come."

Miss Cornelia's face was a study.

"Mr. Palmer," she said, flourishing her crimping fork tragically, "do you mean to say you went and invited Linda Grant here tomorrow? Linda Grant, of all women in this world!"

"I did," said the teacher with penitent wretchedness. "It was very careless of me—I am very sorry. What can I do? I'll go down and tell them I made a mistake if you like."

"You can't do that," groaned Miss Cornelia, sitting down and wrinkling up her forehead in dire perplexity. "It would never do in the world. For pity's sake, let me think for a minute."

Miss Cornelia did think—to good purpose evidently, for her forehead smoothed out as her meditations proceeded and her face brightened. Then she got up briskly. "Well, you've done it and no mistake. I don't know that I'm sorry, either. Anyhow, we'll leave it as it is. But you must go straight down now and invite the Smithsons too. And for pity's sake, don't make any more mistakes."

When he had gone Miss Cornelia opened her heart to Hannah. "I never could have done it myself—never; the Turner is too strong in me. But I'm glad it is done. I've been wanting for years to make up with Linda. And now the chance has come, thanks to that blessed blundering boy, I mean to make the most of it. Mind, Hannah, you never whisper a word about its being a mistake. Linda must never know. Poor Linda! She's had a hard time. Hannah, we must make some more pies, and I must go straight down to the store and get some more Santa Claus stuff; I've only got enough to go around the Smithsons."

When Mrs. Grant and her family arrived at the yellow house next morning Miss Cornelia herself ran out bareheaded to meet them. The two women shook hands a little stiffly and then a rill of long-repressed affection trickled out from some secret spring in Miss Cornelia's heart and she kissed her new-found old friend tenderly. Linda returned the kiss warmly, and both felt that the old-time friendship was theirs again.

The little Smithsons all came and they and the little Grants sat down on the long bright dining room to a dinner that made history in their small lives, and was eaten over again in happy dreams for months.

How those children did eat! And how beaming Miss Cornelia and grim-faced, soft-hearted Hannah and even the absent-minded teacher himself enjoyed watching them!

After dinner Miss Cornelia distributed among the delighted little souls the presents she had bought for them, and then turned them loose in the big shining kitchen to have a taffy pull—and they had it to their hearts' content! And as for the shocking, taffyfied state into which they got their own rosy faces and that once immaculate domain—well, as Miss Cornelia and Hannah never said one word about it, neither will I.

The four women enjoyed the afternoon in their own way, and the schoolteacher buried himself in algebra to his own great satisfaction.

When her guests went home in the starlit December dusk, Miss Cornelia walked part of the way with them and had a long confidential talk with Mrs. Grant. When she returned it was to find Hannah groaning in and over the kitchen and the schoolteacher dreamily trying to clean some molasses off his boots with the kitchen hairbrush. Long-suffering Miss Cornelia rescued her property and despatched Mr. Palmer into the woodshed to find the shoe-brush. Then she sat down and laughed.

"Hannah, what will become of that boy yet? There's no counting on what he'll do next. I don't know how he'll ever get through the world, I'm sure, but I'll look after him while he's here at least. I owe him a huge debt of gratitude for this Christmas blunder. What an awful mess this place is in! But, Hannah, did you ever in the world see anything so delightful as that little Tommy Smithson stuffing himself with plum cake, not to mention Teddy Grant? It did me good just to see them."

A CHRISTMAS INSPIRATION

"Well, I really think Santa Claus has been very good to us all," said Jean Lawrence, pulling the pins out of her heavy coil of fair hair and letting it ripple over her shoulders.

"So do I," said Nellie Preston as well as she could with a mouthful of chocolates. "Those blessed home folks of mine seem to have divined by instinct the very things I most wanted."

It was the dusk of Christmas Eve and they were all in Jean Lawrence's room at No. 16 Chestnut Terrace. No. 16 was a boarding-house, and boarding-houses are not proverbially cheerful places in which to spend Christmas, but Jean's room, at least, was a pleasant spot, and all the girls had brought their Christmas presents in to show each other. Christmas came on Sunday that year and the Saturday evening mail at Chestnut Terrace had been an exciting one.

Jean had lighted the pink-globed lamp on her table and the mellow light fell over merry faces as the girls chatted about their gifts. On the table was a big white box heaped with roses that betokened a bit of Christmas extravagance on somebody's part. Jean's brother had sent them to her from Montreal, and all the girls were enjoying them in common.

No. 16 Chestnut Terrace was overrun with girls generally. But just now only five were left; all the others had gone home for Christmas, but these five could not go and were bent on making the best of it.

Belle and Olive Reynolds, who were sitting on the bed—Jean could never keep them off it—were High School girls; they were said to be always laughing, and even the fact that they could not go home for Christmas because a young brother had measles did not dampen their spirits.

Beth Hamilton, who was hovering over the roses, and Nellie Preston, who was eating candy, were art students, and their homes were too far away to visit. As for Jean Lawrence, she was an orphan, and had no home of her own. She worked on the staff of one of the big city newspapers and the other girls were a little in awe of her cleverness, but her nature was a "chummy" one and her room was a favourite rendezvous. Everybody liked frank, open-handed and hearted Jean.

"It was so funny to see the postman when he came this evening," said Olive. "He just bulged with parcels. They were sticking out in every direction."

"We all got our share of them," said Jean with a sigh of content.

"Even the cook got six—I counted."

"Miss Allen didn't get a thing—not even a letter," said Beth quickly. Beth had a trick of seeing things that other girls didn't.

"I forgot Miss Allen. No, I don't believe she did," answered Jean thoughtfully as she twisted up her pretty hair. "How dismal it must be to be so forlorn as that on Christmas Eve of all times. Ugh! I'm glad I have friends."

"I saw Miss Allen watching us as we opened our parcels and letters," Beth went on. "I happened to look up once, and such an expression as was on her face, girls! It was pathetic and sad and envious all at once. It really made me feel bad—for five minutes," she concluded honestly.

"Hasn't Miss Allen any friends at all?" asked Beth.

"No, I don't think she has," answered Jean. "She has lived here for fourteen years, so Mrs. Pickrell says. Think of that, girls! Fourteen years at Chestnut Terrace! Is it any wonder that she is thin and dried-up and snappy?"

"Nobody ever comes to see her and she never goes anywhere," said Beth. "Dear me! She must feel lonely now when everybody else is being remembered by their friends. I can't forget her face tonight; it actually haunts me. Girls, how would you feel if you hadn't anyone belonging to you, and if nobody thought about you at Christmas?"

"Ow!" said Olive, as if the mere idea made her shiver.

A little silence followed. To tell the truth, none of them liked Miss Allen. They knew that she did not like them either, but considered them frivolous and pert, and complained when they made a racket.

"The skeleton at the feast," Jean called her, and certainly the presence of the pale, silent, discontented-looking woman at the No. 16 table did not tend to heighten its festivity.

Presently Jean said with a dramatic flourish, "Girls, I have an inspiration—a Christmas inspiration!"

"What is it?" cried four voices.

"Just this. Let us give Miss Allen a Christmas surprise. She has not received a single present and I'm sure she feels lonely. Just think how we would feel if we were in her place."

"That is true," said Olive thoughtfully. "Do you know, girls, this evening I went to her room with a message from Mrs. Pickrell, and I do believe she had been crying. Her room looked dreadfully bare and cheerless, too. I think she is very poor. What are we to do, Jean?"

"Let us each give her something nice. We can put the things just outside of her door so that she will see them whenever she opens it. I'll give her some of Fred's roses too, and I'll write a Christmassy letter in my very best style to go with them," said Jean, warming up to her ideas as she talked.

The other girls caught her spirit and entered into the plan with enthusiasm.

"Splendid!" cried Beth. "Jean, it is an inspiration, sure enough. Haven't we been horribly selfish—thinking of nothing but our own gifts and fun and pleasure? I really feel ashamed."

"Let us do the thing up the very best way we can," said Nellie, forgetting even her beloved chocolates in her eagerness. "The shops are open yet. Let us go up town and invest."

Five minutes later five capped and jacketed figures were scurrying up the street in the frosty, starlit December dusk. Miss Allen in her cold little room heard their gay voices and sighed. She was crying by herself in the dark. It was Christmas for everybody but her, she thought drearily.

In an hour the girls came back with their purchases.

"Now, let's hold a council of war," said Jean jubilantly. "I hadn't the faintest idea what Miss Allen would like so I just guessed wildly. I got her a lace handkerchief and a big bottle of perfume and a painted photograph frame—and I'll stick my own photo in it for fun. That was really all I could afford. Christmas purchases have left my purse dreadfully lean."

"I got her a glove-box and a pin tray," said Belle, "and Olive got her a calendar and Whittier's poems. And besides we are going to give her half of that big plummy fruit cake Mother sent us from home. I'm sure she hasn't tasted anything so delicious for years, for fruit cakes don't grow on Chestnut Terrace and she never goes anywhere else for a meal."

Beth had bought a pretty cup and saucer and said she meant to give one of her pretty water-colours too. Nellie, true to her reputation, had invested in a big box of chocolate creams, a gorgeously striped candy cane, a bag of oranges, and a brilliant lampshade of rose-coloured crepe paper to top off with.

"It makes such a lot of show for the money," she explained. "I am bankrupt, like Jean."

"Well, we've got a lot of pretty things," said Jean in a tone of satisfaction. "Now we must do them up nicely. Will you wrap them in tissue paper, girls, and tie them with baby ribbon—here's a box of it—while I write that letter?"

While the others chatted over their parcels Jean wrote her letter, and Jean could write delightful letters. She had a decided talent in that respect, and her correspondents all declared her letters to be things of beauty and joy forever. She put her best into Miss Allen's Christmas letter. Since then she has written many bright and clever things, but I do not believe she ever in her life wrote anything more genuinely original and delightful than that letter. Besides, it breathed the very spirit of Christmas, and all the girls declared that it was splendid.

"You must all sign it now," said Jean, "and I'll put it in one of those big envelopes; and, Nellie, won't you write her name on it in fancy letters?"

Which Nellie proceeded to do, and furthermore embellished the envelope by a border of chubby cherubs, dancing hand in hand around it and a sketch of No. 16 Chestnut Terrace in the corner in lieu of a stamp. Not content with this she hunted out a huge sheet of drawing paper and drew upon it an original pen-and-ink design after her own heart. A dudish[1] cat—Miss Allen was fond of the No. 16 cat if she could be said to be fond of anything—was portrayed seated on a rocker arrayed in smoking jacket and cap with a cigar waved airily aloft in one paw while the other held out a placard bearing the legend "Merry Christmas." A second cat in full street costume bowed politely, hat in paw, and waved a banner inscribed with "Happy New Year," while faintly suggested kittens gambolled around the border. The girls laughed until they cried over it and voted it to be the best thing Nellie had yet done in original work.

All this had taken time and it was past eleven o'clock. Miss Allen had cried herself to sleep long ago and everybody else in Chestnut Terrace was abed when five figures cautiously crept down the hall, headed by Jean with a dim lamp. Outside of Miss Allen's door the procession halted and the girls silently arranged their gifts on the floor.

"That's done," whispered Jean in a tone of satisfaction as they tiptoed back. "And now let us go to bed or Mrs. Pickrell, bless her heart, will be down on us for burning so much midnight oil. Oil has gone up, you know, girls."

It was in the early morning that Miss Allen opened her door. But early as it was, another door down the hall was half open too and five rosy faces were peering cautiously out. The girls had been up for an hour for fear they would miss the sight and were all in Nellie's room, which commanded a view of Miss Allen's door.

That lady's face was a study. Amazement, incredulity, wonder, chased each other over it, succeeded by a glow of pleasure. On the floor before her was a snug little pyramid of parcels topped by Jean's letter. On a chair behind it was a bowl of delicious hot-house roses and Nellie's placard.

Miss Allen looked down the hall but saw nothing, for Jean had slammed the door just in time. Half an hour later when they were going down to breakfast Miss Allen came along the hall with outstretched hands to meet them. She had been crying again, but I think her tears were happy ones; and she was smiling now. A cluster of Jean's roses were pinned on her breast.

"Oh, girls, girls," she said, with a little tremble in her voice, "I can never thank you enough. It was so kind and sweet of you. You don't know how much good you have done me."

Breakfast was an unusually cheerful affair at No. 16 that morning. There was no skeleton at the feast and everybody was beaming. Miss Allen laughed and talked like a girl herself.

"Oh, how surprised I was!" she said. "The roses were like a bit of summer, and those cats of Nellie's were so funny and delightful. And your letter too, Jean! I cried and laughed over it. I shall read it every day for a year."

After breakfast everyone went to Christmas service. The girls went uptown to the church they attended. The city was very beautiful in the morning sunshine. There had been a white frost in the night and the tree-lined avenues and public squares seemed like glimpses of fairyland.

"How lovely the world is," said Jean.

"This is really the very happiest Christmas morning I have ever known," declared Nellie. "I never felt so really Christmassy in my inmost soul before."

"I suppose," said Beth thoughtfully, "that it is because we have discovered for ourselves the old truth that it is more blessed to give than to receive. I've always known it, in a way, but I never realized it before."

"Blessing on Jean's Christmas inspiration," said Nellie. "But, girls, let us try to make it an all-the-year-round inspiration, I say. We can bring a little of our own sunshine into Miss Allen's life as long as we live with her."

"Amen to that!" said Jean heartily. "Oh, listen, girls—the Christmas chimes!"

And over all the beautiful city was wafted the grand old message of peace on earth and good will to all the world. -End-

Note: [1]Dudish-well-dressed, manly

Christmas Carol

SARA TEASDALE

Sara Teasdale, 1884–1933

American Poet

Critics of Teasdale's day considered this to be a simple poem, relegating her to the ranks of less serious poets, even to that of a lyricist for such verse. But she won numerous prizes, one of which later was renamed the Pulitzer Prize for Poetry. Despite detractors, Teasdale was popular with the public and with critics during her lifetime, particularly valued for "musical language and evocative emotion."

CHRISTMAS CAROL

The kings they came from out the south,
All dressed in ermine fine;
They bore Him gold and chrysoprase,
And gifts of precious wine.

**

The shepherds came from out the north,
Their coats were brown and old;

They brought Him little new-born lambs—
They had not any gold.

**

The wise men came from out the east,
And they were wrapped in white;
The star that led them all the way
Did glorify the night.

**

The angels came from heaven high,
And they were clad with wings;
And lo, they brought a joyful song
The host of heaven sings.

**

The kings they knocked upon the door,
The wise men entered in,
The shepherds followed after them
To hear the song begin.

**

The angels sang through all the night
Until the rising sun,
But little Jesus fell asleep
Before the song was done.

Christmas in the Alley

OLIVE THORNE MILLER

Olive Thorne Miller, 1831 – 1918

Author, naturalist and ornithologist

Olive Thorne Miller, the pen name of Harriet Mann Miller, was a prolific writer, penning an estimated 780 articles and 24 books. Besides being an author, she was a naturalist and highly respected ornithologist. As in all of the selections, the spelling and grammar are unchanged from the original.

CHRISTMAS IN THE ALLEY

"I declare for 't, to-morrow is Christmas Day an' I clean forgot all about it," said old Ann, the washerwoman, pausing in her work and holding the flatiron suspended in the air.

"Much good it'll do us," growled a discontented voice from the coarse bed in the corner.

"We haven't much extra, to be sure," answered Ann cheerfully, bringing the iron down onto the shirt-bosom before her, "but at least we've enough to eat, and a good fire, and that's more'n some have, not a thousand miles from here either."

"We might have plenty more," said the fretful voice, "if you didn't think so much more of strangers than you do of your own folk's comfort, keeping a houseful of beggars, as if you was a lady!"

"Now, John," replied Ann, taking another iron from the fire, "you're not half so bad as you pretend. You wouldn't have me turn them poor creatures into the streets to freeze, now, would you?"

"It's none of our business to pay rent for them," grumbled John. "Every one for himself, I say, these hard times. If they can't pay you'd ought to send 'em off; there's plenty as can."

"They'd pay quick enough if they could get work," said Ann. "They're good honest fellows, every one, and paid me regular as long as they had a cent. But when hundreds are out o' work in the city, what can they do?"

"That's none o' your business, you can turn 'em out!" growled John.

"And leave the poor children to freeze as well as starve?" said Ann. "Who'd ever take 'em in without money, I'd like to know? No, John," bringing her iron down as though she meant it, "I'm glad I'm well enough to wash and iron, and pay my rent, and so long as I can do that, and keep the hunger away from you and the child, I'll never turn the poor souls out, leastways, not in this freezing winter weather."

"An' here's Christmas," the old man went on whiningly, "an' not a penny to spend, an' I needin' another blanket so bad, with my rhumatiz, an' haven't had a drop of tea for I don't know how long!"

"I know it," said Ann, never mentioning that she too had been without tea, and not only that, but with small allowance of food of any kind, "and I'm desperate sorry I can't get a bit of something for Katey. The child never missed a little something in her stocking before."

"Yes," John struck in, "much you care for your flesh an' blood. The child ha'n't had a thing this winter."

"That's true enough," said Ann, with a sigh, "an' it's the hardest thing of all that I've had to keep her out o' school when she was doing so beautiful."

"An' her feet all on the ground," growled John.

"I know her shoes is bad," said Ann, hanging the shirt up on a line that stretched across the room, and was already nearly full of freshly ironed clothes, "but they're better than the Parker children's."

"What's that to us?" almost shouted the weak old man, shaking his fist at her in his rage.

"Well, keep your temper, old man," said Ann. "I'm sorry it goes so hard with you, but as long as I can stand on my feet, I sha'n't turn anybody out to freeze, that's certain."

"How much'll you get for them?" said the miserable old man, after a few moments' silence, indicating by his hand the clean clothes on the line.

"Two dollars," said Ann, "and half of it must go to help make up next month's rent. I've got a good bit to make up yet, and only a week to do it in, and I sha'n't have another cent till day after to-morrow."

"Well, I wish you'd manage to buy me a little tea," whined the old man; "seems as if that would go right to the spot, and warm up my old bones a bit."

"I'll try," said Ann, revolving in her mind how she could save a few pennies from her indispensable purchases to get tea and sugar, for without sugar he would not touch it.

Wearied with his unusual exertion, the old man now dropped off to sleep, and Ann went softly about, folding and piling the clothes into a big basket already half full. When they were all packed in, and nicely covered with a piece of clean muslin, she took an old shawl and hood from a nail in the corner, put them on, blew out the candle, for it must not burn one moment unnecessarily, and, taking up her basket, went out into the cold winter night, softly closing the door behind her.

The house was on an alley, but as soon as she turned the corner she was in the bright streets, glittering with lamps and gay people. The shop windows were brilliant with Christmas displays, and thousands of warmly dressed buyers were lingering before them, laughing and chatting, and selecting their purchases. Surely it seemed as if there could be no want here.

As quickly as her burden would let her, the old washerwoman passed through the crowd into a broad street and rang the basement bell of a large, showy house.

"Oh, it's the washerwoman!" said a flashy-looking servant who answered the bell; "set the basket right m here. Mrs. Keithe can't look them over to-night. There's company in the parlour—Miss Carry's Christmas party."

"Ask her to please pay me—at least a part," said old Ann hastily. "I don't see how I can do without the money. I counted on it."

"I'll ask her," said the pert young woman, turning to go upstairs; "but it's no use."

Returning in a moment, she delivered the message. "She has no change to-night; you're to come in the morning."

"Dear me!" thought Ann, as she plodded back through the streets, "it'll be even worse than I expected, for there's not a morsel to eat in the house, and not a penny to buy one with. Well—well—the Lord will provide, the Good Book says, but it's mighty dark days, and it's hard to believe."

Entering the house, Ann sat down silently before the expiring fire. She was tired, her bones ached, and she was faint for want of food.

Wearily she rested her head on her hands, and tried to think of some way to get a few cents. She had nothing she could sell or pawn, everything she could do without had gone before, in similar emergencies. After sitting there some time, and revolving plan after plan, only to find them all impossible, she was forced to conclude that they must go supperless to bed.

Her husband grumbled, and Katey—who came in from a neighbour's—cried with hunger, and after they were asleep old Ann crept into bed to keep warm, more disheartened than she had been all winter.

If we could only see a little way ahead! All this time—the darkest the house on the alley had seen—help was on the way to them. A kind-hearted city missionary, visiting one of the unfortunate families living in the upper rooms of old Ann's house, had learned from them of the noble charity of the humble old washerwoman. It was more than princely charity, for she not only denied herself nearly every comfort, but she endured the reproaches of her husband, and the tears of her child.

Telling the story to a party of his friends this Christmas Eve, their hearts were troubled, and they at once emptied their purses into his hands for her. And the gift was at that very moment in the pocket of the missionary, waiting for morning to make her Christmas happy. Christmas morning broke clear and cold. Ann was up early, as usual, made her fire, with the last of her coal, cleared up her two rooms, and, leaving her husband and Katey in bed, was about starting out to try and get her money to provide a breakfast for them. At the door she met the missionary.

"Good-morning, Ann," said he. "I wish you a Merry Christmas."

"Thank you, sir," said Ann cheerfully; "the same to yourself."

"Have you been to breakfast already?" asked the missionary.

"No, sir," said Ann. "I was just going out for it."

"I haven't either," said he, "but I couldn't bear to wait until I had eaten breakfast before I brought you your Christmas present—I suspect you haven't had any yet."

Ann smiled. "Indeed, sir, I haven't had one since I can remember."

"Well, I have one for you. Come in, and I'll tell you about it."

Too much amazed for words, Ann led him into the room. The missionary opened his purse, and handed her a roll of bills.

"Why—what!" she gasped, taking it mechanically.

"Some friends of mine heard of your generous treatment of the poor families upstairs," he went on, "and they send you this, with their respects and best wishes for Christmas. Do just what you please with it—it is wholly yours. No thanks," he went on, as she struggled to speak. "It's not from me. Just enjoy it—that's all. It has done them more good to give than it can you to receive," and before she could speak a word he was gone.

What did the old washerwoman do?

Well, first she fell on her knees and buried her agitated face in the bedclothes. After a while she became aware of a storm of words from her husband, and she got up, subdued as much as possible her agitation, and tried to answer his frantic questions.

"How much did he give you, old stupid?" he screamed; "can't you speak, or are you struck dumb? Wake up! I just wish I could reach you! I'd shake you till your teeth rattled!"

His vicious looks were a sign, it was evident that he only lacked the strength to be as good as his word. Ann roused herself from her stupour and spoke at last.

"I don't know. I'll count it." She unrolled the bills and began.

"O Lord!" she exclaimed excitedly, "here's ten-dollar bills! One, two, three, and a twenty-that makes five—and five are fifty-five—sixty—seventy—eighty—eighty-five—ninety—one hundred—and two and five are seven, and two and one are ten, twenty—twenty-five—one hundred and twenty-five! Why, I'm rich!" she shouted. "Bless the Lord! Oh, this is the glorious Christmas Day! I knew He'd provide. Katey! Katey!" she screamed at the door of the other room, where the child lay asleep. "Merry Christmas to you, darlin'! Now you can have some shoes! and a new dress! and—and—breakfast, and a regular Christmas dinner! Oh! I believe I shall go crazy!"

But she did not. Joy seldom hurts people, and she was brought back to everyday affairs by the querulous voice of her husband.

"Now I will have my tea, an' a new blanket, an' some tobacco—how I have wanted a pipe!" and he went on enumerating his wants while Ann bustled about, putting away most of her money, and once more getting ready to go out.

"I'll run out and get some breakfast," she said, "but don't you tell a soul about the money."

"No! they'll rob us!" shrieked the old man.

"Nonsense! I'll hide it well, but I want to keep it a secret for another reason. Mind, Katey, don't you tell?"

"No!" said Katey, with wide eyes. "But can I truly have a new frock, Mammy, and new shoes—and is it really Christmas?"

"It's really Christmas, darlin'," said Ann, "and you'll see what mammy'll bring home to you, after breakfast."

The luxurious meal of sausages, potatoes, and hot tea was soon smoking on the table, and was eagerly devoured by Katey and her father. But Ann could not eat much. She was absent-minded, and only drank a cup of tea. As soon as breakfast was over, she left Katey to wash the dishes, and started out again.

She walked slowly down the street, revolving a great plan in her mind.

"Let me see," she said to herself. "They shall have a happy day for once. I suppose John'll grumble, but the Lord has sent me this money, and I mean to use part of it to make one good day for them."

Having settled this in her mind, she walked on more quickly, and visited various shops in the neighbourhood. When at last she went home, her big basket was stuffed as full as it could hold, and she carried a bundle besides.

"Here's your tea, John," she said cheerfully, as she unpacked the basket, "a whole pound of it, and sugar, and tobacco, and a new pipe."

"Give me some now," said the old man eagerly; "don't wait to take out the rest of the things."

"And here's a new frock for you, Katey," old Ann went on, after making John happy with his treasures, "a real bright one, and a pair of shoes, and some real woollen stockings; oh! how warm you'll be!"

"Oh, how nice, Mammy!" cried Katey, jumping about. "When will you make my frock?"

"To-morrow," answered the mother, "and you can go to school again."

"Oh, goody!" she began, but her face fell. "If only Molly Parker could go too!"

"You wait and see," answered Ann, with a knowing look. "Who knows what Christmas will bring to Molly Parker?"

"Now here's a nice big roast," the happy woman went on, still unpacking, "and potatoes and turnips and cabbage and bread and butter and coffee and—"

"What in the world! You goin' to give a party?" asked the old man between the puffs, staring at her in wonder.

"I'll tell you just what I am going to do," said Ann firmly, bracing herself for opposition, "and it's as good as done, so you needn't say a word about it. I'm going to have a Christmas dinner, and I'm going to invite every blessed soul in this house to come. They shall be warm and full for once in their lives, please God! And, Katey," she went on breathlessly, before the old man had sufficiently recovered from his astonishment to speak, "go right upstairs now, and invite every one of 'em from the fathers down to Mrs. Parker's baby to come to dinner at three o'clock; we'll have to keep fashionable hours, it's so late now; and mind, Katey, not a word about the money. And hurry back, child, I want you to help me."

To her surprise, the opposition from her husband was less than she expected. The genial tobacco seemed to have quieted his nerves, and even opened his heart. Grateful for this, Ann resolved that his pipe should never lack tobacco while she could work.

But now the cares of dinner absorbed her. The meat and vegetables were prepared, the pudding made, and the long table spread, though she had to borrow every table in the house, and every dish to have enough to go around.

At three o'clock when the guests came in, it was really a very pleasant sight. The bright warm fire, the long table, covered with a substantial, and, to them, a luxurious meal, all smoking hot. John, in his neatly brushed suit, in an armchair at the foot of the table, Ann in a bustle of hurry and welcome, and a plate and a seat for every one.

How the half-starved creatures enjoyed it; how the children stuffed and the parents looked on with a happiness that was very near to tears; how old John actually smiled and urged them to send back their plates again and again, and how Ann, the washerwoman, was the life and soul of it all, I can't half tell.

After dinner, when the poor women lodgers insisted on clearing up, and the poor men sat down by the fire to smoke, for old John actually passed around his beloved tobacco, Ann quietly slipped out for a few minutes, took four large bundles from a closet under the stairs, and disappeared upstairs. She was scarcely missed before she was back again.

Well, of course it was a great day in the house on the alley, and the guests sat long into the twilight before the warm fire, talking of their old homes in the fatherland, the hard winter, and prospects for work in the spring. When at last they returned to the chilly discomfort of their own rooms, each family found a package containing a new warm dress and pair of shoes for every woman and child in the family.

"And I have enough left," said Ann the washerwoman, to herself, when she was reckoning up the expenses of the day, "to buy my coal and pay my rent till spring, so I can save my old bones a bit. And sure John can't grumble at their staying now, for it's all along of keeping them that I had such a blessed Christmas day at all."

A Christmas Carol

S.T. COLERIDGE

Samuel Taylor Coleridge, 1772 – 1834

English Romantic Poet

Say the name 'Coleridge,' and most people think of famous poems such as "The Tale of the Ancient Mariner," or "Kubla Khan." In secular colleges and universities, you may learn about these but will probably not study the following poem. Its place is earned here, however, not only for its masterful handling of the poetic form, but because it gives homage to the Christmas story and more, the Christian faith itself.

In it, Coleridge, a leader of the British Romantic Movement, makes use of the visit of the Shepherds to pontificate (poetically) upon war through an imaginary dialogue between the shepherds and Mary, first with an idealized view of its supposed glory, followed by a reminder of its brutality. This throws into sharp relief God's message of "Peace, peace on earth" that the birth of the Savior heralds to man.

A CHRISTMAS CAROL

I.

The Shepherds went their hasty way,
And found the lowly stable-shed
Where the Virgin-Mother lay:
And now they checked their eager tread,
For to the Babe, that at her bosom clung,
A Mother's song the Virgin-Mother sung.

II.

They told her how a glorious light,
Streaming from a heavenly throng,
Around them shone, suspending night!
While sweeter than a Mother's song,
Blest Angels heralded the Saviour's birth,
Glory to God on high! and Peace on Earth.

III

She listened to the tale divine,
And closer still the Babe she pressed;
And while she cried, the Babe is mine!
The milk rushed faster to her breast:
Joy rose within her, like a summer's morn;
Peace, Peace on Earth! the Prince of Peace is born.

IV.

Thou Mother of the Prince of Peace,
Poor, simple, and of low estate!
That Strife should vanish, Battle cease,
O why should this thy soul elate?
Sweet Music's loudest note, the Poet's story,
—Did'st thou ne'er love to hear of Fame and Glory?

V.

And is not War a youthful King,
A stately Hero clad in Mail?
Beneath his footsteps laurels spring;
Him Earth's majestic monarchs hail
Their Friend, their Playmate!
and his bold bright eyeCompels
the maiden's love-confessing sigh.

VI.

Tell this in some more courtly scene,
To maids and youths in robes of state!
I am a woman poor and mean,
And therefore is my Soul elate."
War is a ruffian, all with guilt defiled,
That from the aged Father tears his Child!

VII.

A murderous fiend, by fiends adored,
He kills the Sire and starves the Son;
The Husband kills, and from her board
Steals all his Widow's toil had won;
Plunders God's world of beauty; rends away
All safety from the Night, all comfort from the Day.

VIII.

Then wisely is my soul elate,
That Strife should vanish, Battle cease:
I'm poor and of a low estate,
The Mother of the Prince of Peace."
Joy rises in me, like a summer's morn:
Peace, Peace on Earth, the Prince of Peace is born.

Mistletoe

WALTER DE LA MARE

Walter de la Mare, 1873 – 1956

English poet, short story writer and novelist

Best known for his works for children, de la Mare also wrote about nature, war, and the human condition. The following little poem is from Collected Poems, published in 1920.

MISTLETOE

Sitting under the mistletoe
(Pale-green, fairy mistletoe),
One last candle burning low,
All the sleepy dancers gone,
Just one candle burning on,
Shadows lurking everywhere:
Some one came, and kissed me there.

Tired I was; my head would go
Nodding under the mistletoe
(Pale-green, fairy mistletoe),
No footsteps came, no voice, but only,

Just as I sat there, sleepy, lonely,
Stooped in the still and shadowy air
Lips unseen—and kissed me there.

Going Further

(For Children or Adults)

1. What is mistletoe? Look it up, see what it looks like, and write out the definition or draw it.

2. Do you think what the poem describes really happened or was the poet imagining it? Why or why not? And is there any way to know for sure?

3. For how long do you think people have been using mistletoe as it is used in this poem? Take a guess and then look it up to see if you're right. Places you could check offline would be encyclopedias. Online try, Wikipedia, or https://www.etymonline.com/word/mistletoe

4. Extra: One of these sources above mentions other names for mistletoe that have been used in the past. Can you name a few?

Good Christians, Rise, This is the Morn

Anonymous

This anonymous poem first began appearing in hymnals before 1870. Various composers have set it to music over the years.

GOOD CHRISTIANS RISE, THIS IS THE MORN

Good Christians, rise, this is the morn,
When Christ our Saviour, He was born.
All in a stable so lowly,
At Bethlehem in Galilee.

Chorus:
Rejoice! Our Saviour, He was born
On Christmas day in the morning.

There pilgrims who in countries far
Had seen by night Christ's natal Star,
Now, lowly bending, peasants bring,

An offering to their God and King.

Chorus
Rejoice! Our Saviour, He was born
On Christmas day in the morning.

Then rise, good Christians, rise and sing
Hosannas to the new-born King!
And with angelic hosts above
Proclaim to earth God's perfect love.

Chorus
Rejoice! Our Saviour, He was born
On Christmas day in the morning.

The Christmas Tree and Other Selections

CHARLES DICKENS

Charles Dickens, 1812 –1870

English novelist and social critic

There is hardly an author whose work is more iconically associated with Christmas than Dickens. He is considered by many to be the greatest novelist of the Victorian era and the man who, more than anyone else, put Victorian Christmases into the minds and hearts of the world as the definitive old-fashioned celebration, though many of its customs were in fact far older.

Following are three excerpts of his work, the first, written in 1850 as an imaginative 'memoir' of his own boyhood, when Christmas presents were hung on the branches of a table-top tree as opposed to being piled underneath it. The latter two excerpts are from, of course, A Christmas Carol, *1843.*

THE CHRISTMAS TREE

But hark! The Waits are playing, and they break my childish sleep! What images do I associate with the Christmas music as I see them set forth on the Christmas Tree? ...They gather round my little bed. An angel, speaking to a group of shepherds in a field; some travellers, with eyes uplifted, following a star; a baby in a manger; a child in a spacious temple, talking with grave men; a solemn figure, with a mild and beautiful face, raising a dead girl by the hand; again, near a city gate, calling back the son of a widow, on his bier, to life; a crowd of people looking through the opened roof of a chamber where he sits, and letting down a sick person on a bed, with ropes; the same, in a tempest, walking on the water to a ship; again, on a sea-shore, teaching a great multitude; again, with a child upon his knee, and other children round; again, restoring sight to the blind, speech to the dumb, hearing to the deaf, health to the sick, strength to the lame, knowledge to the ignorant; again, dying upon a Cross, watched by armed soldiers, a thick darkness coming on, the earth beginning to shake, and only one voice heard, "Forgive them, for they know not what they do."

...Among the later toys and fancies hanging there—as idle often and less pure—be the images once associated with the sweet old Waits, the softened music in the night, ever unalterable! Encircled by the social thoughts of Christmas-time, still let the benignant figure of my childhood stand unchanged! In every cheerful image and suggestion that the season brings, may the bright star that rested above the poor roof, be the star of all the Christian World! A moment's pause, O vanishing tree, of which the lower boughs are dark to me as yet, and let me look once more! I know there are blank spaces on thy branches, where eyes that I have loved have shone and smiled; from which they are departed. But, far above, I see the raiser of the dead girl, and the Widow's Son; and God is good! If Age be hiding for me in the unseen portion of thy downward growth, O may I, with a grey head, turn a child's heart to that figure yet, and a child's trustfulness and confidence!

Now, the tree is decorated with bright merriment, and song, and dance, and cheerfulness. And they are welcome. Innocent and welcome be they ever held, beneath the branches of the Christmas Tree, which cast no gloomy shadow! But, as it sinks into the ground, I hear a whisper going through the leaves.

"This, in commemoration of the law of love and kindness, mercy and compassion. This, in remembrance of Me!"

Notes:
[1] *The complete story is available from Google Books, public domain.*

CHRISTMAS AT FEZZIWIG'S WAREHOUSE

"Yo Ho! my boys," said Fezziwig. "No more work to-night! Christmas Eve, Dick! Christmas, Ebenezer! Let's have the shutters up!" cried old Fezziwig with a sharp clap of his hands, "before a man can say Jack Robinson...."

"Hilli-ho!" cried old Fezziwig, skipping down from the high desk with wonderful agility. "Clear away, my lads, and let's have lots of room here! Hilli-ho, Dick! Cheer-up, Ebenezer!"

Clear away! There was nothing they wouldn't have cleared away, or couldn't have cleared away with old Fezziwig looking on. It was done in a minute. Every movable was packed off, as if it were dismissed from public life forevermore; the floor was swept and watered, the lamps were trimmed, fuel was heaped upon the fire; and the warehouse was as snug, and warm, and dry, and bright a ballroom as you would desire to see on a winter's night.

In came a fiddler with a music book, and went up to the lofty desk and made an orchestra of it and tuned like fifty stomach-aches. In came Mrs. Fezziwig, one vast substantial smile. In came the three Misses Fezziwig, beaming and lovable. In came the six followers whose hearts they broke.

In came all the young men and women employed in the business. In came the housemaid with her cousin the baker. In came the cook with her brother's particular friend the milkman. In came the boy from over the way, who was suspected of not having board enough from his master, trying to hide himself behind the girl from next door but one who was proved to have had her ears pulled by her mistress; in they all came, anyhow and everyhow.

Away they all went, twenty couple at once; hands half round and back again the other way; down the middle and up again; round and round in various stages of affectionate grouping, old top couple always turning up in the wrong place; new top couple starting off again, as soon as they got there; all top couples at last, and not a bottom one to help them.

When this result was brought about the fiddler struck up "Sir Roger de Coverley."

Then old Fezziwig stood out to dance with Mrs. Fezziwig. Top couple, too, with a good stiff piece of work cut out for them; three or four and twenty pairs of partners; people who were not to be trifled with; people who would dance and had no notion of walking.

But if they had been thrice as many—oh, four times as many—old Fezziwig would have been a match for them, and so would Mrs. Fezziwig. As to her, she was worthy to be his partner in every sense of the term. If that's not high praise, tell me higher and I'll use it. A positive light appeared to issue from Fezziwig's calves. They shone in every part of the dance like moons. You couldn't have predicted at any given time what would become of them next. And when old Fezziwig and Mrs. Fezziwig had gone all through the dance, advance and retire; both hands to your partner, bow and courtesy, corkscrew, thread the needle, and back again to your place; Fezziwig "cut"—cut so deftly that he appeared to wink with his legs, and came upon his feet again with a stagger.

When the clock struck eleven the domestic ball broke up. Mr. and Mrs. Fezziwig took their stations, one on either side of the door, and shaking hands with every person individually, as he or she went out, wished him or her a Merry Christmas!

THE CRATCHIT'S CHRISTMAS

Scrooge and the Ghost of Christmas Present stood in the city streets on Christmas morning, where (for the weather was severe) the people made a rough but brisk and not unpleasant kind of music, in scraping the snow from the pavement in front of their dwellings, and from the tops of their houses, whence it was mad delight to the boys to see it come plumping down into the road below, and splitting into artificial little snowstorms.

The house fronts looked black enough, and the windows blacker, contrasting with the smooth white sheet of snow upon the roofs, and with the dirtier snow upon the ground, which last deposit had been ploughed up in deep furrows by the heavy wheels of carts and wagons; furrows that crossed and recrossed each other hundreds of times where the great streets branched off, and made intricate channels, hard to trace, in the thick yellow mud and icy water. The sky was gloomy, and the shortest streets were choked up with a dingy mist, half thawed, half frozen, whose heavier particles descended in a shower of sooty atoms, as if all the chimneys in Great Britain had, by one consent, caught fire, and were blazing away to their dear heart's content. There was nothing very cheerful in the climate or the town, and yet was there an air of cheerfulness abroad that the dearest summer air and brightest summer sun might have endeavoured to diffuse in vain.

For the people who were shovelling away on the housetops were jovial and full of glee, calling out to one another from the parapets, and now and then exchanging a facetious snowball—better-natured missile far than many a wordy jest—laughing heartily if it went right, and not less heartily if it went wrong. The poulterers' shops were still half open, and the fruiterers' were radiant in their glory. There were great, round, potbellied baskets of chestnuts, shaped like the waistcoats of jolly old gentlemen, lolling at the doors, and tumbling out into the street in their apoplectic opulence.

There were ruddy, brown-faced, broad-girthed Spanish onions, shining in the fatness of their growth like Spanish friars, and winking, from their shelves, in wanton slyness at the girls as they went by, and glanced demurely at the hung-up mistletoe. There were pears and apples, clustering high in blooming pyramids; there were bunches of grapes, made, in the shop-keeper's benevolence, to dangle from conspicuous hooks, that people's mouths might water gratis as they passed; there were piles of filberts, mossy and brown, recalling, in their fragrance, ancient walks among the woods, and pleasant shufflings ankle deep through withered leaves; there were Norfolk biffins, squab and swarthy, setting off the yellow of the oranges and lemons, and, in the great compactness of their juicy persons, urgently entreating and beseeching to be carried home in paper bags and eaten after dinner.

The very gold and silver fish, set forth among these choice fruits in a bowl, though members of a dull and stagnant-blooded race, appeared to know that there was something going on; and, to a fish, went gasping round and round their little world in slow and passionless excitement.

The grocers'! oh, the grocers'! nearly closed, with perhaps two shutters down, or one; but through those gaps such glimpses! It was not alone that the scales descending on the counter made a merry sound, or that the twine and roller parted company so briskly, or that the canisters were rattled up and down like juggling tricks, or even that the blended scents of tea and coffee were so grateful to the nose, or even that the raisins were so plentiful and rare, the almonds so extremely white, the sticks of cinnamon so long and straight, the other spices so delicious, the candied fruits so caked and spotted with molten sugar as to make the coldest lookers-on feel faint, and subsequently bilious.

Nor was it that the figs were moist and pulpy, or that the French plums blushed in modest tartness from their highly decorated boxes, or that everything was good to eat and in its Christmas dress; but the customers were all so hurried and so eager in the hopeful promise of the day that they tumbled up against each other at the door, crashing their

wicker baskets wildly, and left their purchases upon the counter, and came running back
to fetch them, and committed hundreds of the like mistakes, in the best humour possible;
while the grocer and his people were so frank and fresh that the polished hearts with which
they fastened their aprons behind might have been their own, worn outside for general
inspection, and for Christmas daws to peck at, if they chose.

But soon the steeples called good people all to church and chapel, and away they
came, flocking through the streets in their best clothes, and with their gayest faces. And
at the same time there emerged from scores of by-streets, lanes, and nameless turnings,
innumerable people, carrying their dinners to the bakers' shops. The sight of these poor
revellers appeared to interest the Spirit very much, for he stood, with Scrooge beside him,
in a baker's doorway, and, taking off the covers as their bearers passed, sprinkled incense
on their dinners from his torch. And it was a very uncommon kind of torch, for once or
twice when there were angry words between some dinner-carriers who had jostled each
other, he shed a few drops of water on them from it, and their good-humour was restored
directly. For they said it was a shame to quarrel upon Christmas Day. And so it was! God
love it, so it was!

In time the bells ceased, and the bakers were shut up; and yet there was a genial
shadowing forth of all these dinners, and the progress of their cooking, in the thawed
blotch of wet above each baker's oven, where the pavement smoked as if its stones were
cooking too.

"Is there a peculiar flavour in what you sprinkle from your torch?" asked Scrooge.

"There is. My own."

"Would it apply to any kind of dinner on this day?" asked Scrooge.

"To any kindly given. To a poor one most."

"Why to a poor one most?" asked Scrooge.

"Because it needs it most."

They went on, invisible, as they had been before, into the suburbs of the town. It
was a remarkable quality of the Ghost (which Scrooge had observed at the baker's) that,
notwithstanding his gigantic size, he could accommodate himself to any place with ease;
and that he stood beneath a low roof quite as gracefully, and like a supernatural creature,
as it was possible he could have done in any lofty hall.

And perhaps it was the pleasure the good Spirit had in showing off this power of his,
or else it was his own kind, generous, hearty nature, and his sympathy with all poor men,
that led him straight to Scrooge's clerk's; for there he went, and took Scrooge with him,

holding to his robe; and on the threshold of the door the Spirit smiled, and stopped to bless Bob Cratchit's dwelling with the sprinklings of his torch. Think of that! Bob had but fifteen "bob" a week himself; he pocketed on Saturdays but fifteen copies of his Christian name; and yet the Ghost of Christmas Present blessed his four-roomed house!

Then up rose Mrs. Cratchit, Cratchit's wife, dressed out but poorly in a twice-turned gown, but brave in ribbons, which are cheap and make a goodly show for sixpence; and she laid the cloth, assisted by Belinda Cratchit, second of her daughters, also brave in ribbons; while Master Peter Cratchit plunged a fork into the saucepan of potatoes, and getting the corners of his monstrous shirt-collar (Bob's private property, conferred upon his son and heir in honour of the day) into his mouth, rejoiced to find himself so gallantly attired, and yearned to show his linen in the fashionable parks.

And now two smaller Cratchits, boy and girl, came tearing in, screaming that outside the baker's they had smelt the goose, and known it for their own, and, basking in luxurious thoughts of sage and onion, these young Cratchits danced about the table, and exalted Master Peter Cratchit to the skies, while he (not proud, although his collar nearly choked him) blew the fire, until the slow potatoes, bubbling up, knocked loudly at the saucepan lid to be let out and peeled.

"What has ever got your precious father, then?" said Mrs. Cratchit. "And your brother, Tiny Tim? And Martha warn't as late last Christmas Day by half an hour!"

"Here's Martha, mother!" said a girl, appearing as she spoke.

"Here's Martha, mother!" cried the two young Cratchits. "Hurrah! There's such a goose, Martha!"

"Why, bless your heart alive, my dear, how late you are!" said Mrs. Cratchit, kissing her a dozen times, and taking off her shawl and bonnet for her with officious zeal.

"We'd a deal of work to finish up last night," replied the girl, "and had to clear away this morning, mother!"

"Well, never mind so long as you are come," said Mrs. Cratchit. "Sit ye down before the fire, my dear, and have a warm, Lord bless ye!"

"No, no! There's father coming!" cried the two young Cratchits, who were everywhere at once. "Hide, Martha, hide!"

So Martha hid herself, and in came little Bob, the father, with at least three feet of comforter, exclusive of the fringe, hanging down before him, and his threadbare clothes darned up and brushed, to look seasonable; and Tiny Tim upon his shoulder. Alas for

Tiny Tim, he bore a little crutch, and had his limbs supported by an iron frame!

"Why, where's our Martha?" cried Bob Cratchit, looking around.

"Not coming," said Mrs. Cratchit.

"Not coming?" said Bob, with a sudden declension in his high spirits; for he had been Tim's blood horse all the way from the church, and had come home rampant. "Not coming upon Christmas Day?"

Martha didn't like to see him disappointed, if it were only in joke; so she came out prematurely from behind the closet door, and ran into his arms, while the two young Cratchits hustled Tiny Tim, and bore him off into the wash-house, that he might hear the pudding singing in the copper.

"And how did little Tim behave?" asked Mrs. Cratchit, when she had rallied Bob on his credulity, and Bob had hugged his daughter to his heart's content.

"As good as gold," said Bob, "and better. Somehow he gets thoughtful, sitting by himself so much, and thinks the strangest things you ever heard. He told me, coming home, that he hoped the people saw him in the church, because he was a cripple, and it might be pleasant to them to remember, upon Christmas Day, who made lame beggars walk, and blind men see."

Bob's voice was tremulous when he told them this, and trembled more when he said that Tiny Tim was growing strong and hearty.

His active little crutch was heard upon the floor, and back came Tiny Tim before another word was spoken, escorted by his brother and sister to his stool beside the fire; and while Bob, turning up his cuffs—as if, poor fellow, they were capable of being made more shabby—compounded some hot mixture in a jug with gin and lemons, and stirred it round and round, and put it on the hob to simmer, Master Peter and the two ubiquitous young Cratchits went to fetch the goose, with which they soon returned in high procession.

Such a bustle ensued that you might have thought a goose the rarest of all birds—a feathered phenomenon, to which a black swan was a matter of course—and in truth it was something very like it in that house. Mrs. Cratchit made the gravy (ready beforehand in a little saucepan) hissing hot; Master Peter mashed the potatoes with incredible vigour; Miss Belinda sweetened up the apple-sauce; Martha dusted the hot plates; Bob took Tiny Tim beside him in a tiny corner at the table; the two young Cratchits set chairs for everybody, not forgetting themselves, and, mounting guard upon their posts, crammed spoons into their mouths, lest they should shriek for goose before their turn came to be helped.

At last the dishes were set on and grace was said. It was succeeded by a breathless pause, as Mrs. Cratchit, looking slowly all along the carving knife, prepared to plunge it into the breast; but when she did, and when the long expected gush of stuffing issued forth, one murmur of delight arose all round the board, and even Tiny Tim, excited by the two young Cratchits, beat on the table with the handle of his knife, and feebly cried, "Hurrah!"

There never was such a goose. Bob said he didn't believe there ever was such a goose cooked. Its tenderness and flavour, size and cheapness, were the themes of universal admiration. Eked out by apple-sauce and mashed potatoes, it was a sufficient dinner for the whole family; indeed, as Mrs. Cratchit said with great delight (surveying one small atom of a bone upon the dish), they hadn't ate it all at last! Yet every one had had enough, and the youngest Cratchits in particular were steeped in sage and onion to the eyebrows! But now, the plates being changed by Miss Belinda, Mrs. Cratchit left the room alone—too nervous to bear witnesses—to take the pudding up, and bring it in.

Suppose it should not be done enough? Suppose it should break in turning out? Suppose somebody should have got over the wall of the backyard and stolen it, while they were merry with the goose—a supposition at which the two young Cratchits became livid! All sorts of horrors were supposed.

Hallo! A great deal of steam! The pudding was out of the copper. A smell like a washing-day! That was the cloth. A smell like an eating house and a pastry-cook's next door to each other, with a laundress's next door to that! That was the pudding! In half a minute Mrs. Cratchit entered—flushed, but smiling proudly—with the pudding, like a speckled cannon-ball, so hard and firm, blazing in half of half-a-quartern of ignited brandy, and bedight with Christmas holly stuck into the top.

Oh, a wonderful pudding! Bob Cratchit said, and calmly, too, that he regarded it as the greatest success achieved by Mrs. Cratchit since their marriage. Mrs. Cratchit said that, now the weight was off her mind, she would confess she had her doubts about the quantity of flour. Everybody had something to say about it, but nobody thought or said it was at all a small pudding for a large family. It would have been flat heresy to do so. Any Cratchit would have blushed to hint at such a thing.

At last the dinner was all done, the cloth was cleared, the hearth swept, and the fire made up. The compound in the jug being tasted, and considered perfect, tipples and oranges were put upon the table, and a shovelful of chestnuts on the fire. Then all the Cratchit family drew round the hearth in what Bob Cratchit called a circle, meaning half a one; and at Bob Cratchit's elbow stood the family display of glass—two tumblers and a custard-cup without a handle.

These held the hot stuff from the jug, however, as well as golden goblets would have done; and Bob served it out with beaming looks, while the chestnuts on the fire sputtered and cracked noisily. Then Bob proposed:

"A Merry Christmas to us all, my dears. God bless us!"

Which all the family reechoed.

"God bless us every one!" said Tiny Tim, the last of all.

The Three Kings

HENRY WADSWORTH LONGFELLOW

Henry Wadsworth Longfellow, 1807–1882

American poet

Longfellow was one of the best-loved American poets of the 19th century. His most famous poem is probably "Paul Revere's Ride."

The galloping, steady rhythm of this poem wonderfully emphasizes the journey of the three kings from the East to Bethlehem, here given horses rather than camels for their mounts. The fast-paced lines carry the reader along much like the steeds carrying the Wise Men in this imagined version of their quest.

The rhyme scheme-a-b-a-a-b in each verse also draws the reader along, as the ear waits through two lines of 'a' beats for the completion of the 'b' rhyme. When it comes, the satisfaction of it further mimics completed movement, progress, much like the journey in the poem.

The hurry of the riders is not paramount, however, as Longfellow, with full stanzas, stops to allow us to gaze at the star, and later, at the baby King and his mother.

THE THREE KINGS

Three Kings came riding from far away,
Melchior and Gaspar and Baltasar;
Three Wise Men out of the East were they,
And they travelled by night and they slept by day,
For their guide was a beautiful, wonderful star.

The star was so beautiful, large and clear,
That all the other stars of the sky
Became a white mist in the atmosphere,
And by this they knew that the coming was near
Of the Prince foretold in the prophecy.

Three caskets they bore on their saddle-bows,
Three caskets of gold with golden keys;
Their robes were of crimson silk with rows
Of bells and pomegranates and furbelows,
Their turbans like blossoming almond-trees.

And so the Three Kings rode into the West,
Through the dusk of the night, over hill and dell,
And sometimes they nodded with beard on breast,
And sometimes talked, as they paused to rest,
With the people they met at some wayside well.

"Of the child that is born," said Baltasar,
"Good people, I pray you, tell us the news;
For we in the East have seen his star,
And have ridden fast, and have ridden far,
To find and worship the King of the Jews."

And the people answered, "You ask in vain;
We know of no King but Herod the Great!"

They thought the Wise Men were men insane,
As they spurred their horses across the plain,
Like riders in haste, who cannot wait.

And when they came to Jerusalem,
Herod the Great, who had heard this thing,
Sent for the Wise Men and questioned them;
And said, "Go down unto Bethlehem,
And bring me tidings of this new king."

So they rode away; and the star stood still,
The only one in the grey of morn;
Yes, it stopped—it stood still of its own free will,
Right over Bethlehem on the hill,
The city of David, where Christ was born.

And the Three Kings rode through the gate and the guard,
Through the silent street, till their horses turned
And neighed as they entered the great inn-yard;
But the windows were closed, and the doors were barred,
And only a light in the stable burned.

And cradled there in the scented hay,
In the air made sweet by the breath of kine,
The little child in the manger lay,
The child, that would be king one day
Of a kingdom not human, but divine.

His mother Mary of Nazareth
Sat watching beside his place of rest,
Watching the even flow of his breath,
For the joy of life and the terror of death
Were mingled together in her breast.

They laid their offerings at his feet:
The gold was their tribute to a King,
The frankincense, with its odor sweet,
Was for the Priest, the Paraclete,
The myrrh for the body's burying.

And the mother wondered and bowed her head,
And sat as still as a statue of stone,
Her heart was troubled yet comforted,
Remembering what the Angel had said
Of an endless reign and of David's throne.

Then the Kings rode out of the city gate,
With a clatter of hoofs in proud array;
But they went not back to Herod the Great,
For they knew his malice and feared his hate,
And returned to their homes by another way.

In the Bleak Midwinter, and, A Christmas Carol

CHRISTINA ROSSETTI

Christina Rossetti, 1830–1894

English Victorian writer of romantic, devotional, and children's poems.

Rossetti was an important female Victorian poet for both the range and quality of her work, which included fantasy and religious poems. She was a High Church Anglican and rejected at least two suitors because they were not. The author of numerous books of poetry, her work is characterized by intensity of feeling, metrical excellence and lyrical beauty. You'll recognize her first poem, below, as a popular song at Christmas.

IN THE BLEAK MIDWINTER

In the bleak midwinter, frosty wind made moan,

Earth stood hard as iron, water like a stone;
Snow had fallen, snow on snow, snow on snow,
In the bleak midwinter, long ago.

Our God, Heaven cannot hold Him, nor earth sustain;
Heaven and earth shall flee away when He comes to reign.
In the bleak midwinter a stable place sufficed
The Lord God Almighty, Jesus Christ.

Enough for Him, whom cherubim, worship night and day,
Breastful of milk, and a mangerful of hay;
Enough for Him, whom angels fall before,
The ox and ass and camel which adore.

Angels and archangels may have gathered there,
Cherubim and seraphim thronged the air;
But His mother only, in her maiden bliss,
Worshipped the beloved with a kiss.

What can I give Him, poor as I am?
If I were a shepherd, I would bring a lamb;
If I were a Wise Man, I would do my part;
Yet what I can I give Him: give my heart.

A CHRISTMAS CAROL

Less well known than the former poem, this little carol is no less deserving of a spot in this collection. It has an unusual rhyme scheme, a-b-c-b-d-b.

The Shepherds had an Angel,

Wise Men had a star,
But what have I, a little child,
To guide me home from far,
Where glad stars sing together
And singing angels are?

Those Shepherds through the lonely night
Sat watching by their sheep,
Until they saw the heavenly host
Who neither tire nor sleep,
All singing "Glory, glory,"
In festival they keep.

The Wise Men left their country
To journey morn by morn,
With gold and frankincense and myrrh,
Because the Lord was born:
God sent a star to guide them
And sent a dream to warn.

My life is like their journey,
Their star is like God's book;
I must be like those good Wise Men
With heavenward heart and look:
But shall I give no gifts to God?
—What precious gifts they took!

The Unexpected Christmas

Grace Margaret Gallaher

Grace Margaret Gallaher

(ca. late 19th – 20th century)

American writer of short stories, many for children.

Gallaher's work often shows up in Christmas collections, and she wrote her own collection of college stories, but other information on her life and writing is vague.

While the theme of this story is unoriginal, the treatment is sweet for readers of American historical fiction.

THE UNEXPECTED CHRISTMAS

Betty stood at her door, gazing drearily down the long, empty corridor in which the breakfast gong echoed mournfully. All the usual brisk scenes of that hour, groups of girls in Peter Thomson suits or starched shirt-waists, or a pair of energetic ones, red-cheeked and shining-eyed from a run in the snow, had vanished as by the hand of some evil magician. Silent and lonely was the corridor.

"And it's the day before Christmas!" groaned Betty. Two chill little tears hung on her eyelashes.

The night before, in the excitement of getting the girls off with all their trunks and packages intact, she had not realized the homesickness of the deserted school. Now it seemed to pierce her very bones.

"Oh, dear, why did father have to lose his money? 'Twas easy enough last September to decide I wouldn't take the expensive journey home these holidays, and for all of us to promise we wouldn't give each other as much as a Christmas card. But now!" The two chill tears slipped over the edge of her eyelashes. "Well, I know how I'll spend this whole day; I'll come right up here after breakfast and cry and cry and cry!" Somewhat fortified by this cheering resolve, Betty went to breakfast.

Whatever the material joys of that meal might be, it certainly was not "a feast of reason and a flow of soul." Betty, whose sense of humour never perished, even in such a frost, looked round the table at the eight grim-faced girls doomed to a Christmas in school, and quoted mischievously to herself: "On with the dance, let joy be unconfined."

Breakfast bolted, she lagged back to her room, stopping to stare out of the corridor windows.

She saw nothing of the snowy landscape, however. Instead, a picture, the gayest medley of many colours and figures, danced before her eyes: Christmas-trees thumping in through the door, mysterious bundles scurried into dark corners, little brothers and sisters flying about with festoons of mistletoe, scarlet ribbon and holly, everywhere sound and laughter and excitement. The motto of Betty's family was: "Never do to-day what you can put off till to-morrow"; therefore the preparations of a fortnight were always crowded into a day.

The year before, Betty had rushed till her nerves were taut and her temper snapped, had shaken the twins, raged at the housemaid, and had gone to bed at midnight weeping with weariness. But in memory only the joy of the day remained.

"I think I could endure this jail of a school, and not getting one single present, but it breaks my heart not to give one least little thing to any one! Why, who ever heard of such a Christmas!"

"Won't you hunt for that blue—"

"Broken my thread again!"

"Give me those scissors!"

Betty jumped out of her day-dream. She had wandered into "Cork" and the three O'Neills surrounded her, staring.

"I beg your pardon—I heard you—and it was so like home the day before Christmas—"

"Did you hear the heathen rage?" cried Katherine.

"Dolls for Aunt Anne's mission," explained Constance.

"You're so forehanded that all your presents went a week ago, I suppose," Eleanor swept clear a chair. "The clan O'Neill is never forehanded."

"You'd think I was from the number of thumbs I've grown this morning. Oh, misery!" Eleanor jerked a snarl of thread out on the floor.

Betty had never cared for "Cork" but now the hot worried faces of its girls appealed to her. "Let me help. I'm a regular silkworm."

The O'Neills assented with eagerness, and Betty began to sew in a capable, swift way that made the others stare and sigh with relief.

The dolls were many, the O'Neills slow. Betty worked till her feet twitched on the floor; yet she enjoyed the morning, for it held an entirely new sensation, that of helping some one else get ready for Christmas.

"Done!"

"We never should have finished if you hadn't helped! Thank you, Betty Luther, very, VERY much! You're a duck! Let's run to luncheon together, quick."

Somehow the big corridors did not seem half so bleak echoing to those warm O'Neill voices.

"This morning's just spun by, but, oh, this long, dreary afternoon!" sighed Betty, as she wandered into the library. "Oh, me, there goes Alice Johns with her arms loaded with presents to mail, and I can't give a single soul anything!"

"Do you know where 'Quotations for Occasions' has gone?" Betty turned to face pretty Rosamond Howitt, the only senior left behind.

"Gone to be rebound. I heard Miss Dyce say so."

"Oh, dear, I needed it so."

"Could I help? I know a lot of rhymes and tags of proverbs and things like that."

"Oh, if you would help me, I'd be so grateful! Won't you come to my room? You see, I promised a friend in town, who is to have a Christmas dinner, and who's been very kind to me, that I'd paint the place cards and write some quotation appropriate to each guest.

I'm shamefully late over it, my own gifts took such a time; but the painting, at least, is done."

Rosamond led the way to her room, and there displayed the cards which she had painted.

"You can't think of my helplessness! If it were a Greek verb now, or a lost and strayed angle—but poetry!"

Betty trotted back and forth between the room and the library, delved into books, and even evolved a verse which she audaciously tagged "old play," in imitation of Sir Walter Scott.

"I think they are really and truly very bright, and I know Mrs. Fernell will be delighted." Rosamond wrapped up the cards carefully. "I can't begin to tell you how you've helped me. It was sweet in you to give me your whole afternoon."

The dinner-bell rang at that moment, and the two went down together.

"Come for a little run; I haven't been out all day," whispered Rosamond, slipping her hand into Betty's as they left the table.

A great round moon swung cold and bright over the pines by the lodge.

"Down the road a bit—just a little way—to the church," suggested Betty.

They stepped out into the silent country road.

"Why, the little mission is as gay as—as Christmas! I wonder why?"

Betty glanced at the bright windows of the small plain church. "Oh, some Christmas-eve doings," she answered.

Some one stepped quickly out from the church door.

"Oh, Miss Vernon, I am relieved! I had begun to fear you could not come."

The girls saw it was the tall old rector, his white hair shining silver bright in the moonbeams.

"We're just two girls from the school, sir," said Rosamond.

"Dear, dear!" His voice was both impatient and distressed. "I hoped you were my organist. We are all ready for our Christmas-eve service, but we can do nothing without the music."

"I can play the organ a little," said Betty. "I'd be glad to help."

"You can? My dear child, how fortunate! But—do you know the service?"

"Yes, sir, it's my church."

No vested choir stood ready to march triumphantly chanting into the choir stalls. Only a few boys and girls waited in the dim old choir loft, where Rosamond seated herself quietly.

Betty's fingers trembled so at first that the music sounded dull and far away; but her courage crept back to her in the silence of the church, and the organ seemed to help her with a brave power of its own. In the dark church only the altar and a great gold star above it shone bright. Through an open window somewhere behind her she could hear the winter wind rattling the ivy leaves and bending the trees. Yet, somehow, she did not feel lonesome and forsaken this Christmas eve, far away from home, but safe and comforted and sheltered. The voice of the old rector reached her faintly in pauses; habit led her along the service, and the star at the altar held her eyes.

Strange new ideas and emotions flowed in upon her brain. Tears stole softly into her eyes, yet she felt in her heart a sweet glow. Slowly the Christmas picture that had flamed and danced before her all day, painted in the glory of holly and mistletoe and tinsel, faded out, and another shaped itself, solemn and beautiful in the altar light.

"My dear child, I thank you very much!" The old rector held Betty's hand in both his. "I cannot have a Christmas morning service—our people have too much to do to come then—but I was especially anxious that our evening service should have some message, some inspiration for them, and your music has made it so. You have given me great aid. May your Christmas be a blessed one."

"I was glad to play, sir. Thank you!" answered Betty, simply.

"Let's run!" she cried to Rosamond, and they raced back to school.

She fell asleep that night without one smallest tear.

The next morning Betty dressed hastily, and catching up her mandolin, set out into the corridor.

Something swung against her hand as she opened the door. It was a great bunch of holly, glossy green leaves and glowing berries, and hidden in the leaves a card: "Betty, Merry Christmas," was all, but only one girl wrote that dainty hand.

"A winter rose," whispered Betty, happily, and stuck the bunch into the ribbon of her mandolin.

Down the corridor she ran until she faced a closed door. Then, twanging her mandolin, she burst out with all her power into a gay Christmas carol. High and sweet sang her voice in the silent corridor all through the gay carol. Then, sweeter still, it changed into a Christmas hymn. Then from behind the closed doors sounded voices:

"Merry Christmas, Betty Luther!"

Then Constance O'Neill's deep, smooth alto flowed into Betty's soprano; and at the last all nine girls joined in "Adeste Fideles." Christmas morning began with music and laughter.

"This is your place, Betty. You are lord of Christmas morning."

Betty stood, blushing, red as the holly in her hand, before the breakfast table. Miss Hyle, the teacher at the head of the table, had given up her place.

The breakfast was a merry one. After it somebody suggested that they all go skating on the pond.

Betty hesitated and glanced at Miss Hyle and Miss Thrasher, the two sad-looking teachers.

She approached them and said, "Won't you come skating, too?"

Miss Thrasher, hardly older than Betty herself, and pretty in a white frightened way, refused, but almost cheerfully. "I have a Christmas box to open and Christmas letters to write. Thank you very much."

Betty's heart sank as she saw Miss Hyle's face. "Goodness, she's coming!"

Miss Hyle was the most unpopular teacher in school. Neither ill-tempered nor harsh, she was so cold, remote and rigid in face, voice, and manner that the warmest blooded shivered away from her, the least sensitive shrank.

"I have no skates, but I should like to borrow a pair to learn, if I may. I have never tried," she said.

The tragedies of a beginner on skates are to the observers, especially if such be school-girls, subjects for unalloyed mirth. The nine girls choked and turned their backs and even giggled aloud as Miss Hyle went prone, now backward with a whack, now forward in a limp crumple.

But amusement became admiration. Miss Hyle stumbled, fell, laughed merrily, scrambled up, struck out, and skated. Presently she was swinging up the pond in stroke with Betty and Eleanor O'Neill.

"Miss Hyle, you're great!" cried Betty, at the end of the morning. "I've taught dozens and scores to skate, but never anybody like you. You've a genius for skating."

Miss Hyle's blue eyes shot a sudden flash at Betty that made her whole severe face light up. "I've never had a chance to learn—at home there never is any ice—but I have always been athletic."

"Where is your home, Miss Hyle?" asked Betty.

"Cawnpore, India."

"India?" gasped Eleanor. "How delightful! Oh, won't you tell us about it, Miss Hyle?"

So it was that Miss Hyle found herself talking about something besides triangles to girls who really wanted to hear, and so it was that the flash came often into her eyes.

"I have had a happy morning, thank you, Betty—and all." She said it very simply, yet a quick throb of pity and liking beat in Betty's heart.

"How stupid we are about judging people!" she thought. Yet Betty had always prided herself on her character-reading.

"Hurrah, the mail and express are in!" The girls ran excitedly to their rooms.

Betty alone went to hers without interest. "Why, Hilma, what's happened?"

The little round-faced Swedish maid mopped the big tears with her duster, and choked out:

"Nothings, ma'am!"

"Of course there is! You're crying like everything."

Hilma wept aloud. "Christmas Day it is, and mine family and mine friends have party, now, all day."

"Where?"

Hilma jerked her head toward the window.

"Oh, you mean in town? Why can't you go?"

"I work. And never before am I from home Christmas day."

Betty shivered. "Never before am *I* from home Christmas day," she whispered.

She went close to the girl, very tall and slim and bright beside the dumpy, flaxen Hilma.

"What work do you do?"

"The cook, he cooks the dinner and the supper; I put it on and wait it on the young ladies and wash the dishes. The others all are gone."

Betty laughed suddenly. "Hilma, go put on your best clothes, quick, and go down to your party. I'm going to do your work."

Hilma's eyes rounded with amazement. "The cook, he be mad."

"No, he won't. He won't care whether it's Hilma or Betty, if things get done all right. I know how to wait on table and wash dishes. There's no housekeeper here to object. Run along, Hilma; be back by nine o'clock—and—Merry Christmas!"

Hilma's face beamed through her tears. She was speechless with joy, but she seized Betty's slim brown hand and kissed it loudly.

"What larks!"

"Is it a joke?"

"Betty, you're the handsomest butler!"

Betty, in a white shirt-waist suit, a jolly red bow pinned on her white apron, and a little cap cocked on her dark hair, waved them to their seats at the holly-decked table.

"Merry Christmas! Merry Christmas!"

"Nobody is ill, Betty?" Rosamond asked, anxiously.

"If I had three guesses, I should use every one that our maid wanted to go into town for the day, and Betty took her place." It was Miss Hyle's calm voice.

Betty blushed. It was her turn now to flash back a glance; and those two sparks kindled the fire of friendship.

It was a jolly Christmas dinner, with the "butler" eating with the family.

"And now the dishes!" thought Betty. It must be admitted the "washing up" after a Christmas dinner of twelve is not a subject for much joy.

"I propose we all help Betty wash the dishes!" cried Rosamond Howitt.

Out in the kitchen everyone laughed and talked and got in the way, and had a good time; and if the milk pitcher was knocked on the floor and the pudding bowl emptied in Betty's lap—why, it was all "Merry Christmas."

After that they all skated again. When they came in, little Miss Thrasher, looking almost gay in a rose-red gown, met them in the corridor.

"I thought it would be fun," she said, shyly, "to have supper in my room. I have a big box from home. I couldn't possibly eat all the things myself, and if you'll bring chafing-dishes and spoons, and those things, I'll cook it, and we can sit round my open fire."

Miss Thrasher's room was homelike, with its fire of white-birch and its easy chairs, and Miss Thrasher herself proved to be a pleasant hostess.

After supper Miss Hyle told a tale of India, Miss Thrasher gave a Rocky Mountain adventure, and the girls contributed ghost and burglar stories till each guest was in a thrill of delightful horror.

"We've had really a fine day!"

"I expected to die of homesickness, but it's been jolly!"

"So did I, but I have actually been happy."

Thus the girls commented as they started for bed.

"I have enjoyed my day," said little Miss Thrasher, "very much."

"Yes, indeed, it's been a merry Christmas." Miss Hyle spoke almost eagerly.

Betty gave a little jump; she realized each one of them was holding her hand and pressing it a little. "Thank you, it's been a lovely evening. Goodnight."

Rosamond had invited Betty to share her roommate's bed, but both girls were too tired and sleepy for any confidence.

"It's been the queerest Christmas!" thought Betty, as she drifted toward sleep. "Why, I haven't given one single soul one single present!"

Yet she smiled, drowsily happy, and then the room seemed to fill with a bright, warm light, and round the bed there danced a great Christmas wreath, made up of the faces of the three O'Neills, and the thin old rector, with his white hair, and pretty Rosamond, and frightened Miss Thrasher and the homesick girls, and lonely Miss Hyle, and tear-dimmed Hilma.

And all the faces smiled and nodded, and called, "Merry Christmas, Betty, Merry Christmas!"

Not to Jerusalem's Palm-Welcomed King...

EDNAH PROCTOR CLARKE

Ednah Proctor Clarke, born 1870's

Poet

Not much could be unearthed about Miss Clarke other than that she was born in NYC and then spent much of her youth in Washington, D. C. She appears to have begun publishing poetry in the 1890's, got married in 1899 and moved to Hawaii. You may find some of her works online with her married name, Ednah Proctor Clarke Hayes.

NOT TO JERUSALEM'S PALM-WELCOMED KING

Not to Jerusalem's palm-welcomed King,
Not to the Man reviled on Calvary's height,
Not to the risen God, my heart doth lift
In wondering awe to-night:

But to the Baby, shut from Bethlehem's Inn,

About whose feet the wise, dumb creatures pressed,—
The downy head, the little nestling hands,
On Mary's breast.

There were so many ways Thou could have come,—
Lord of incarnate life and form Thou art,—
That Thou shouldst (sic) choose to be a helpless Babe,
Held to a woman's heart,

Doth seem Thy tenderest miracle of love;
For this, more wondrous than Love sacrificed,
All women, till the utmost stars grow dim
Must love Thee, Christ!

The Burning Babe

ROBERT SOUTHWELL

Robert Southwell, 1561–1595

British Jesuit Priest, contemporary of Shakespeare, and eventually a Catholic martyr.

Southwell's work is thought to have had an influence on his much more famous contemporary, Shakespeare.

His poetry is noted for clarity of expression, precision, and rhythmic beauty. Another feature is passion as in depth of emotion. This short but powerful poem, probably meant to serve as a lesson or reminder, is an apt display of all of the above.

THE BURNING BABE

As I in hoary winter's night stood shivering in the snow,
    Surpris'd I was with sudden heat which made my heart to glow;
    And lifting up a fearful eye to view what fire was near,
    A pretty Babe all burning bright did in the air appear;
    Who, scorched with excessive heat, such floods of tears did shed
    As though his floods should quench his flames which with his tears were fed.

"Alas!" quoth he, "but newly born, in fiery heats I fry,
Yet none approach to warm their hearts or feel my fire but I!
My faultless breast the furnace is, the fuel wounding thorns,
Love is the fire, and sighs the smoke, the ashes shame and scorns;
The fuel Justice layeth on, and Mercy blows the coals,
The metal in this furnace wrought are men's defiled souls,
For which, as now on fire I am to work them to their good,
So will I melt into a bath to wash them in my blood."
With this he vanish'd out of sight and swiftly shrunk away,
And straight I called unto mind that it was Christmas day.

Going Further: "The Burning Babe"

1. Do you think this vision really happened or did the poet invent it? Tell why you think which it was. (If he invented it, what was his possible motive?)

2.   Much of the imagery in this poem is unpleasant, but how does the last line put it into perspective and affect the reading of the poem?

3.   Despite the unsavory image of a "burning babe," what message of hope does the poem convey?

The Set of Poe

GEORGE ADE

George Ade, 1866 – 1944

American writer, newspaper columnist, humorist, and playwright

---

Written in 1903, this selection is an example of when the best in a man is not brought out by Christmas alone, but at least we get to see him eat humble pie. My middle daughter's opinion of the story was "really cute!" and I think, in the end, you will agree. Fans of Edgar Allan Poe may especially sympathize with Mr. Waterby.

THE SET OF POE

Waterby remarked to his wife: "I'm still tempted by that set of Poe. I saw it in the window today, marked down to fifteen dollars."

"Yes?" said Mrs. Waterby, with a sudden gasp of emotion, it seemed to him.

"Yes--I believe I'll have to get it."

"I wouldn't if I were you, Alfred." she said. "You have so many books now."

"I know I have, my dear, but I haven't any set of Poe; and that's what I've been wanting for a long time. This edition I was telling you about is beautifully gotten up."

"Oh, I wouldn't buy it, Alfred," she repeated, and there was a note of pleading earnestness in her voice. "It's so much money to spend for a few books."

"Well, I know, but--" and then he paused for the lack of words to express his mortified surprise.

Mr. Waterby had tried to be an indulgent husband. He took a selfish pleasure in giving, and found it more blessed than receiving. Every salary day he turned over to Mrs. Waterby a fixed sum for household expenses. He added to this an allowance for her spending money. He set aside a small amount for his personal expenses and deposited the remainder in the bank. He flattered himself that he approximated the model husband.

Mr. Waterby had no costly habits and no prevailing appetite for anything expensive. Like every other man, he had one or two hobbies, and one of his particular hobbies was Edgar Allan Poe. He believed that Poe, of all American writers, was the one unmistakable "genius."

The word "genius" has been bandied around the country until it has come to be applied to a long-haired man out of work or a stout lady who writes poetry. In the case of Poe, Mr. Waterby maintained that "genius" meant one who was not governed by the common mental processes, but "who spoke from inspiration, his mind involuntarily taking superhuman flight into the realm of pure imagination"--or something of that sort. At any rate, Mr. Waterby liked Poe, and he wanted a set of Poe. He allowed himself not more than one luxury a year and he determined that this year the luxury should be a set of Poe.

Therefore, imagine the hurt to his feelings when his wife objected to his expending fifteen dollars for that which he coveted above anything else in the world.

As he went to work that day he reflected on Mrs. Waterby's conduct. Did she not have her allowance of spending money? Did he ever find fault with her extravagance? Was he an unreasonable husband in asking that he be allowed to spend this small sum for that which would give him many hours of pleasure and which would belong to Mrs. Waterby as much to him?

He told himself that many a husband would have bought the books without consulting his wife. But he (Waterby) had deferred to his wife in all matters touching family finances, and he said to himself, with a tincture of bitterness in his thoughts, that probably he had put himself into the attitude of a mere dependent.

For had she not forbidden him to buy a few books for himself? Well, no, she had not forbidden him, but it amounted to the same thing. She had declared that she was firmly opposed to the purchase of Poe. Mr. Waterby wondered if it were possible that he was just beginning to know his wife. Was she a selfish woman at heart? Was she complacent and good-natured only while she was having her own way? Wouldn't she prove to be an entirely different sort of woman if he should do as many husbands do—spend his income on clubs and cigars and private amusements; and give her the pickings of small change?

Nothing in Mr. Waterby's experience as a married man had so wrenched his sensibilities and disturbed his faith as Mrs. Waterby's objection to the purchase of a set of Poe. There was but one way to account for it. She wanted all the money for herself or else she wanted him to put it into the bank so that she could come into it after he--but this was too monstrous.

However, Mrs. Waterby's conduct helped to give strength to Mr. Waterby's meanest suspicions. Two or three days after the first conversation she asked: "You didn't buy that set of Poe, did you Alfred?"

"No, I didn't buy it," he answered as coldly and with as much hauteur as possible.

He hoped to hear her say: "Well, why don't you go and get it? I'm sure that you want it, and I'd like to see you buy something for yourself once in awhile."

That would have shown the spirit of a loving and unselfish wife.

But she merely said: "That's right; don't buy it," and he was utterly unhappy, for he realized that he had married a woman who did not love him and who simply desired to use him as a pack horse for all household burdens.

As soon as Mr. Waterby had learned the horrible truth about his wife he began to recall little episodes dating back years, and now he pieced them together to convince himself that he was a deeply wronged person.

Small at the time and almost unnoticed, they were now accumulating to prove that Mrs. Waterby had no real anxiety for her husband's happiness. Also, Mr. Waterby began to observe her closely, and he believed that he found new evidences of her unworthiness. For one thing, while he was in gloom over his discovery and harassed by doubts of what the future might reveal to him, she was content and even-tempered.

The holiday season approached and Mr. Waterby had made a resolution. He decided that if she would not permit him to spend a little money on himself he would not buy the customary Christmas present for her.

"Selfishness is a game at which two can play," he said.

Furthermore, he determined that if she asked him for any extra money for Christmas he would say: "I'm sorry, my dear, but I can't spare any. I am so hard up that I can't even afford to buy a few books that I've been wanting along time. Don't you remember that you told me that I couldn't afford to buy that set of Poe?"

Could anything be more biting as to sarcasm or more crushing as to logic?

He rehearsed this speech and had it all ready for her, as he pictured to himself her humiliation and surprise at discovering that he had some spirit after all and a considerable say-so whenever money was involved.

Unfortunately for his plan, she did not ask for any extra spending money and so he had to rely on the other mode of punishment. He would withhold the expected Christmas present. In order that she might fully understand his purpose, he would give presents to both of the children.

It was a harsh measure, he admitted, but perhaps it would teach her to have some consideration for the wishes of others.

It must be said that Mr. Waterby was not wholly proud of his revenge when he arose on Christmas morning. He felt that he had accomplished his purpose and he told himself that his motives had been good and pure, but still he was not satisfied with himself.

He went to the dining room and there on the table in front of his plate was a long paper box containing ten books each marked "Poe." It was the edition he had coveted.

"What's this?" he asked, winking slowly, for his mind could not grasp in one moment the fact of his awful shame.

"I should think you ought to know, Alfred," said Mrs. Waterby, flushed and giggling like a school girl.

"Oh, it was you—"

"My goodness, you've had me so frightened. That day when you spoke of buying them and I told you not to, I was just sure that you suspected something. I bought them a week before that."

"Yes--yes," said Mr. Waterby, feeling the salt water in his eyes. At that moment he had the soul of a wretch being whipped at the stake.

"I was determined not to ask you for any money to pay for your own presents," Mrs. Waterby continued. "Do you know I had to save for you and the children out of my regular allowance. Why, last week I nearly starved you and you never noticed it as I was afraid you would."

"No, I didn't notice it," said Mr. Waterby brokenly, for he was confused and giddy. This self-sacrificing angel--and he had bought no Christmas present for her! It was a fearful situation, and he lied his way out of it.

"How did you like your present?" he asked.

"Why, I haven't seen it yet," she responded, looking across at him in surprise.

"You haven't? I told them to send it up yesterday."

The children were shouting and laughing over their gifts in the next room and he felt it his duty to lie for their sake.

"Well, don't tell me what it is," interrupted Mrs. Waterby. "Wait until it comes."

"I'll go after it."

He did go after it, although he had to drag a jeweler away from his home on Christmas Day and have him open his great safe. The ring which he selected was beyond his means, it is true, but when a man has to buy back his self-respect the price is never too high.

Ye Simple Men of Heart Sincere

CHARLES WESLEY

Charles Wesley, 1707 – 1788

English leader of the Methodist movement, poet and hymn writer.

Wesley was astoundingly prolific and wrote over 6500 hymns, putting the gospel into music form, an effective means of evangelism. George Fridric Handel wrote music for some of them. Among Wesley's best known are "Hark, the Herald Angels Sing, 'and "Christ the Lord is Ris'n Today." Below are two lesser known but beautiful hymns.

YE SIMPLE MEN OF HEART SINCERE

Ye simple men of heart sincere,
Shepherds who watch your flocks by night,
Start not to see an angel near,
Nor tremble at this glorious light.

An herald from the heavenly King,

I come your every fear to chase:
Good tidings of great joy I bring,
Great joy to all the fallen race!

To you is born on this glad day
A Saviour, by our host adored;
Our God in *Bethlehem* survey,
Make haste to worship Christ the Lord.

By this the Saviour of mankind,
The incarnate God, shall be display'd,
The Babe ye wrapp'd in swathes shall find
And humbly in a manger laid.

O MERCY DIVINE

O Mercy Divine,
How couldst Thou incline,
My God, to become such an infant as *mine?*

What a wonder of grace,
The Ancient of Days
Is found in the likeness of *Adam's* frail race!

He comes from on high,
Who fashion'd the sky,
And meekly vouchsafes in a manger to lie.

Our God, ever blest,
With oxen doth rest,

Is nursed by His creature, and hangs at the breast.

So heavenly mild

His innocence smiled,

No wonder the mother should worship the Child.

The angels she knew

Had worshipp'd Him too,

And still they confess adoration His due.

On Jesus's face

With eager amaze,

And pleasures ecstatic, the cherubim gaze.

Their newly born King

Transported they sing,

And heaven and earth with the triumph doth ring.

The shepherds behold

Him promised of old

By angels attended, by prophets foretold.

The wise men adore,

And bring Him their store,

The rich are permitted to follow the poor.

To the inn they repair,

To see the young Heir;

The inn is a palace, for Jesus is there.

Who now would be great,

And not rather wait

On Jesus, their Lord, in His humble estate?

Like Him would I be,
My Master I see
In a stable; a stable shall satisfy me.

With Him I reside;
The manger shall hide
Mine honour, the manger shall bury my pride.

And here will I lie,
Till raised up on high,
With Him on the cross, I recover the sky.

The Tale of the Little Mummers

JULIANA HORIATIA EWING

JULIANA HORATIA EWING, 1841 – 1885

English writer of children's stories, artist, and editor

Ewing only lived 44 years but left a beautiful legacy of poems and stories, most highly reflective of a deep Christian faith. Her works were called the "first outstanding child-novels," [1] probably for their realism, but also because adults enjoyed them too. She was much admired by later writers including Rudyard Kipling.

This story was originally titled "The Peace Egg, Or, The Tale of the Little Mummers."

THE TALE OF THE LITTLE MUMMERS

Every one ought to be happy at Christmas. But there are many things which ought to be, and yet are not; and people are sometimes sad even in the Christmas holidays.

The Captain and his wife were sad, though it was Christmas Eve. Sad, though they were in the prime of life, blessed with good health, devoted to each other and to their children, with competent means, a comfortable house on a little freehold property of their own, and, one might say, everything that heart could desire. Sad, though they were good people, whose peace of mind had a firmer foundation than their earthly goods alone; contented people, too, with plenty of occupation for mind and body. Sad—and in the nursery this was held to be past all reason—though the children were performing that ancient and most entertaining play or Christmas mystery, known as "The Peace Egg," for their benefit and behoof alone.

The play was none the worse that most of the actors were too young to learn parts, so that there was very little of the rather tedious dialogue, only plenty of dress and ribbons, and of fighting with the wooden swords. But though Robert, the eldest of the five children, looked bonny enough to warm any father's heart, as he marched up and down with an air learned by watching many a parade in barrack-square and drill ground, and though Nicholas did not cry in spite of falling hard, and Dora, who took the part of the Doctor, treading accidentally on his little finger in picking him up, still the Captain and his wife sighed nearly as often as they smiled, and the mother dropped tears as well as pennies into the cap which Tom, as the King of Egypt, brought round after the performance.

II.

Many, many years back the Captain's wife had been a child herself, and had laughed to see the village mummers act "The Peace Egg," and had been quite happy on Christmas Eve. Happy, though she had no mother. Happy, though her father was a stern man, very fond of his only child, but with an obstinate will that not even she dared thwart. She had lived to thwart it, and he had never forgiven her. It was when she married the Captain. The old man had a prejudice against soldiers, which was quite reason enough, in his opinion, for his daughter to sacrifice the happiness of her future life by giving up the soldier she loved. At last he gave her her choice between the Captain and his own favor and money. She chose the Captain, and was disowned and disinherited.

The Captain bore a high character, and was a good and clever officer, but that went for nothing against the old man's whim. He made a very good husband too; but even this did not move his father-in-law, who had never held any intercourse with him or his wife since the day of their marriage, and who had never seen his own grand-children.

Amid the ups and downs of their wanderings, the discomforts of shipboard and of stations in the colonies, bad servants, and unwonted sicknesses, the Captain's tenderness never failed. If the life was rough the Captain was ready. He had been, by turns, in one strait or another, sick-nurse, doctor, carpenter, nursemaid and cook to his family, and had, moreover, an idea that nobody filled these offices quite so well as himself. Withal, his very profession kept him neat, well-dressed, and active. In the roughest of their ever-changing quarters he was a smart man, and never changed his manner from that of the lover of his wife's young days.

As years went and children came, the Captain and his wife grew tired of traveling. New scenes were small comfort when they heard of the death of old friends. One foot of the dear, old, dull home sky was dearer, after all, than miles of the unclouded heavens of the South. The grey hills and over-grown lanes of her old home haunted the Captain's wife by night and day, and home-sickness (that weariest of all sicknesses) began to take the light out of her eyes before their time.

It preyed upon the Captain too. Now and then he would say, fretfully, "I *should* like a resting-place in our own country, however small, before *every*body is dead! But the children's prospects have to be considered." The continued estrangement from the old man was an abiding sorrow also, and they had hopes that, if only they could get home, he might be persuaded to peace and charity this time.

At last they were sent home. But the hard old father still would not relent. He returned their letters unopened. This bitter disappointment made the Captain's wife so ill that she almost died, and in one month the Captain's hair became iron gray. He reproached himself for having ever taken the daughter from her father, "to kill her at last," as he said. And (thinking of his own children) he even reproached himself for having robbed the old widower of his only child.

After two years at home his regiment was ordered again on foreign duty. He failed to effect an exchange, and they prepared to move once more—from Chatham to Calcutta. Never before had the packing to which she was so well accustomed, been so bitter a task to the Captain's wife.

It was at the darkest hour of this gloomy time that the Captain came in, waving above his head a letter which changed all their plans.

Now close by the old home of the Captain's wife there had lived a man, much older than herself, who yet had loved her with a devotion as great as that of the young Captain. She never knew it, for when he saw that she had given her heart to his younger rival, he kept silence, and he never asked for what he knew he might have had—the old man's authority in his favor. So generous was the affection which he could never conquer, that he constantly tried to reconcile the father to his children whilst he lived, and, when he died, he bequeathed his house and small estate to the woman he had loved.

"It will be a legacy of peace," he thought, on his death bed. "The old man cannot hold out when she and her children are constantly in sight. And it may please God that I shall know of the reunion I have not been permitted to see with my eyes."

And thus it came about that the Captain's regiment went to India without him, and that the Captain's wife and her father lived on opposite sides of the same road.

III.

The eldest of the Captain's children was a boy. He was named Robert, after his grandfather, and seemed to have inherited a good deal of the old gentleman's character, mixed with gentler traits. He was a fair, fine boy, tall and stout for his age, with the Captain's regular features, and (he flattered himself) the Captain's firm step and martial bearing. He was apt—like his grandfather—to hold his own will to be other people's law, and (happily for the peace of the nursery) this opinion was devoutly shared by his brother Nicholas.

Though the Captain had left the army, Robin continued to command an irregular force of volunteers in the nursery, and never was colonel more despotic. His brothers and sisters were by turn infantry, cavalry, engineers, and artillery, according to his whim.

The Captain alone was a match for his strong-willed son.

"If you please, sir," said Sarah, one morning, flouncing in upon the Captain, just as he was about to start for the neighboring town,—"If you please, sir, I wish you'd speak to Master Robert. He's past my powers."

"I've no doubt of it," thought the Captain, but he only said, "Well, what's the matter?"

"Night after night do I put him to bed," said Sarah, "and night after night does he get up as soon as I'm out of the room, and says he's orderly officer for the evening, and goes about in his night-shirt and his feet as bare as boards."

The Captain fingered his heavy moustache to hide a smile, but he listened patiently to Sarah's complaints.

"It ain't so much *him* I should mind, sir," she continued, "but he goes round the beds and wakes up the other young gentlemen and Miss Dora, one after another, and when I speak to him, he gives me all the sauce he can lay his tongue to, and says he's going round the guards. The other night I tried to put him back in his bed, but he got away and ran all over the house, me hunting him everywhere, and not a sign of him, till he jumps out on me from the garret stairs and nearly knocks me down. 'I've visited the outposts, Sarah,' says he; 'all's well.' And off he goes to bed as bold as brass."

"Have you spoken to your mistress?" asked the Captain.

"Yes, sir," said Sarah. "And missis spoke to him, and he promised not to go round the guards again."

"Has he broken his promise?" asked the Captain, with a look of anger, and also of surprise.

"When I opened the door last night, sir," continued Sarah, in her shrill treble, "what should I see in the dark but Master Robert a-walking up and down with the carpet-brush stuck in his arm. 'Who goes there?' says he. 'You awdacious boy!' says I, 'Didn't you promise your ma you'd leave off them tricks?' 'I'm not going round the guards,' says he; 'I promised not. But I'm for sentry-duty to-night.' And say what I would to him, all he had for me was, 'You mustn't speak to a sentry on duty.' So I says, 'As sure as I live till morning, I'll go to your pa,' for he pays no more attention to his ma than to me, nor to any one else."

"Please to see that the bed is taken out of my dressing-room," said the Captain. "I will attend to Master Robert."

With this Sarah had to content herself, and she went back to the nursery. Robert was nowhere to be seen, and made no reply to her summons. On this the unwary nursemaid flounced into the bed-room to look for him, when Robert, who was hidden beneath a table, darted forth, and promptly locked her in.

"You're under arrest," he shouted, through the keyhole.

"Let me out!" shrieked Sarah.

"I'll send a file of the guard to fetch you to the orderly-room, by-and-by," said Robert, "for 'preferring frivolous complaints.'" And he departed to the farmyard to look at the ducks.

That night, when Robert went up to bed, the Captain quietly locked him into his dressing-room, from which the bed had been removed.

"You're for sentry duty, to-night," said the Captain. "The carpet-brush is in the corner. Good-evening."

As his father anticipated, Robert was soon tired of the sentry game in these new circumstances, and long before the night had half worn away he wished himself safely undressed and in his own comfortable bed. At half-past twelve o'clock he felt as if he could bear it no longer, and knocked at the Captain's door.

"Who goes there?" said the Captain.

"Mayn't I go to bed, please?" whined poor Robert.

"Certainly not," said the Captain. "You're on duty."

And on duty poor Robert had to remain, for the Captain had a will as well as his son. So he rolled himself up in his father's railway rug, and slept on the floor.

The next night he was very glad to go quietly to bed, and remain there.

IV.

The Captain's children sat at breakfast in a large, bright nursery. It was the room where the old bachelor had died, and now *her* children made it merry. This was just what he would have wished.

They all sat round the table, for it was breakfast-time. There were five of them, and five bowls of boiled bread-and-milk smoked before them. Sarah (a foolish, gossiping girl, who acted as nurse till better could be found) was waiting on them, and by the table sat Darkie, the black retriever, his long, curly back swaying slightly from the difficulty of holding himself up, and his solemn hazel eyes fixed very intently on each and all of the breakfast bowls. He was as silent and sagacious as Sarah was talkative and empty-headed. Though large, he was unassuming.

Pax, the pug, on the contrary, who came up to the first joint of Darkie's leg, stood defiantly on his dignity (and his short stumps). He always placed himself in front of the bigger dog, and made a point of hustling him in doorways and of going first downstairs.

Robert's tongue was seldom idle, even at meals. "Sarah, who is that tall old gentleman at church, in the seat near the pulpit?" he asked. "He wears a cloak like what the Blues wear, only all blue, and is tall enough for a Life-guardsman. He stood when we were kneeling down, and said, *Almighty and most merciful Father,* louder than anybody."

Sarah knew who the old gentleman was, and knew also that the children did not know, and that their parents did not see fit to tell them as yet. But she had a passion for telling and hearing news, and would rather gossip with a child than not gossip at all. "Never you mind, Master Robin," she said, nodding sagaciously. "Little boys aren't to know everything."

"Ah, then, I know you don't know," replied Robert; "if you did, you'd tell."

"I do," said Sarah.

"You don't," said Robin.

"Your ma's forbid you to contradict, Master Robin," said Sarah; "and if you do I shall tell her. I know well enough who the old gentleman is, and perhaps I might tell you, only you'd go straight off and tell again."

"No, no, I wouldn't!" shouted Robin. "I can keep a secret, indeed I can! Pinch my little finger, and try. Do, do tell me, Sarah, there's a dear Sarah, and then I shall know you know." And he danced round her, catching at her skirts.

To keep a secret was beyond Sarah's powers.

"Do let my dress be, Master Robin," she said, "you're ripping out all the gathers, and listen while I whisper. As sure as you're a living boy, that gentleman's your own grandpapa."

Robin lost his hold on Sarah's dress; his arms fell by his side, and he stood with his brows knit for some minutes, thinking. Then he said, emphatically, "What lies you do tell, Sarah!"

"Oh, Robin!" cried Nicholas, who had drawn near, his thick curls standing stark with curiosity, "Mamma said 'lies' wasn't a proper word, and you promised not to say it again."

"I forgot," said Robin, "I didn't mean to break my promise. But she does tell—ahem!—*you know what*."

"You wicked boy!" cried the enraged Sarah; "how dare you say such a thing, and everybody in the place knows he's your ma's own pa."

"I'll go and ask her," said Robin, and he was at the door in a moment; but Sarah, alarmed by the thought of getting into a scrape herself, caught him by the arm.

"Don't you go, love; it'll only make your ma angry. There; it was all my nonsense."

"Then it's not true?" said Robin, indignantly. "What did you tell me so for?"

"It was all my jokes and nonsense," said the unscrupulous Sarah, "But your ma wouldn't like to know I've said such a thing. And Master Robert wouldn't be so mean as to tell tales, would he, love?"

"I'm not mean," said Robin stoutly; "and I don't tell tales; but you do, and you tell *you know what*, besides. However, I won't go this time; but I'll tell you what—if you tell tales of me to papa any more, I'll tell him what you said about the old gentleman in the blue cloak." With which parting threat Robin strode off to join his brothers and sisters.

V.

After Robert left the nursery he strolled out of doors, and, peeping through the gate at the end of the drive, he saw a party of boys going through what looked like a military exercise with sticks and a good deal of stamping; but, instead of mere words of command, they all spoke by turns, as in a play. Not being at all shy, he joined them, and asked so many questions that he soon got to know all about it.

They were practicing a Christmas mumming-play, called "The Peace Egg." Why it was called thus they could not tell him, as there was nothing whatever about eggs in it, and so far from being a play of peace, it was made up of a series of battles between certain valiant knights and princes.

The rehearsal being over, Robin went with the boys to the sexton's house (he was father to one of the characters called the "King of Egypt") where they showed him the dresses they were to wear. These were made of gay-colored materials, and covered with ribbons, except that of the "Black Prince of Paradine," which was black, as became his title. The boys also showed him the book from which they learned their parts, and which was to be bought at the post-office store.

"Then are you the mummers who come round at Christmas, and act in people's kitchens, and people give them money, that mamma used to tell us about?" said Robin.

The boy hesitated a moment and then said, "Well, I suppose we are."

"And do you go out in the snow from one house to another at night; and oh, don't you enjoy it?" cried Robin.

"We like it well enough," the lad admitted.

Robin bought a copy of "The Peace Egg." He was resolved to have a nursery performance, and to take the chief part himself. The others were willing for what he wished, but there were difficulties. In the first place, there are eight characters in the play, and there were only five children.

They decided among themselves to leave out the "Fool," and Mamma said that another character was not to be acted by any of them, or indeed mentioned; "the little one who comes in at the end," Robin explained.

Mamma had her reasons, and these were always good. She had not been altogether pleased that Robin had bought the play. It was a very old thing, she said, and very queer; not adapted for a child's play. If Mamma thought the parts not quite fit for the children to learn, they found them much too long: so in the end she picked out some bits for each, which they learned easily, and which, with a good deal of fighting, made quite as good a story of it as if they had done the whole. What may have been wanting otherwise was made up for by the dresses, which were charming.

Robin was St. George, Nicholas the valiant Slasher, Dora the Doctor, and the other two Hector and the King of Egypt. "And now we've no Black Prince!" cried Robin in dismay.

"Let Darkie be the Black Prince," said Nicholas.

"When you wave your stick he'll jump for it, and then you can pretend to fight with him."

"It's not a stick, it's a sword," said Robin.

"However, Darkie may be the Black Prince."

"And what's Pax to be?" asked Dora; "for you know he will come if Darkie does, and he'll run in before everybody else too."

"Then he must be the Fool," said Robin, "and it will do very well, for the Fool comes in before the rest, and Pax can have his red coat on, and the collar with the little bells."

VI.

Robin thought that Christmas would never come. To the Captain and his wife it seemed to come too fast. They had hoped it might bring reconciliation with the old man, but it seemed they had hoped in vain.

There were times now when the Captain almost regretted the old bachelor's bequest. The familiar scenes of her old home sharpened his wife's grief. To see her father every Sunday in church, with marks of age and infirmity upon him, but with not a look of tenderness for his only child, this tried her sorely.

"She felt it less abroad," thought the Captain. "A home in which she frets herself to death, is after all, no great boon."

Christmas Eve came.

"I'm sure it's quite Christmas enough now," said Robin. "We'll have 'The Peace Egg' to-night."

So as the Captain and his wife sat sadly over their fire, the door opened, and Pax ran in shaking his bells, and followed by the nursery mummers. The performance was most successful. It was by no means pathetic, and yet, as has been said, the Captain's wife shed tears.

"What is the matter, mamma?" said Robert, abruptly dropping his sword and running up to her.

"Don't tease mamma with questions," said the Captain; "she is not very well, and rather sad. We must all be very kind and good to poor dear mamma;" and the Captain raised his wife's hand to his lips as he spoke. Robin seized the other hand and kissed it tenderly. He was very fond of his mother. At this moment Pax took a little run, and jumped on to mamma's lap, where, sitting facing the company, he opened his black mouth and yawned, with a ludicrous inappropriateness worthy of any clown. It made everybody laugh.

"And now we'll go and act in the kitchen," said Nicholas.

"Supper at nine o'clock, remember," shouted the Captain. "And we are going to have real frumenty and Yule cakes, such as mamma used to tell us of when we were abroad."

"Hurray!" shouted the mummers, and they ran off, Pax leaping from his seat just in time to hustle the Black Prince in the doorway. When the dining-room door was shut, Robert raised his hand, and said "Hush!"

The mummers pricked their ears, but there was only a distant harsh and scraping sound, as of stones rubbed together.

"They're cleaning the passages," Robert went on, "and Sarah told me they meant to finish the mistletoe, and have everything cleaned up by supper-time. They don't want us, I know. Look here, we'll go *real mumming* instead. That *will* be fun!"

Nicholas grinned with delight.

"But will mamma let us?" he enquired.

"Oh, it will be all right if we're back by supper-time," said Robert, hastily. "Only of course we must take care not to catch cold. Come and help me to get some wraps."

The old oak chest in which spare shawls, rugs, and coats were kept was soon ransacked, and the mummers' gay dresses hidden by motley wrappers. But no sooner did Darkie and Pax behold the coats, etc., than they at once began to leap and bark, as it was their custom to do when they saw any one dressing to go out. Robin was sorely afraid that this would betray them; but though the Captain and his wife heard the barking they did not guess the cause.

So the front door being very gently opened and closed, the nursery mummers stole away.

VII.

It was a very fine night. The snow was well-trodden on the drive, so that it did not wet their feet, but on the trees and shrubs it hung soft and white.

"It's much jollier being out at night than in the daytime," said Robin.

"Much," responded Nicholas, with intense feeling.

"We'll go a wassailing next week," said Robin. "I know all about it, and perhaps we shall get a good lot of money, and then we'll buy tin swords with scabbards for next year. I don't like these sticks. Oh, dear, I wish it wasn't so long between one Christmas and another."

"Where shall we go first?" asked Nicholas, as they turned into the high road.

"This is the first house," he said. "We'll act here;" and all pressed in as quickly as possible. Once safe within the grounds, they shouldered their sticks, and marched with composure.

"You're going to the front door," said Nicholas. "Mummers ought to go to the back."

"We don't know where it is," said Robin, and he rang the front-door bell. There was a pause. Then lights shone, steps were heard, and at last a sound of much unbarring, unbolting, and unlocking. It might have been a prison. Then the door was opened by an elderly, timid-looking woman, who held a tallow candle above her head.

"Who's there?" she said, "at this time of night."

"We're Christmas mummers," said Robin, stoutly; "we didn't know the way to the back door, but——"

"And don't you know better than to come here?" said the woman. "Be off with you, as fast as you can."

"You're only the servant," said Robin. "Go and ask your master and mistress if they wouldn't like to see us act. We do it very well."

"You impudent boy, be off with you!" repeated the woman. "Master'd no more let you nor any other such rubbish set foot in this house——"

"Woman!" shouted a voice close behind her, which made her start as if she had been shot, "who authorizes you to say what your master will or will not do, before you've asked him? The boy is right. You *are* the servant, and it is not your business to choose for me whom I shall or shall not see."

"I meant no harm, sir, I'm sure," said the housekeeper; "but I thought you'd never——"

"My good woman," said her master, "if I had wanted somebody to think for me, you're the last person I should have employed. I hire you to obey orders, not to think."

"I'm sure, sir," said the housekeeper, whose only form of argument was reiteration, "I never thought you would have seen them——"

"Then you were wrong," shouted her master. "I will see them. Bring them in."

He was a tall, gaunt old man, and Robin stared at him for some minutes, wondering where he could have seen somebody very like him. At last he remembered. It was the old gentleman of the blue cloak.

The children threw off their wraps, the housekeeper helping them, and chattering ceaselessly, from sheer nervousness.

"Well, to be sure," said she, "their dresses are pretty, too. And they seem quite a better sort of children, they talk quite genteel. I might ha' knowed they weren't like common mummers, but I was so flusterated hearing the bell go so late, and——"

"Are they ready?" said the old man, who had[Pg 305] stood like a ghost in the dim light of the flaring tallow candle, grimly watching the proceedings.

"Yes, sir. Shall I take them to the kitchen, sir?"

"——for you and the other idle hussies to gape and grin at? No. Bring them to the library," he snapped, and then stalked off, leading the way.

The housekeeper accordingly led them to the library, and then withdrew, nearly falling on her face as she left the room by stumbling over Darkie, who slipped in last like a black shadow.

The old man was seated in a carved oak chair by the fire.

"I never said the dogs were to come in," he said.

"But we can't do without them, please," said Robin, boldly. "You see there are eight people in 'The Peace Egg,' and there are only five of us; and so Darkie has to be the Black Prince, and Pax has to be the Fool, and so we have to have them."

"Five and two make seven," said the old man, with a grim smile; "what do you do for the eighth?"

"Oh, that's the little one at the end," said Robin, confidently. "Mamma said we weren't to mention him, but I think that's because we're children.—You're grown up, you know, so I'll show you the book, and you can see for yourself," he went on, drawing "The Peace Egg" from his pocket: "there, that's the picture of him, on the last page; black, with horns and a tail."

The old man's stern face relaxed into a broad smile as he examined the grotesque woodcut; but when he turned to the first page the smile vanished in a deep frown, and his eyes shone like hot coals with anger. He had seen Robin's name.

"Who sent you here?" he asked, in a hoarse voice. "Speak, and speak the truth! Did your mother send you here?"

Robin thought the old man was angry with them for playing truant. He said, slowly, "N—no. She didn't exactly send us; but I don't think she'll mind our having come if we get back in time for supper. Mamma never *forbid* our going mumming, you know."

"I don't suppose she ever thought of it," Nicholas said candidly, wagging his curly head from side to side.

"She knows we're mummers," said Robin, "for she helped us. When we were abroad, you know, she used to tell us about the mummers acting at Christmas, when she was a little girl; and so we thought we'd be mummers, and so we acted to papa and mamma, and so we thought we'd act to the maids, but they were cleaning the passages, and so we thought we'd really go mumming; and we've got several other houses to go to before supper-time; we'd better begin, I think," said Robin; and without more ado he began to march round and round, raising his sword, and the performance went off quite as creditably as before.

As the children acted the old man's anger wore off. He watched them with an interest he could not repress. When Nicholas took some hard thwacks from Robert without flinching, the old man clapped his hands; and after the encounter was over, he said he would not have had the dogs excluded on any consideration. It was just at the end, when they were all marching round and round, holding on by each other's swords "over the shoulder," and singing "A mumming we will go, etc.," that Nicholas suddenly brought the circle to a stand-still by stopping dead short, and staring up at the wall before him.

"What *are* you stopping for?" said Robert, turning indignantly around.

"Look there!" cried Nicholas, pointing to a little painting which hung above the old man's head.

Robin looked, and said abruptly, "It's Dora."

"Which is Dora?" asked the old man in a strange, sharp tone.

"Here she is," said Robin and Nicholas in one breath, as they dragged her forward.

"She's the Doctor," said Robin, "and you can't see her face for her things. Dor, take off your cap and pull back that hood. There! Oh, it *is* like her!"

It was the portrait of her mother as a child; but of this the nursery mummers knew nothing. The old man looked as the peaked cap and hood fell away from Dora's face and fair curls, and then he uttered a sharp cry, and buried his head upon his hands. The boys stood stupefied, but Dora ran up to him, and putting her little hands on his arms, said, in childish pitying tones, "Oh, I am so sorry! Have you got a headache? May Robin put the shovel in the fire for you? Mamma has hot shovels for her headaches." And though the old man did not speak or move, she went on coaxing him, and stroking his head, on which the hair was white. At this moment Pax took one of his unexpected runs, and jumped on to the old man's knee, in his own particular fashion, and then yawned at the company. The old man was startled, and lifted his face suddenly. It was wet with tears.

"Why, you're crying!" exclaimed the children with one breath.

"It's very odd," said Robin, fretfully. "I can't think what's the matter to-night. Mamma was crying too when we were acting, and papa said we weren't to tease her with questions, and he kissed her hand, and I kissed her hand too. And papa said we must all be very good and kind to poor dear mamma, and so I mean to be, she's so good. And I think we'd better go home, or perhaps she'll be frightened," Robin added.

"She's so good, is she?" asked the old man.[Pg 308] He had put Pax off his knee, and taken Dora on to it.

"Oh, isn't she!" said Nicholas, swaying his curly head from side to side as usual.

"She's always good," said Robin, emphatically; "and so's papa. But I'm always doing something I oughtn't to," he added, slowly. "But then, you know, I don't pretend to obey Sarah. I don't care a fig for Sarah; and I won't obey any woman but mamma."

"Who's Sarah?" asked the grandfather.

"She's our nurse," said Robin, "and she tells—I mustn't say what she tells—but it's not the truth. She told one about *you* the other day," he added.

"About me?" said the old man.

"She said you were our grandpapa. So then I knew she was telling *you know what*."

"How did you know it wasn't true?" the old man asked.

"Why, of course," said Robin, "if you were our mamma's father, you'd know her, and be very fond of her, and come to see her. And then you'd be our grandfather, too, and you'd have us to see you, and perhaps give us Christmas-boxes. I wish you were," Robin added with a sigh. "It would be very nice."

"Would *you* like it?" asked the old man of Dora.

And Dora, who was half asleep and very comfortable, put her little arms about his neck as she was wont to put them around the Captain's, and said, "Very much."

He put her down at last, very tenderly, almost unwillingly, and left the children alone. By-and-by he returned, dressed in the blue cloak, and took Dora up again.

"I will see you home," he said.

The children had not been missed. The clock had only just struck nine when there came a knock[Pg 309] on the door of the dining-room, where the Captain and his wife still sat by the Yule log. She said "Come in," wearily, thinking it was the frumenty and the Christmas cakes.

But it was her father, with her child in his arms!

VIII.

The Captain had many friends who knew of the sad estrangement between his wife and her father. Some of them were in church the next day, which was Christmas Day, when the Captain's wife came in. They would have hid their faces, but for the startling sight that met the gaze of the congregation. The old grandfather walked into church abreast of the Captain.

"They've met in the porch," whispered one under the shelter of his hat.

"They can't quarrel publicly in a place of worship," said another, turning pale.

"She's gone into his seat," cried a girl in a shrill whisper.

"And the children after her," added her sister, incautiously aloud.

There was now no doubt about the matter. The old man in his blue cloak stood for a few moments politely disputing the question of precedence with his handsome son-in-law. Then the Captain bowed and passed in, and the old man followed him.

By the time that the service was ended everybody knew of the happy peacemaking, and was glad. One old friend after another came up with blessings and good wishes. This was a proper Christmas, indeed, they said. There was a general rejoicing.

But only the grandfather and his children knew that it was hatched from "The Peace Egg."

The Burglar's Christmas

WILLA CATHER

Willa Cather, 1873 – 1947

Pulitzer Prize-winning American novelist

Cather wrote the following story at the age of 23, using the pseudonym Elizabeth L. Seymour. Pathos, sentimentality, a tug at the heart—call it what you will—but the story works, and who can resist a happy ending?

THE BURGLAR'S CHRISTMAS

TWO very shabby-looking young men stood at the corner of Prairie Avenue and Eightieth Street, looking despondently at the carriages that whirled by. It was Christmas Eve, and the streets were full of vehicles; florists' wagons, grocers' carts and carriages. The streets were in that half-liquid, half-congealed condition peculiar to the streets of Chicago at that season of the year. The swift wheels that spun by sometimes threw the slush of mud and snow over the two young men who were talking on the corner.

"Well," remarked the elder of the two, "I guess we are at our rope's end, sure enough. How do you feel?"

"Pretty shaky. The wind's sharp tonight. If I had had anything to eat I mightn't mind it so much. There is simply no show. I'm sick of the whole business. Looks like there's nothing for it but the lake."

"O, nonsense, I thought you had more grit. Got anything left you can hock?"

"Nothing but my beard, and I am afraid they wouldn't find it worth a pawn ticket," said the younger man ruefully, rubbing the week's growth of stubble on his face.

"Got any folks anywhere? Now's your time to strike 'em if you have."

"Never mind if I have, they're out of the question."

"Well, you'll be out of it before many hours if you don't make a move of some sort. A man's got to eat. See here, I am going down to Longtin's saloon. I used to play the banjo in there with a couple of coons, and I'll bone him for some of his free lunch stuff. You'd better come along, perhaps they'll fill an order for two."

"How far down is it?"

"Well, it's clear down town, of course, way down on Michigan avenue."

"Thanks, I guess I'll loaf around here. I don't feel equal to the walk, and the cars—well, the cars are crowded." His features drew themselves into what might have been a smile under happier circumstances.

"No, you never did like street cars, you're too aristocratic. See here, Crawford, I don't like leaving you here. You ain't good company for yourself to-night."

"Crawford? O, yes, that's the last one. There have been so many I forget them."

"Have you got a real name, anyway?"

"O, yes, but it's one of the ones I've forgotten. Don't you worry about me. You go along and get your free lunch. I think I had a row in Longtin's place once. I'd better not show myself there again." As he spoke the young man nodded and turned slowly up the avenue.

He was miserable enough to want to be quite alone. Even the crowd that jostled by him annoyed him. He wanted to think about himself. He had avoided this final reckoning with himself for a year now. He had laughed it off and drunk it off. But now, when all those artificial devices which are employed to turn our thoughts into other channels and shield us from ourselves had failed him, it must come. Hunger is a powerful incentive to introspection.

It is a tragic hour, that hour when we are finally driven to reckon with ourselves, when every avenue of mental distraction has been cut off and our own life and all its ineffaceable failures closes about us like the walls of that old torture chamber of the Inquisition.

To-night, as this man stood stranded in the streets of the city, his hour came. It was not the first time he had been hungry and desperate and alone. But always before there had been some outlook, some chance ahead, some pleasure yet untasted that seemed worth the effort, some face that he fancied was, or would be, dear. But it was not so tonight. The unyielding conviction was upon him that he had failed in everything, had outlived everything. It had been near him for a long time, that Pale Spectre. He had caught its shadow at the bottom of his glass many a time, at the head of his bed when he was sleepless at night, in the twilight shadows when some great sunset broke upon him. It had made life hateful to him when he awoke in the morning before now.

But now it settled slowly over him, like night, the endless Northern nights that bid the sun a long farewell. It rose up before him like granite. From this brilliant city with its glad bustle of Yuletide he was shut off as completely as though he were a creature of another species. His days seemed numbered and done, sealed over like the little coral cells at the bottom of the sea. Involuntarily he drew that cold air through his lungs slowly, as though he were tasting it for the last time.

Yet he was but four and twenty, this man—he looked even younger—and he had a father some place down East who had been very proud of him once. Well, he had taken his life into his own hands, and this was what he had made of it. That was all there was to be said.

He could remember the hopeful things they used to say about him at college in the old days, before he had cut away and begun to live by his wits, and he found courage to smile at them now. They had read him wrongly. He knew now that he never had the essentials of success, only the superficial agility that is often mistaken for it. He was tow without the tinder, and he had burnt himself out at other people's fires. He had helped other people to make it win, but he himself—he had never touched an enterprise that had not failed eventually. Or, if it survived his connection with it, it left him behind.

His last venture had been with some ten-cent specialty company, a little lower than all the others, that had gone to pieces in Buffalo, and he had worked his way to Chicago by boat. When the boat made up its crew for the outward voyage, he was dispensed with as usual. He was used to that. The reason for it? O, there are so many reasons for failure! His was a very common one.

As he stood there in the wet under the street light he drew up his reckoning with the world and decided that it had treated him as well as he deserved. He had overdrawn his account once too often. There had been a day when he thought otherwise; when he had said he was unjustly handled, that his failure was merely the lack of proper adjustment between himself and other men, that some day he would be recognized and it would all come right. But he knew better than that now, and he was still man enough to bear no grudge against any one—man or woman.

Tonight was his birthday, too. There seemed something particularly amusing in that. He turned up a limp little coat collar to try to keep a little of the wet chill from his throat, and instinctively began to remember all the birthday parties he used to have. He was so cold and empty that his mind seemed unable to grapple with any serious question. He kept thinking about ginger bread and frosted cakes like a child. He could remember the splendid birthday parties his mother used to give him, when all the other little boys in the block came in their Sunday clothes and creaking shoes, with their ears still red from their mother's towel, and the pink and white birthday cake, and the stuffed olives and all the dishes of which he had been particularly fond, and how he would eat and eat and then go to bed and dream of Santa Claus.

And in the morning he would awaken and eat again, until by night the family doctor arrived with his castor oil, and poor William used to dolefully say that it was altogether too much to have your birthday and Christmas all at once. He could remember, too, the royal birthday suppers he had given at college, and the stag dinners, and the toasts, and the music, and the good fellows who had wished him happiness and really meant what they said.

And since then there were other birthday suppers that he could not remember so clearly; the memory of them was heavy and flat, like cigarette smoke that has been shut in a room all night, like champagne that has been a day opened, a song that has been too often sung, an acute sensation that has been overstrained. They seemed tawdry and garish, discordant to him now. He rather wished he could forget them altogether.

Whichever way his mind now turned there was one thought that it could not escape, and that was the idea of food. He caught the scent of a cigar suddenly, and felt a sharp pain in the pit of his abdomen and a sudden moisture in his mouth. His cold hands clenched angrily, and for a moment he felt that bitter hatred of wealth, of ease, of everything that is well-fed and well-housed that is common to starving men.

At any rate he had a right to eat! He had demanded great things from the world once: fame and wealth and admiration. Now it was simply bread—and he would have it! He looked about him quickly and felt the blood begin to stir in his veins. In all his straits he had never stolen anything, his tastes were above it. But to-night there would be no tomorrow. He was amused at the way in which the idea excited him. Was it possible there was yet one more experience that would distract him, one thing that had power to excite his jaded interest? Good! He had failed at everything else, now he would see what his chances would be as a common thief.

It would be amusing to watch the beautiful consistency of his destiny work itself out even in that role. It would be interesting to add another study to his gallery of futile attempts, and then label them all: "the failure as a journalist," "the failure as a lecturer," "the failure as a business man," "the failure as a thief," and so on, like the titles under the pictures of the Dance of Death. It was time that Childe Roland came to the dark tower.

A girl hastened by him with her arms full of packages. She walked quickly and nervously, keeping well within the shadow, as if she were not accustomed to carrying bundles and did not care to meet any of her friends. As she crossed the muddy street, she made an effort to lift her skirt a little, and as she did so one of the packages slipped unnoticed from beneath her arm. He caught it up and overtook her. "Excuse me, but I think you dropped something."

She started, "O, yes, thank you, I would rather have lost anything than that."

The young man turned angrily upon himself. The package must have contained something of value. Why had he not kept it? Was this the sort of thief he would make? He ground his teeth together. There is nothing more maddening than to have morally consented to crime and then lack the nerve force to carry it out.

A carriage drove up to the house before which he stood. Several richly dressed women alighted and went in. It was a new house, and must have been built since he was in Chicago last. The front door was open and he could see down the hall-way and up the stair case. The servant had left the door and gone with the guests. The first floor was brilliantly lighted, but the windows upstairs were dark. It looked very easy, just to slip upstairs to the darkened chambers where the jewels and trinkets of the fashionable occupants were kept.

Still burning with impatience against himself he entered quickly. Instinctively he removed his mud-stained hat as he passed quickly and quietly up the stair case. It struck him as being a rather superfluous courtesy in a burglar, but he had done it before he had thought. His way was clear enough, he met no one on the stairway or in the upper hall. The gas was lit in the upper hall. He passed the first chamber door through sheer cowardice. The second he entered quickly, thinking of something else lest his courage should fail him, and closed the door behind him. The light from the hall shone into the room through the transom.

The apartment was furnished richly enough to justify his expectations. He went at once to the dressing case. A number of rings and small trinkets lay in a silver tray. These he put hastily in his pocket. He opened the upper drawer and found, as he expected, several leather cases. In the first he opened was a lady's watch, in the second a pair of old-fashioned bracelets; he seemed to dimly remember having seen bracelets like them before, somewhere. The third case was heavier, the spring was much worn, and it opened easily. It held a cup of some kind. He held it up to the light and then his strained nerves gave way and he uttered a sharp exclamation. It was the silver mug he used to drink from when he was a little boy.

The door opened, and a woman stood in the doorway facing him. She was a tall woman, with white hair, in evening dress. The light from the hall streamed in upon him but she was not afraid. She stood looking at him a moment, then she threw out her hand and went quickly toward him.

"Willie, Willie! Is it you!"

He struggled to loose her arms from him, to keep her lips from his cheek. "Mother—you must not! You do not understand!"

*The door opened and a woman stood in the
doorway facing him. She was a tall woman
with white hair in evening dress.*

"O, my G__, this is worst of all!" Hunger, weakness, cold, shame, all came back to him, and shook his self-control completely. Physically he was too weak to stand a shock like this. Why could it not have been an ordinary discovery, arrest, the station house and all the rest of it. Anything but this! A hard dry sob broke from him. Again he strove to disengage himself.

"Who is it says I shall not kiss my son? O, my boy, we have waited so long for this! You have been so long in coming, even I almost gave you up."

Her lips upon his cheek burnt him like fire. He put his hand to his throat, and spoke thickly and incoherently: "You do not understand. I did not know you were here. I came here to rob—it is the first time—I swear it—but I am a common thief. My pockets are full of your jewels now. Can't you hear me? I am a common thief!"

"Hush, my boy, those are ugly words. How could you rob your own house? How could you take what is your own? They are all yours, my son, as wholly yours as my great love—and you can't doubt that, Will, do you?"

That soft voice, the warmth and fragrance of her person stole through his chill, empty veins like a gentle stimulant. He felt as though all his strength were leaving him and even consciousness. He held fast to her and bowed his head on her strong shoulder, and groaned aloud.

"O, mother, life is hard, hard!"

She said nothing, but held him closer. And O, the strength of those white arms that held him! O, the assurance of safety in that warm bosom that rose and fell under his cheek! For a moment they stood so, silently. Then they heard a heavy step upon the stair. She led him to a chair and went out and closed the door. At the top of the staircase she met a tall, broad-shouldered man, with iron gray hair, and a face alert and stern. Her eyes were shining and her cheeks on fire, her whole face was one expression of intense determination.

"James, it is William in there, come home. You must keep him at any cost. If he goes this time, I go with him. O, James, be easy with him, he has suffered so." She broke from a command to an entreaty, and laid her hand on his shoulder. He looked questioningly at her a moment, then went in the room and quietly shut the door.

She stood leaning against the wall, clasping her temples with her hands and listening to the low indistinct sound of the voices within. Her own lips moved silently. She waited a long time, scarcely breathing. At last the door opened, and her husband came out. He stopped to say in a shaken voice,

"You go to him now, he will stay. I will go to my room. I will see him again in the morning."

She put her arm about his neck, "O, James, I thank you, I thank you! This is the night he came so long ago, you remember? I gave him to you then, and now you give him back to me!"

"Don't, Helen," he muttered. "He is my son, I have never forgotten that. I failed with him. I don't like to fail, it cuts my pride. Take him and make a man of him." He passed on down the hall.

She flew into the room where the young man sat with his head bowed upon his knee. She dropped upon her knees beside him. Ah, it was so good to him to feel those arms again!

"He is so glad, Willie, so glad! He may not show it, but he is as happy as I. He never was demonstrative with either of us, you know."

"O, my G, he was good enough," groaned the man. "I told him everything, and he was good enough. I don't see how either of you can look at me, speak to me, touch me." He shivered under her clasp again as when she had first touched him, and tried weakly to throw her off.

But she whispered softly,

"This is my right, my son."

Presently, when he was calmer, she rose. "Now, come with me into the library, and I will have your dinner brought there."

As they went down stairs she remarked apologetically, "I will not call Ellen to-night; she has a number of guests to attend to. She is a big girl now, you know, and came out last winter. Besides, I want you all to myself to-night."

When the dinner came, and it came very soon, he fell upon it savagely. As he ate she told him all that had transpired during the years of his absence, and how his father's business had brought them there. "I was glad when we came. I thought you would drift West. I seemed a good deal nearer to you here."

There was a gentle unobtrusive sadness in her tone that was too soft for a reproach.

"Have you everything you want? It is a comfort to see you eat."

He smiled grimly, "It is certainly a comfort to me. I have not indulged in this frivolous habit for some thirty-five hours."

She caught his hand and pressed it sharply, uttering a quick remonstrance.

"Don't say that! I know, but I can't hear you say it,—it's too terrible! My boy, food has choked me many a time when I have thought of the possibility of that. Now take the old lounging chair by the fire, and if you are too tired to talk, we will just sit and rest together."

He sank into the depths of the big leather chair with the lion's heads on the arms, where he had sat so often in the days when his feet did not touch the floor and he was half afraid of the grim monsters cut in the polished wood. That chair seemed to speak to him of things long forgotten. It was like the touch of an old familiar friend. He felt a sudden yearning tenderness for the happy little boy who had sat there and dreamed of the big world so long ago. Alas, he had been dead many a summer, that little boy!

He sat looking up at the magnificent woman beside him. He had almost forgotten how handsome she was; how lustrous and sad were the eyes that were set under that serene brow, how impetuous and wayward the mouth even now, how superb the white throat and shoulders! Ah, the wit and grace and fineness of this woman! He remembered how proud he had been of her as a boy when she came to see him at school. Then in the deep red coals of the grate he saw the faces of other women who had come since then into his vexed, disordered life. Laughing faces, with eyes artificially bright, eyes without depth or meaning, features without the stamp of high sensibilities. And he had left this face for such as those!

He sighed restlessly and laid his hand on hers. There seemed refuge and protection in the touch of her, as in the old days when he was afraid of the dark. He had been in the dark so long now, his confidence was so thoroughly shaken, and he was bitterly afraid of the night and of himself.

"Ah, mother, you make other things seem so false. You must feel that I owe you an explanation, but I can't make any, even to myself. Ah, but we make poor exchanges in life. I can't make out the riddle of it all. Yet there are things I ought to tell you before I accept your confidence like this."

"I'd rather you wouldn't, Will. Listen: Between you and me there can be no secrets. We are more alike than other people. Dear boy, I know all about it. I am a woman, and circumstances were different with me, but we are of one blood. I have lived all your life before you. You have never had an impulse that I have not known, you have never touched a brink that my feet have not trod. This is your birthday night. Twenty-four years ago I foresaw all this. I was a young woman then and I had hot battles of my own, and I felt your likeness to me. You were not like other babies. From the hour you were born you were restless and discontented, as I had been before you. You used to brace your strong little limbs against mine and try to throw me off as you did to-night. To-night you have come back to me, just as you always did after you ran away to swim in the river that was forbidden you, the river you loved because it was forbidden. You are tired and sleepy, just as you used to be then, only a little older and a little paler and a little more foolish. I never asked you where you had been then, nor will I now. You have come back to me, that's all in all to me. I know your every possibility and limitation, as a composer knows his instrument."

He found no answer that was worthy to give to talk like this. He had not found life easy since he had lived by his wits. He had come to know poverty at close quarters. He had known what it was to be gay with an empty pocket, to wear violets in his button hole when he had not breakfasted, and all the hateful shams of the poverty of idleness. He had been a reporter on a big metropolitan daily, where men grind out their brains on paper until they have not one idea left—and still grind on. He had worked in a real estate office, where ignorant men were swindled. He had sung in a comic opera chorus and played Harris in an Uncle Tom's Cabin Company, and edited a Socialist weekly. He had been dogged by debt and hunger and grinding poverty, until to sit here by a warm fire without concern as to how it would be paid for seemed unnatural.

He looked up at her questioningly. "I wonder if you know how much you pardon?"

"O, my poor boy, much or little, what does it matter? Have you wandered so far and paid such a bitter price for knowledge and not yet learned that love has nothing to do with pardon or forgiveness, that it only loves, and loves—and loves? They have not taught you well, the women of your world." She leaned over and kissed him, as no woman had kissed him since he left her.

He drew a long sigh of rich content. The old life, with all its bitterness and useless antagonism and flimsy sophistries, its brief delights that were always tinged with fear and distrust and unfaith, that whole miserable, futile, swindled world of Bohemia seemed immeasurably distant and far away, like a dream that is over and done.

And as the chimes rang joyfully outside and sleep pressed heavily upon his eyelids, he wondered dimly if the Author of this sad little riddle of ours were not able to solve it after all, and if the Potter would not finally mete out his all comprehensive justice, such as none but he could have, to his Things of Clay, which are made in his own patterns, weak or strong, for his own ends; and if some day we will not awaken and find that all evil is a dream, a mental distortion that will pass when the dawn shall break.

The Christmas Babe

MARGARET E. SANGSTER

Margaret E. Sangster, 1838 – 1912

American poet, author, journalist and editor

Sangster's work was most popular in the late 19th to the early 20th century but her work is still appealing today. She wore many hats in the publishing world, a testament to the fact that women were able to use their literary skills in a period many have called a "man's world."

THE CHRISTMAS BABE

We love to think of Bethlehem,
That little mountain town,
To which, on earth's first Christmas Day,
Our blessed Lord came down.

A lowly manger for His bed,
The cattle near in stall,

There, cradled close in Mary's arms,
He slept, the Lord of all.

If we had been in Bethlehem,
We too had hasted fain

To see the Babe whose little face
Knew neither care nor pain.

Like any little child of ours,
He came unto His own,
Through Cross and shame before Him stretched,
—His pathway to His Throne.

If we had dwelt in Bethlehem,
We would have followed fast,
And where the Star had led our feet
Have knelt ere dawn was past.

Our gifts, our songs, our prayers had been
An offering, as He lay,
The blessed Babe of Bethlehem,
In Mary's arms that day.

Now breaks the latest Christmas Morn!
Again the angels sing,
And far and near the children throng
Their happy hymns to bring.

All heaven is stirred! All earth is glad!
For down the shining way,
The Lord who came to Bethlehem,
Comes yet, on Christmas Day.

King John's Christmas

A. A. Milne

A.A. Milne. 1882 – 1956

English writer best known for *Winnie the Pooh Tales* in the Hundred Acre Wood.

We are likely all familiar with the Winnie the Pooh stories. Not many are familiar with this whimsical poem by the same author, however. Ready for a bit of fun? Read on!

KING JOHN'S CHRISTMAS

King John was not a good man—
He had his little ways.
And sometimes no one spoke to him
For days and days and days.
And men who came across him,
When walking in the town,
Gave him a supercilious stare,
Or passed with noses in the air—
And bad King John stood dumbly there,
Blushing beneath his crown.

King John was not a good man,
And no good friends had he.
He stayed in every afternoon...
But no one came to tea.
And, round about December,
The cards upon his shelf
Which wished him lots of Christmas cheer,
And fortune in the coming year,
Were never from his near and dear,
But only from himself.

King John was not a good man,
Yet had his hopes and fears.
They'd given him no present now
For years and years and years.
But every year at Christmas,
While minstrels stood about,
Collecting tribute from the young
For all the songs they might have sung,
He stole away upstairs and hung
A hopeful stocking out.

King John was not a good man,
He lived his life aloof;
Alone he thought a message out
While climbing up the roof.
He wrote it down and propped it
Against the chimney stack:
"TO ALL AND SUNDRY—NEAR AND FAR—
F. CHRISTMAS IN PARTICULAR."
And signed it not "Johannes R."
But very humbly, "JACK."

"I want some crackers,
And I want some candy;
I think a box of chocolates
Would come in handy;
I don't mind oranges,
I do like nuts!
And I SHOULD like a pocket-knife
That really cuts.
And, oh! Father Christmas, if you love me at all,
Bring me a big, red india-rubber ball!"

King John was not a good man—
He wrote this message out,
And gat him to his room again,
Descending by the spout.
And all that night he lay there,
A prey to hopes and fears.

"I think that's him a-coming now,"
(Anxiety bedewed his brow.)
"He'll bring one present, anyhow—
The first I've had for years."

"Forget about the crackers,
And forget about the candy;
I'm sure a box of chocolates
Would never come in handy;
I don't like oranges,
I don't want nuts,
And I HAVE got a pocket-knife
That almost cuts.
But, oh! Father Christmas, if you love me at all,
Bring me a big, red india-rubber ball!"

King John was not a good man—
Next morning when the sun
Rose up to tell a waiting world
That Christmas had begun,

And people seized their stockings,
And opened them with glee,
And crackers, toys and games appeared,
And lips with sticky sweets were smeared,
King John said grimly: "As I feared, Nothing again for me!"

"I did want crackers,
And I did want candy;
I know a box of chocolates
Would come in handy;
I do love oranges,
I did want nuts.
I haven't got a pocket-knife—
Not one that cuts.
And, oh! if Father Christmas had loved me at all,
He would have brought a big, red india-rubber ball!"

King John stood by the window,
And frowned to see below
The happy bands of boys and girls
All playing in the snow.
A while he stood there watching,
And envying them all...
When through the window big and red
There hurtled by his royal head,
And bounced and fell upon the bed,
An india-rubber ball!

AND OH, FATHER CHRISTMAS,
MY BLESSINGS ON YOU FALL
FOR BRINGING HIM
A BIG, RED, INDIA-RUBBER BALL!

On Christmas Day in the Morning

GRACE S. RICHMOND

Grace S. Richmond, 1866 – 1959

Romance novelist, story writer

The daughter of a Baptist clergyman, Richmond was a romance novelist but apparently best known for writing this story, first published in 1905. The set up seems a little wordy, perhaps, but the payoff is sweet. Six grown siblings remember their roots and discover one really can go home for Christmas. And, because Richmond was a romance writer, there's even something here for the romantic in each of us. As the mother of five grown children myself, this tale holds a special place in my heart. Also, the original illustrations are a nice touch, as good artwork always is.

On CHRISTMAS DAY IN THE MORNING

And all the angels in heaven do sing,

On Christmas Day, on Christmas Day
And all the bells on earth do ring,
On Christmas Day in the morning
—Old Song

That Christmas Day virtually began a whole year beforehand, with a red-hot letter written by Guy Fernald to his younger sister, Nan, who had been married to Samuel Burnett just two and one-half years. The letter was read aloud by Mrs. Burnett to her husband at the breakfast table, the second day after Christmas. From start to finish it was upon one subject, and it read as follows:

Dear Nan,

It's a confounded, full-grown shame that not a soul of us all got home for Christmas—except yours truly, and he only for a couple of hours. What have the blessed old folks done to us that we treat them like this?

I was invited to the Sewalls' for the day, and went, of course—you know why. We had a ripping time, but along toward evening I began to feel worried. I really thought Ralph was home—he wrote me that he might swing round that way by the holidays—but I knew the rest of you were all wrapped up in your own Christmas trees and weren't going to get there.

Well, I took the seven-thirty down and walked in on them. Sitting all alone by the fire, by George. I felt gulpish in my throat, on my honour I did, when I looked at them. Mother just gave one gasp and flew into my arms, and Dad got up more slowly—he has that darned rheumatism worse than ever this winter—and came over and I thought he'd shake my hand off.

Well—I sat down between them by the fire, and pretty soon I got down in the old way on a cushion by mother, and let her run her fingers through my hair, the way she used to—and Nan, I'll be indicted for perjury if her hand wasn't trembly. They were so glad to see me it made my throat ache.

Of course you'd all written and sent them things—jolly things, and they appreciated them. But—blame it all—they were just dead lonesome—and the whole outfit of us within three hundred miles, most within thirty!

Nan—next Christmas it's going to be different. That's all I say. I've got it all planned out. The idea popped into my head when I came away last night. Not that they had a word of blame—not they. They understood all about the children, and the cold snap, and Ed's being under the weather, and Oliver's wife's neuralgia, and Ralph's girl in the West, and all that. But that didn't make the thing any easier for them.

As I say, next year—But you'll all hear from me then. Meanwhile—run down and see them once or twice this winter, will you, Nan? Somehow it struck me they aren't so young as—they used to be.

Splendid winter weather. Margaret Sewall's a peach, but I don't seem to make much headway.

My best to Sam.

Your affectionate brother,

Guy

Nan had felt a slight choking in her own throat as she read this letter. "We really must make an effort to be there Christmas next year, Sam," she said to her husband, and Sam assented cheerfully. He only wished there were a father and mother somewhere in the world for him to go home to.

Guy wrote the same sort of thing, with more or less detail, to Edson and Oliver, his married elder brothers; to Ralph, his unmarried brother; and to Carolyn—Mrs. Charles Wetmore, his other—and elder—married sister. He received varied and more or less sympathetic responses, to the effect that with so many little children, and such snowdrifts as always blocked the roads leading toward North Estabrook, it really was not strange—and of course somebody would go next year.

But they had all sent the nicest gifts they could find. Didn't Guy think mother liked those beautiful Russian sables Ralph sent her? And wasn't father pleased with his gold-headed cane from Oliver? Surely with such presents pouring in from all the children, Father and Mother Fernald couldn't feel so awfully neglected.

"Gold-headed cane be hanged!" Guy exploded when he read this last sentence from the letter of Marian, Oliver's wife. "I'll bet she put him up to it. If anybody dares give me a gold-headed cane before I'm ninety-five I'll thrash him with it on the spot. He wasn't using it, either—bless him. He had his old hickory stick, and he wouldn't have had that if that abominable rheumatism hadn't gripped him so hard. He isn't old enough to use a cane, by jolly, and Ol ought to know it, if Marian doesn't.

I'm glad I sent him that typewriter. He liked that, I know he did, and it'll amuse him, too—not make him think he's ready to die!"

Guy was not the fellow to forget anything which had taken hold of him as that pathetic Christmas home-coming had done. When the year had nearly rolled around, the first of December saw him at work getting his plans in train. He began with his eldest brother, Oliver, because he considered Mrs. Oliver the hardest proposition he had to tackle in the carrying out of his idea.

"You see," he expounded patiently, as they sat and stared at him, "it isn't that they aren't always awfully glad to see the whole outfit, children and all, but it just struck me it would do 'em a lot of good to revive old times.

I thought if we could make it just as much as possible like one of the old Christmases before anybody got married—hang up the stockings and all, you know—it would give them a mighty jolly surprise. I plan to have us all creep in in the night and go to bed in our old rooms. And then in the morning—See?"

Mrs. Oliver looked at him. An eager flush lit his still boyish face—Guy was twenty-eight—and his blue eyes were very bright. His lithe, muscular figure bent toward her pleadingly; all his arguments were aimed at her. Oliver sat back in his impassive way and watched them both. It could not be denied that it was Marian's decisions which usually ruled in matters of this sort.

"It seems to me a very strange plan," was Mrs. Oliver's comment, when Guy had laid the whole thing before her in the most tactful manner he could command.

She spoke rather coldly. "It is not usual to think that families should be broken up like this on Christmas Day, of all days in the year. Four families, with somebody gone—a mother or a father—just to please two elderly people who expect nothing of the sort, and who understand just why we can't all get home at once. Don't you think you are really asking a good deal?"

Guy kept his temper, though it was hard work. "It doesn't seem to me I am," he answered quite gently. "It's only for once. I really don't think father and mother would care much what sort of presents we brought them, if we only came ourselves. Of course, I know I'm asking a sacrifice of each family, and it may seem almost an insult not to invite the children and all, yet—perhaps next year we'll try a gathering of all the clans. But just for this year—honestly—I do awfully wish you'd give me my way. If you'd seen those two last Christmas—"

He broke off, glancing appealingly at Oliver himself. To his surprise, that gentleman shifted his pipe to the corner of his mouth and put a few pertinent questions to his younger brother. Had he thought it all out? What time should they arrive there? How early on the day after Christmas could they get away? Was he positive they could all crowd into the house without rousing and alarming the pair?

"Sure thing," Guy declared, quickly. "Marietta—well, you know I've had the soft side of her old heart ever since I was born, somehow. I talked it all over with her last year, and I'm solid with her, all right. She'll work the game. You see, father's quite a bit deaf now—"

"Father deaf?"

"Sure. Didn't you know it?"

"Forgotten. But mother'd hear us."

"No, she wouldn't. Don't you know how she trusts everything about the house to Marietta since she got that fall—"

"Mother get a fall?"

"Why, *yes*!" Guy stared at his brother with some impatience. "Don't you remember she fell down the back stairs a year ago last October, and hurt her knee?"

"Certainly, Oliver," his wife interposed. "I wrote for you to tell her how sorry we were. But I supposed she had entirely recovered."

"She's a little bit lame, and always will be," said Guy, a touch of reproach in his tone. "Her knee stiffens up in the night, and she doesn't get up and go prowling about at the least noise, the way she used to. Marietta won't let her. So if we make a whisper of noise Marietta'll tell her it's the cat or something.

Good Lord! yes—it can be worked all right. The only thing that worries me is the fear that I can't get you all to take hold of the scheme. On my word, Ol,"—he turned quite away from his sister-in-law's critical gaze and faced his brother with something like indignation in his frank young eyes—"don't we owe the old home anything but a present tied up in tissue paper once a year?"

Marian began to speak. She thought Guy was exceeding his rights in talking as if they had been at fault. It was not often that elderly people had so many children within call—loyal children who would do anything within reason. But certainly a man owed something to his own family. And at Christmas! Why not carry out this plan at some other—

Her husband abruptly interrupted her. He took his pipe quite out of his mouth and spoke decidedly.

"Guy, I believe you're right. I'll be sorry to desert my own kids, of course, but I rather think they can stand it for once. If the others fall into line, you may count on me."

Guy got away, feeling that the worst of his troubles was over. In his younger sister, Nan, he hoped to find an ardent ally and he was not disappointed. Carolyn—Mrs. Charles Wetmore—also fell in heartily with the plan. Ralph, from somewhere in the far West, wrote that he would get home or break a leg. Edson thought the idea rather a foolish one, but was persuaded by Jessica, his wife—whom Guy privately declared a trump[1]—that he must go by all means.

And so they all fell into line, and there remained for Guy only the working out of the details.

"Mis' Fernald"—Marietta Cooley strove with all the decision of which she was capable to keep her high-pitched, middle-aged voice in order—"'fore you get to bed I'm most forgettin' what I was to ask you. I s'pose you'll laugh, but Guy—he wrote me partic'lar he wanted you and his father to"—Marietta's rather stern, thin face took on a curious expression—"to hang up your stockin's."

Mrs. Fernald paused in the door-way of the bedroom opening from the sitting-room downstairs. She looked back at Marietta with her gentle smile.

"Guy wrote that?" she asked. "Then—it almost looks as if he might be coming himself, doesn't it, Marietta?"

"Well, I don't know's I'd really expect him," Marietta replied, turning her face away and busying herself about the hearth. "I guess what he meant was more in the way of a surprise for a Christmas present—something that'll go into a stockin', maybe."

"It's rather odd he should have written you to ask me," mused Mrs. Fernald, as she looked out the stockings.

Marietta considered rapidly. "Well, I s'pose he intended for me to get 'em on the sly without mentionin' it to you, an' put in what he sent, but I sort of guessed you might like to fall in with his idee by hangin' 'em up yourself, here by the chimbley, where the children all used to do it. Here's the nails, same as they always was."

Mrs. Fernald found the stockings, and touched her husband on the shoulder, as he sat unlacing his shoes. "Father, Guy wrote he wanted us to hang up our stockings," she said, raising her voice a little and speaking very distinctly. The elderly man beside her looked up, smiling.

"Well, well," he said, "anything to please the boy. It doesn't seem more than a year since he was a little fellow hanging up his own stocking, does it, mother?"

The stockings were hung in silence. They looked thin and lonely as they dangled beside the dying fire. Marietta hastened to make them less lonely. "Well," she said, in a shame-faced way, "the silly boy said I was to hang mine, too. Goodness knows what he'll find to put into it that'll fit, 'less it's a poker."

They smiled kindly at her, wished her good night, and went back into their own room. The little episode had aroused no suspicions. It was very like Guy's affectionate boyishness.

"I presume he'll be down," said Mrs. Fernald, as she limped quietly about the room, making ready for bed. "Don't you remember how he surprised us last year? I'm sorry the others can't come. Of course, I sent them all the invitation, just as usual—I shall always do that—but it *is* pretty snowy weather, and I suppose they don't quite like to risk it."

Presently, as she was putting out the light, she heard Marietta at the door.

"Mis' Fernald, Peter Piper's got back in this part o' the house, somehow, and I can't lay hands on him. Beats all how cute that cat is. Seem's if he knows when I'm goin' to put him out in the wood-shed.I don't think likely he'll do no harm, but I thought I'd tell you, so 'f you heard any queer noises in the night you'd know it was Peter."

"Very well, Marietta"—the soft voice came back to the schemer on the other side of the door. "Peter will be all right, wherever he is. I shan't be alarmed if I hear him."

"All right, Mis' Fernald; I just thought I'd let you know," and the guileful one went grinning away.

There was a long silence in the quiet sleeping-room. Then, out of the darkness, came this little colloquy:

"Emeline, you aren't getting to sleep."

"I—know I'm not, John. I—Christmas Eve keeps one awake, somehow. It always did."

"Yes.... I don't suppose the children realise at all, do they?"

"Oh, no—oh, no! They don't realise—they never will, till—they're here themselves. It's all right. I think—I think at least Guy will be down to-morrow, don't you?"

"I guess maybe he will." Then, after a short silence. "Mother—you've got me, you know. You know—you've always got me, dear."

"Yes." She would not let him hear the sob in her voice. She crept close, and spoke cheerfully in his best ear. "And you've got me, Johnny Boy!"

"Thank the Lord, I have!"

So, counting their blessings, they fell asleep at last. But, even in sleep, one set of lashes was strangely wet.

"Christopher Jinks, what a drift!"

"Lucky we weren't two hours later."

"Sh-h—they might hear us."

"Nan, stop laughing, or I'll drop a snowball down your neck!"

"Here, Carol, give me your hand. I'll plough you through. Large bodies move slowly, of course, but go elbows first and you'll get there."

"Gee *whiz*! Can't you get that door open? I'll bet it's frozen fast."

"Stumbling over their own feet and bundles...th e crew poured into the warm kitchen."

A light showed inside the kitchen. The storm-door swung open, propelled by force from inside. A cautious voice said low: "That the Fernald family?"

A chorus of whispers came back at Miss Marietta Cooley:

"Yes, yes—let us in, we're freezing."

"You bet we're the Fernald family—every man-Jack ofus—not one missing."

"Oh, Marietta—you dear old thing!"

"Hurry up—this is their side of the house."

"*Sh-h-h—*"

"Carol, your *sh-h-ishes* would wake the dead!"

Stumbling over their own feet and bundles in the endeavour to be preternaturally quiet, the crew poured into the warm kitchen. Bearded Oliver, oldest of the clan; stout Edson, big Ralph, tall and slender Guy—and the two daughters of the house, Carolyn, growing plump and rosy at thirty; Nan, slim and girlish at twenty-four—they were all there. Marietta heaved a sigh of content as she looked them over.

"Well, I didn't really think you'd get here—all of you. Thank the Lord, you have. I s'pose you're tearin' hungry, bein' past 'leven. If you think you can eat quiet as cats, I'll feed you up, but if you're goin' to make as much rumpus as you did comin' round the corner o' the wood-shed I'll have to pack you straight off to bed up the back stairs."

They pleaded for mercy and hot food. They got it—everything that could be had that would diffuse no odour of cookery through the house. Smoking clam-broth, a great pot of baked beans, cold meats, and jellies—they had no reason to complain of their reception. They ate hungrily with the appetites of winter travel.

"Say, but this is great," exulted Ralph, the stalwart, consuming a huge wedge of mince pie with a fine disregard for any consequences that might overtake him. "This alone is worth it. I haven't eaten such pie in a century. What a jolly place this old kitchen is! Let's have a candy-pull to-morrow. I haven't been home Christmas in—let me see—by Jove, I believe it's six—seven—yes, seven years. Look here: there's been some excuse for me, but what about you people that live near?"

He looked accusingly about. Carolyn got up and came around to him. "Don't talk about it to-night," she whispered. "We haven't any of us realised how long it's been."

"We'll get off to bed now," Guy declared, rising. "I can't get over the feeling that they may catch us down here. If either of them should want some hot water or anything—"

"The dining-room door's bolted," Marietta assured him, "but it might need explainin' if I had to bring 'em hot water by way of the parlour. Now, go awful careful up them stairs. They're pretty near over your ma's head, but I don't dare have you tramp through the settin'-room to the front ones. Now, remember that seventh stair creaks like Ned—you've got to step right on the outside edge of it to keep it quiet. I don't know but what you boys better step right up over that seventh stair without touchin' foot to it."

"All right—we'll step!"

"Who's going to fix the bundles?" Carolyn paused to ask as she started up the stairs.

"Marietta," Guy answered. "I've labeled every one, so it'll be easy. If they hear paper rattle, they'll think it's the usual presents we've sent on, and if they come out they'll see Marietta, so it's all right. Quiet, now. Remember the seventh stair!"

They crept up, one by one, each to his or her old room. There needed to be no "doubling up," for the house was large, and each room had been left precisely as its owner had left it. It was rather ghostly, this stealing silently about with candles, and in the necessity for the suppression of speech the animation of the party rather suffered eclipse. It was late, and they were beginning to be sleepy, so they were soon in bed. But, somehow, once composed for slumber, more than one grew wakeful again.

Guy, lying staring at a patch of wintry moonlight on the odd striped paper of his wall—it had stopped snowing since they had come into the house, and the clouds had broken away, leaving a brilliant sky—discovered his door to be softly opening. The glimmer of a candle filtered through the crack, a voice whispered his name.

"Who is it?" he answered under his breath.

"It's Nan. May I come in?"

"Of course. What's up?"

"Nothing. I wanted to talk a minute." She came noiselessly in, wrapped in a woolly scarlet kimono, scarlet slippers on her feet, her brown braids hanging down her back. The frost-bloom lately on her cheeks had melted into a ruddy glow, her eyes were stars. She set her candle on the little stand, and sat down on the edge of Guy's bed. He raised himself on his elbow and lay looking appreciatively at her.

"This is like old times," he said. "But won't you be cold?"

"Not a bit. I'm only going to stay a minute. Anyhow, this thing is warm as toast.... Yes, isn't it like old times?"

"Got your lessons for to-morrow?"

She laughed. "All but my Cæsar. You'll help me with that, in the morning, won't you?"

"Sure—if you'll make some cushions for my bobs."

"I will. Guy—how's Lucy Harper?"

"She's all right. How's Bob Fields?"

"Oh, I don't care for him, now!" She tossed her head.

He kept up the play. "Like Dave Strong better, huh? He's a softy."

"He isn't. Oh, Guy—I heard you had a new girl."

"New girl nothing. Don't care for girls."

"Yes, you do. At least I think you do. Her name's—Margaret."

The play ceased abruptly. Guy's face changed. "Perhaps I do," he murmured, while his sister watched him in the candle-light.

"She won't answer yet?" she asked very gently.

"Not a word."

"You've cared a good while, haven't you, dear?"

"Seems like ages. Suppose it isn't."

"No—only two years, really caring hard. Plenty of time left."

He moved his head impatiently. "Yes, if I didn't mind seeing her smile on Tommy Gower—de'il take him—just as sweetly as she smiles on me. If she ever held out the tip of her finger to me, I'd seize it and hold on to it for fair. But she doesn't. She won't. And she's going South next week for the rest of the winter, and there's a fellow down there in South Carolina where she goes—oh, he—he's red-headed after her, like the rest of us. And, well—I'm up against it good and hard, Nan, and that's the truth."

"Poor boy. And you gave up going to see her on Christmas Day, and came down here into the country just to—"

"Just to get even with myself for the way I've neglected 'em these two years while my head's been so full of—her. It isn't fair. After last year I'd have come home to-day if it had meant I had to lose—well—Margaret knows I'm here. I don't know what she thinks."

"I don't believe, Guy, boy, she thinks the less of you. Yes—I must go. It will all come right in the end, dear—I'm sure of it. No, I don't know how Margaret feels—Good night—good night!"

Christmas morning, breaking upon a wintry world—the Star in the East long set. Outside the house a great silence of drift-wrapped hill and plain;—inside, a crackling fire upon a wide hearth, and a pair of elderly people waking to a lonely holiday.

Mrs. Fernald crept to the door of her room—the injured knee always made walking difficult after a night's quiet. She meant to sit down by the fire which she had lately heard Marietta stirring and feeding into activity, and warm herself at its flame. She remembered with a sad little smile that she and John had hung their stockings there, and looked to see what miracle had been wrought in the night.

"*Father!*"—Her voice caught in her throat.... What was all this?... By some mysterious influence her husband learned that she was calling him, though he had not really heard. He came to the door and looked at her, then at the chimneypiece where the stockings hung—a long row of them, as they had not hung since the children grew up—stockings of quality: one of brown silk, Nan's; a fine[gray sock with scarlet clocks,[2] Ralph's,—all stuffed to the top, with bundles overflowing upon the chimneypiece and even to the floor below.

"The children!" she was saying.
"They—they—John—they must be here!"

"Father!"—Her voice caught in her throat.... What was all this?... By some mysterious influence her husband learned that she was calling him, though he had not really heard. He came to the door and looked at her, then at the chimneypiece where the stockings hung—a long row of them, as they had not hung since the children grew up—stockings of quality: one of brown silk, Nan's; a fine[gray sock with scarlet clocks,[2] Ralph's,—all stuffed to the top, with bundles overflowing upon the chimneypiece and even to the floor below.

"What's this—what's this?" John Fernald's voice was puzzled. "Whose are these?" He limped closer. He put on his spectacles and stared hard at a parcel protruding from the sock with the scarlet clocks.

"'*Merry Christmas to Ralph from Nan*,'" he read. "'To Ralph from Nan,'" he repeated vaguely. His gaze turned to his wife. His eyes were wide like a child's. But she was getting to her feet from the chair into which she had dropped.

"The children!" she was saying. "They—they—John—they must be *here*!"

He followed her through the chilly hall to the front staircase, seldom used now, and up—as rapidly as those slow, stiff joints would allow. Trembling, Mrs. Fernald pushed open the first door at the top.

A rumpled brown head raised itself from among the pillows, a pair of sleepy but affectionate brown eyes smiled back at the two faces peering in, and a voice brimful of mirth cried softly: "Merry Christmas, mammy and daddy!" They stared at her, their eyes growing misty. *It was their little daughter Nan, not yet grown up!*

They could not believe it. Even when they had been to every room;—had seen their big son Ralph, still sleeping, his yet youthful face, full of healthy colour, pillowed on his brawny arm, and his mother had gently kissed him awake to be half-strangled in his hug;—when they had met Edson's hearty laugh as he fired a pillow at them—carefully, so that his father could catch it;—when they had seen plump pretty Carol pulling on her stockings as she sat on the floor smiling up at them;—Oliver, advancing to meet them in his bath-robe and slippers;—Guy, holding out both arms from above his blankets, and shouting "Merry Christmas!—and how do you like your children?"—even then it was difficult to realise that not one was missing—and that no one else was there.

Unconsciously Mrs. Fernald found herself looking about for the sons' wives and daughters' husbands and children. She loved them all;—yet—to have her own, and no others, just for this one day—it was happiness indeed.

When they were all downstairs, about the fire, there was great rejoicing. They had Marietta in; indeed, she had been hovering continuously in the background, to the apparently frightful jeopardy of the breakfast in preparation, upon which, nevertheless, she had managed to keep a practised eye.

"And you were in it, Marietta?" Mr. Fernald said to her in astonishment, when he first saw her. "How in the world did you get all these people into the house and to bed without waking us?"

"It was pretty consid'able of a resk," Marietta replied, with modest pride, "'seein' as how they was inclined to be middlin' lively. But I kep' a-hushin' 'em up, and I filled 'em up so full of victuals they couldn't talk. I didn't know's there'd be any eatables left for to-day," she added—which last remark, since she had been slyly baking for a week, Guy thought might be considered pure bluff.

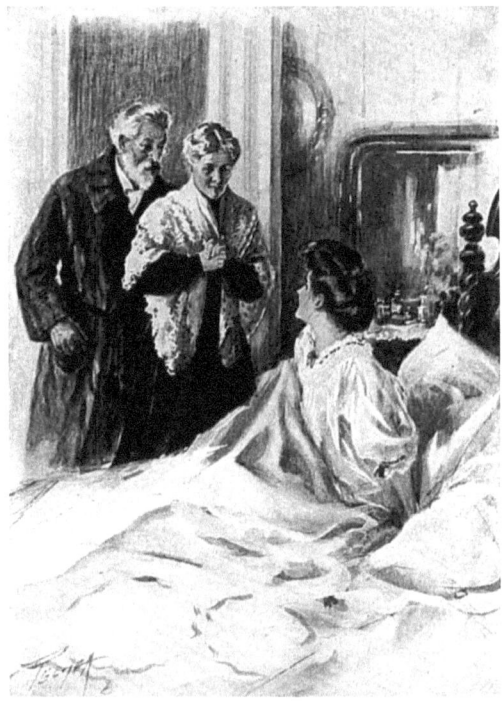

"Merry Christmas, Mammy and Daddy!"

At the breakfast table, while the eight heads were bent, this thanksgiving arose, as the master of the house, in a voice not quite steady, offered it to One Unseen:

> *Thou who camest to us on that first Christmas Day, we bless Thee for this good and perfect gift Thou sendest us to-day, that Thou forgettest us not in these later years, but givest us the greatest joy of our lives in these our loyal children.*

Nan's hand clutched Guy's under the table. "Doesn't that make it worth it?" his grasp said to her, and hers replied with a frantic pressure, "Indeed it does, but we don't deserve it."

... It was late in the afternoon, a tremendous Christmas dinner well over, and the group scattered, when Guy and his mother sat alone by the fire. The "boys" had gone out to the great stock barn with their father to talk over with him every detail of the prosperous business he, with the help of an invaluable assistant, was yet able to manage. Carolyn and Nan had ostensibly gone with them, but in reality the former was calling upon an old friend of her childhood, and the latter had begged a horse and sleigh and driven merrily away alone upon an errand she would tell no one but her mother.

Mrs. Fernald sat in her low chair at the side of the hearth, her son upon a cushion at her feet, his head resting against her knee. Her slender fingers were gently threading the thick locks of his hair, as she listened while he talked to her of everything in his life, and, at last, of the one thing he cared most about.

"Sometimes I get desperate and think I may as well give her up for good and all," he was saying. "She's so—so—*elusive*—I don't know any other word for it. I never can tell how I stand with her. She's going South next week. I've asked her to answer me before she goes. Somehow I've clung to the hope that I'd get my answer to-day. You'll laugh, but I left word with my office-boy to wire me if a note or anything from her came. It's four o'clock, and I haven't heard. She—you see, I can't help thinking it's because she's going to—turn me down—and—hates to do it—Christmas Day!"

He turned suddenly and buried his face in his mother's lap; his shoulders heaved a little in spite of himself. His mother's hand caressed his head more tenderly than ever, but, if he could have seen, her eyes were very bright.

They were silent for a long time. Then suddenly a jingle of sleigh bells approached through the falling winter twilight, drew near, and stopped at the door. Guy's mother laid her hands upon his shoulders. "Son," she said, "there's some one stopping now. Perhaps it's the boy with a message from the station."

He was on his feet in an instant. Her eyes followed him as he rushed away through the hall. Then she rose and quietly closed the sitting-room door behind him.

As Guy flung open the front door, a tall and slender figure in gray furs and a wide gray hat was coming up the walk. Eyes whose glance had long been his dearest torture met Guy Fernald's and fell. Lips like which there were no others in the world smiled tremulously in response to his eager exclamation. And over the piquant young face rose an exquisite colour which was not altogether born of the wintry air. The girl who for two years had been only "elusive" had taken the significant step of coming to North Estabrook in response to an eloquent telephone message sent that morning by Nan.

Holding both her hands fast, Guy led her up into the house—and found himself alone with her in the shadowy hall. With one gay shout Nan had driven away toward the barn. The inner doors were all closed. Blessing the wondrous sagacity of his womankind, Guy took advantage of his moment.

"Nan brought you—I see that. I know you're very fond of her, but—you didn't come wholly to please her, did you—Margaret?"

"Not wholly."

"I've been looking all day for my answer. I—oh—I wonder if—" he was gathering courage from her aspect, which for the first time in his experience failed to keep him at a distance—"*dare* I think you—*bring it*?"

She slowly lifted her face. "I thought it was so—so dear of you," she murmured, "to come home to your people instead of—staying with me. I thought you deserved—what you say—you want—"

"*Margaret*—you—"

"I haven't given you any Christmas present. Will—I—do?"

"Will *you* do!... *Oh!*"—It was a great explosive sigh of relief and joy, and as he gave vent to it he caught her close. "Will—*you*—do!... Good Lord!... I rather *think you will*!"

"I haven't given you any Christmas
present. Will-I-do?"

"*Emeline*—"

"*Yes, John dear?*"

"*You're not—crying?*"

"*Oh, no—no, no, John!*" *What a blessing deafness is sometimes! The ear cannot detect the delicate tremolo which might tell the story too plainly. And in the darkness of night, the eye cannot see.*

"It's been a pretty nice day, hasn't it?"

"A beautiful day!"

"I guess there's no doubt but the children care a good deal for the old folks yet."

"No doubt at all, dear."

"It's good to think they're all asleep under the roof once more, isn't it?—And one extra one. We like her, don't we?"

"Oh, very, very much!"

"Yes, Guy's done well. I always thought he'd get her, if he hung on. The Fernalds always hang on, but Guy's got a mite of a temper—I didn't know but he might let go a little too soon. Well—it's great to think they all plan to spend every Christmas Day with us, isn't it, Emeline?"

"Yes, dear—it's—great."

"Well—I must let you go to sleep. It's been a big day, and I guess you're tired. Emeline, we've not only got each other—we've got the children too. That's a pretty happy thing at our age, isn't it, now?"

"Yes—yes."

"Good night—Christmas Night, Emeline."

"Good night, dear."

1 *"a trump" as in a trump card, the best*

2 *Clocking was lavishly embroidered sections (called "clocks") on hosiery, Early fireplace stockings were literally the type to be worn, not the special Christmas-time-only ones we have now.*

Washington Irving
Christmas Selections

Washington Irving, 1783 – 1859

Writer, historian, diplomat

Irving was one of the first American writers to receive critical acclaim in Europe and is also the author of "Rip Van Winkle" and "Sleepy Hollow." The following four abridged excerpts, "Christmas," "Christmas Eve," "Christmas Day," and "Christmas Dinner" are from Irving's book, Bracebridge Hall, *written in England in 1821 and published in 1822. Pre-dating Dickens, Irving's book brought to readers old customs that had already been long forgotten, considered quaint or antique. They were appreciated then—and now—for precisely that reason.*

CHRISTMAS

Amidst the general call to happiness, the bustle of the spirits, and stir of the affections which prevail at this period what bosom can remain insensible? It is, indeed, the season of regenerated feeling—the season for kindling not merely the fire of hospitality in the hall, but the genial flame of charity in the heart; and the idea of home, fraught with the fragrance of home-dwelling joys, reanimates the drooping spirit...

Stranger and sojourner as I am in the land, though for me no social hearth may blaze, no hospitable roof throw open its doors, nor the warm grasp of friendship welcome me at the threshold, yet I feel the influence of the season beaming into my soul from the happy looks of those around me. Surely happiness is reflective, like the light of heaven, and every countenance, bright with smiles and glowing with innocent enjoyment, is a mirror transmitting to others the rays of a supreme and ever-shining benevolence.

He who can turn churlishly away from contemplating the felicity of his fellow-beings, and sit down darkling and repining in his loneliness when all around is joyful, may have his moments of strong excitement and selfish gratification, but he wants[1] the genial and social sympathies which constitute the charm of a merry Christmas.

[1]*Lacks*

II. CHRISTMAS EVE

...As we approached the house we heard the sound of music, and now and then a burst of laughter from one end of the building. This, Bracebridge said, must proceed from the servants' hall, where a great deal of revelry was permitted, and even encouraged by the squire throughout the twelve days of Christmas, provided everything was done conformably to ancient usage.

Here were kept up the old games of hoodman blind, shoe the wild mare, hot cockles, steal the white loaf, bob apple, and snap dragon; the Yule-clog and Christmas candle were regularly burnt, and the mistletoe with its white berries hung up, to the imminent peril of all the pretty housemaids [1]

So intent were the servants upon their sports that we had to ring repeatedly before we could make ourselves heard. On our arrival being announced the squire came out to receive us, accompanied by his two other sons—one a young officer in the army, home on a leave of absence; the other an Oxonian, just from the university. The squire was a fine healthy-looking old gentleman, with silver hair curling lightly round an open florid countenance, a singular mixture of whim and benevolence.

The family meeting was warm and affectionate; as the evening was far advanced, the squire would not permit us to change our travelling dresses, but ushered us at once to the company, which was assembled in a large old-fashioned hall. ...Where there were the usual proportion of old uncles and aunts, comfortable married dames, superannuated spinsters, blooming country cousins, half-fledged striplings, and bright-eyed boarding-school hoydens.

They were variously occupied—some at a round game of cards; others conversing around the fireplace; at one end of the hall was a group of the young folks, some nearly grown up, others of a more tender and budding age, fully engrossed by a merry game; and a profusion of wooden horses, penny trumpets, and tattered dolls about the floor showed traces of a troop of little fairy beings who, having frolicked through a happy day, had been carried off to slumber through a peaceful night.

The grate had been removed from the wide overwhelming fireplace to make way for a fire of wood, in the midst of which was an enormous log glowing and blazing, and sending forth a vast volume of light and heat: this, I understood, was the Yule-clog,[2] which the squire was particular in having brought in and illumined on a Christmas Eve, according to ancient custom.

Supper was announced... It was served up in a spacious oaken chamber, the panels of which shone with wax, and around which were several family portraits decorated with holly and ivy. Besides the accustomed lights, two great wax tapers, called Christmas candles, wreathed with greens, were placed on a highly polished beaufet[3] among the family plate.

The table was abundantly spread with substantial fare; but the squire made his supper of frumenty, a dish made of wheat cakes boiled in milk with rich spices, being a standing dish in old times for Christmas Eve. I was happy to find my old friend, minced pie, in the retinue of the feast and, finding him to be perfectly orthodox, and that I need not be ashamed of my predilection, I greeted him with all the warmth wherewith we usually greet an old and very genteel acquaintance.

No sooner was supper removed and spiced wines and other beverages peculiar to the season introduced, than Master Simon was called on for a good old Christmas song. He quavered forth a quaint old ditty:

The supper had disposed everyone to gayety, and an old harper was summoned from the servants' hall. The dance, like most dances after supper, was a merry one: some of the older folks joined in it, and the squire himself figured down with a partner with whom he affirmed he had danced at every Christmas for nearly half a century.

Master Simon ... a little antiquated in the taste of his accomplishments, evidently piqued himself on his dancing, and was endeavoring to gain credit by the heel and toe, rigadoon,[4] and other graces of the ancient school; but he had unluckily assorted himself with a little romping girl from boarding-school, who by her wild vivacity...defeated all his sober attempts at elegance: such are the ill-sorted matches to which antique gentlemen are unfortunately prone.

The young Oxonian had led out one of his maiden aunts, on whom the rogue played a thousand little knaveries with impunity: he was full of practical jokes, and his delight was to tease his aunts and cousins, yet, like all madcap youngsters, he was a universal favorite among the women.

The most interesting couple in the dance was the young officer and a ward of the squire's, a beautiful blushing girl of seventeen. From several shy glances which I had noticed in the course of the evening I suspected there was a little kindness growing up between them; and indeed the young soldier was just the hero to captivate a romantic girl.

He was tall, slender, and handsome, and, like most young British officers of late years, had picked up various small accomplishments on the Continent: he could talk French and Italian, draw landscapes, sing very tolerably, dance divinely, but, above all, he had been wounded at Waterloo. What girl of seventeen, well read in poetry and romance, could resist such a mirror of chivalry and perfection?

...The party now broke up for the night with the kind-hearted old custom of shaking hands. As I passed through the hall on my way to my chamber, the dying embers of the Yule-clog still sent forth a dusky glow, and had it not been the season when "no spirit dares stir abroad," I should have been half tempted to steal from my room at midnight and peep whether the fairies might not be at their revels about the hearth.... I had scarcely got into bed when a strain of music seemed to break forth in the air just below the window. I listened, and found it proceeded from a band which I concluded to be the Waits[5] from some neighboring village.

They went round the house, playing under the windows. I drew aside the curtains to hear them more distinctly. The sounds, as they receded, became more soft and aerial, and seemed to accord with the quiet and moonlight. I listened and listened—they became more and more tender and remote, and, as they gradually died away, my head sunk upon the pillow and I fell asleep.

1. *The mistletoe is still hung up in farm-houses and kitchens at Christmas, and the young men have the privilege of kissing the girls under it, plucking each time a berry from the bush. When the berries are all plucked the privilege ceases]*

2. *The Yule-clog is a great log of wood, sometimes the root of a tree, brought into the house with great ceremony on Christmas Eve, laid in the fireplace, and lighted with the brand of last year's clog. While it lasted there was great drinking, singing, and telling of tales. Sometimes it was accompanied by Christmas candles; but in the cottages the only light was from the ruddy blaze of the great wood fire. The Yule-clog was to burn all night; if it went out, it was considered a sign of ill luck.*

3 *A niche, cupboard, or sideboard for plate, china, glass, etc.; a buffet.*

4 *The Rigadoon is a lively French dance or its music*

5 *The Waits were an organized band of carolers or musicians who usually played or sang expecting tips. They were often territorial, banning other groups from doing the same in their village or town.*

III. CHRISTMAS DAY

When I woke the next morning it seemed as if all the events of the preceding evening had been a dream. While I lay musing on my pillow I heard the sound of little feet pattering outside of the door, and a whispering consultation. Presently a choir of small voices chanted forth an old (song), which was

Rejoice, our Saviour he was born
On Christmas Day in the morning.[1]

I rose softly, slipt on my clothes, opened the door suddenly, and beheld one of the most beautiful little fairy groups that a painter could imagine. It consisted of a boy and two girls, the eldest not more than six, and lovely as seraphs. They were going the rounds of the house and singing at every chamber door, but my sudden appearance frightened them into mute bashfulness.

I had scarcely dressed myself when a servant appeared to invite me to family prayers. He showed me the way to a small chapel in the old wing of the house, where I found the principal part of the family already assembled with cushions, hassocks, and large prayer-books; the servants were seated on benches below. The old gentleman read prayers from a desk, and Master Simon acted as clerk and made the responses...

The service was followed by a Christmas carol, which Mr. Bracebridge himself had constructed from a poem of his favorite author, Herrick[3], and it had been adapted to an old church melody by Master Simon. As there were several good voices among the household, the effect was extremely pleasing, but I was particularly gratified by the exaltation of heart and sudden sally of grateful feeling with which the worthy squire delivered one stanza, his eye glistening and his voice rambling out of all the bounds of time and tune:

> "'Tis Thou that crown'st my glittering hearth
> With guiltless mirth,
> And givest me Wassaile bowles to drink
> Spiced to the brink,
> Lord, 'tis Thy plenty-dropping hand
> That soiles my land.
> And giv'st me for my bushell sowne,
> Twice ten for one.

I afterwards understood that early morning service was read on every Sunday and saint's day throughout the year. It was once almost universally the case at the seats of the nobility and gentry of England, and it is much to be regretted that the custom is falling into neglect; for the dullest observer must be sensible of the order and serenity prevalent in those households where the occasional exercise of a beautiful form of worship in the morning gives, as it were, the keynote to every temper for the day and attunes every spirit to harmony.

...Master Simon had now to hurry off, having an appointment at the parish church with the village choristers, who were to perform some music of his selection... While we were talking we heard the distant toll of the village bell, and I was told that the squire was a little particular in having his household at church on a Christmas morning, considering it a day of pouring out of thanks and rejoicing; for, as old Tusser observed,

> "At Christmas be merry, and thankful withal,
> And feast thy poor neighbors, the great with the small."

...As the morning, though frosty, was remarkably fine and clear, most of the family walked to the church, which was a very old building of gray stone. Adjoining it was a low snug parsonage which seemed coeval[1] with the church. As we passed this sheltered nest the parson issued forth and preceded us.

...On reaching the church-porch we found the parson rebuking the gray-headed sexton for having used mistletoe among the greens with which the church was decorated. It was, he observed, an unholy plant, profaned by having been used by the Druids in their mystic ceremonies; and, though it might be innocently employed in the festive ornamenting of halls and kitchens, yet it had been deemed by the Fathers of the Church as unhallowed and totally unfit for sacred purposes. So tenacious was he on this point that the poor sexton was obliged to strip down a great part of the humble trophies of his taste before the parson would consent to enter upon the service of the day.

[He then] gave us a most erudite sermon on the rites and ceremonies of Christmas, and the propriety of observing it not merely as a day of thanksgiving but of rejoicing, supporting the correctness of his opinions by the earliest usages of the Church, and enforcing them by the authorities of Theophilus of Caesarea, St. Cyprian, St. Chrysostom, St. Augustine, and a cloud more of saints and fathers, from whom he made copious quotations.

(He) concluded by urging his hearers, in the most solemn and affecting manner, to stand to the traditional customs of their fathers and feast and make merry on this joyful anniversary of the Church. ..

The villagers doffed their hats to the squire as he passed, giving him the good wishes of the season with every appearance of heartfelt sincerity, and were invited by him to the hall to take something to keep out the cold of the weather; and I heard blessings uttered by several of the poor, which convinced me that, in the midst of his enjoyments, the worthy old cavalier had not forgotten the true Christmas virtue of charity.

On our way homeward [the squire's] heart seemed overflowed with generous and happy feelings... it was, as the squire observed, an emblem of Christmas hospitality breaking through the chills of ceremony and selfishness and thawing every heart into a flow. He pointed with pleasure to the indications of good cheer reeking from the chimneys of the comfortable farm-houses and low thatched cottages.

"I love," said he, "to see this day well kept by rich and poor; it is a great thing to have one day in the year, at least, when you are sure of being welcome wherever you go, and of having, as it were, the world all thrown open to you."

1 From, "Good Christians, Rise, This is the Morn," Anonymous
2 coeval—existing during the same time period; of the same age.
3 Robert Herrick, 1591 – 1694. Poet and vicar.

IV. CHRISTMAS DINNER

Lo, now is come our joyful'st feast!
Let every man be jolly.
Eache roome with yvie leaves is drest,
And every post with holly.

The dinner was served up in the great hall, where the squire always held his Christmas banquet. A blazing crackling fire of logs had been heaped on to warm the spacious apartment, and the flame went sparkling and wreathing up the wide-mouthed chimney. The great picture of the crusader and his white horse had been profusely decorated with greens for the occasion, and holly and ivy had likewise been wreathed round the helmet and weapons on the opposite wall.

A sideboard was set out on which was a display of plate that might have vied (at least in variety) with Belshazzar's parade of the vessels of the temple: "flagons, cans, cups, beakers, goblets, basins, and ewers," the gorgeous utensils of good companionship that had gradually accumulated through many generations of jovial housekeepers. Before these stood the two Yule candles, beaming like two stars of the first magnitude; other lights were distributed in branches, and the whole array glittered like a firmament of silver.

We were ushered into this banqueting scene with the sound of minstrelsy, the old harper being seated on a stool beside the fireplace and twanging his instrument with a vast deal more power than melody.

Never did Christmas board display a more goodly and gracious assemblage of countenances; those who were not handsome were at least happy, and happiness is a rare improver of your hard-favored visage.

The parson said grace... Suddenly the butler entered the hall ... attended by a servant on each side and bore a silver dish on which was an enormous pig's head decorated with rosemary, with a lemon in its mouth, which was placed with great formality at the head of the table.[1]

The table was literally loaded with good cheer, and presented an epitome of country abundance in this season of overflowing larders.

...When the cloth was removed the butler brought in a huge silver vessel of rare and curious workmanship, which he placed before the squire...being the Wassail Bowl, so renowned in Christmas festivity. ...It was a potation...being composed of the richest and raciest wines, highly spiced and sweetened, with roasted apples bobbing about the surface.[2]

The old gentleman's whole countenance beamed ... Having raised it to his lips, with a hearty wish of a merry Christmas to all present, he sent it brimming round the board, for every one to follow his example, according to the primitive style, pronouncing it "the ancient fountain of good feeling, where all hearts met together."[3]

There was much laughing and rallying as the honest emblem of Christmas joviality circulated and was kissed rather coyly by the ladies... How easy it is for one benevolent being to diffuse pleasure around him! and how truly is a kind heart a fountain of gladness, making everything in its vicinity to freshen into smiles! The joyous disposition of the worthy squire was perfectly contagious; he was happy himself, and disposed to make all the world happy...

The parson, too, began to show the effects of good cheer, having gradually settled down into a doze and his wig sitting most suspiciously on one side. Just at this juncture we were summoned to the drawing room.

After the dinner-table was removed the hall was given up to the younger members of the family... (who) made its old walls ring with their merriment as they played at romping games.

But enough of Christmas and its gambols; it is time for me to pause in this garrulity. Methinks I hear the questions asked by my graver readers, "To what purpose is all this? how is the world to be made wiser by this talk?"

But in writing to amuse, if I can by any lucky chance, in these days of evil, rub out one wrinkle from the brow of care or beguile the heavy heart of one moment of sorrow; if I can now and then prompt a benevolent view of human nature, and make my reader more in good-humor with his fellow-beings and himself—surely, surely, I shall not then have written entirely in vain.

1. The tradition of the Boar's Head, served with great pomp, is an ancient English custom. "The Boars Head Carol"
from 1521 includes this verse: Our steward hath provided this/ In honour of the King of bliss,/ Which on this day to be
served is / In reginensi atrio, / Caput apri defero, / Reddens laudes Domino. Translated, the Latin is "In the royal court/
I will bring the boar's head/ Giving praise to the Lord. The author of the carol is unknown.

2. [Original note from Irving] "The Wassail Bowl was sometimes composed of ale instead of wine, with nutmeg,
sugar, toast, ginger, and roasted crabs; in this way the nut-brown beverage is still prepared in some old families and
round the hearths of substantial farmers at Christmas. It is also called Lamb's wool ."

3 *"According to the primitive style" meant that everyone passed the one bowl and sipped from it.*

Good King Wenceslas

John Mason Neale, 1818-1866

British Anglican Priest and Hymnist

Neale was a priest, scholar and hymn writer. "Good King Wenceslas," written in 1853, is among his most famous hymns and is set on the second day of Christmas, the Feast of Stephen, better known today as Boxing Day. Based on the life of the Duke of Vaclav of Bohemia, the song may be more legend than fact, but the duke really was a good, generous man, "noted for his piety and devotion to the strengthening of Christianity."[1] The music was borrowed by Neale from a collection of hymns from 1582. He also wrote, "O Come, O Come, Emmanuel."

GOOD KING WENCESLAS

Good King Wenceslas look'd out,
On the Feast of Stephen;
When the snow lay round about,
Deep, and crisp, and even:
Brightly shone the moon that night,
Though the frost was cruel,
When a poor man came in sight,

Gath'ring winter fuel.

"Hither page and stand by me,
If thou know'st it, telling,
Yonder peasant, who is he?
Where and what his dwelling?"
"Sire, he lives a good league hence.
Underneath the mountain;
Right against the forest fence,
By Saint Agnes' fountain."

"Bring me flesh, and bring me wine,
Bring me pine-logs hither:
Thou and I will see him dine,
When we bear them thither."
Page and monarch forth they went,
Forth they went together;
Through the rude wind's wild lament,
And the bitter weather.

"Sire, the night is darker now,
And the wind blows stronger;
Fails my heart, I know now how,
I can go no longer."
"Mark my footsteps, good my page;
Tread thou in them boldly;
Thou shalt find the winter's rage
Freeze thy blood less coldly."

In his master's steps he trod,
Where the snow lay dinted;
Heat was in the very sod
Which the Saint had printed.
Therefore, Christian men, be sure,

Wealth or rank possessing,
Ye who now will bless the poor,
Shall yourselves find blessing.

The Oxen

THOMAS HARDY

Thomas Hardy, 1840 – 1928

English novelist and poet

While Hardy is best known as a Victorian novelist and realist, he regarded himself primarily as a poet and wrote poetry throughout his lifetime. Published on Christmas Eve, 1915, in The Times, this poem is sometimes called by its first line, "Christmas Eve, and twelve of the clock."

THE OXEN

Christmas Eve and twelve of the clock,
"Now they are all on their knees,"
An elder said as we sat in a flock
By the embers in hearthside ease.[1]

We pictured the meek mild creatures where

They dwelt in their strawy pen,
Nor did it occur to one of us there
To doubt they were kneeling then.

So fair a fancy few would weave
In these years! Yet, I feel,
If someone said on Christmas Eve,
"Come; see the oxen kneel,

"In the lonely barton by yonder coomb[2]
Our childhood used to know,"
I should go with him in the gloom,
Hoping it might be so.

[1] *Based on an English legend that every Christmas Day, farm animals kneel in their stalls in homage to Christ.*
[2] *A barton is a farm building and a coomb, a small valley*

The Adventure of the Blue Carbuncle: A Christmas Mystery

ARTHUR CONAN DOYLE

Arthur Conan Doyle, 1859 – 1930

British writer, physician, and creator of Sherlock Holmes

It may seem strange to find Sherlock Holmes in a Christmas anthology, but this little mystery ends on a sweet note, giving homage to the mercy and generosity that Christmas, at its best, engenders, and which even unsentimental Sherlock cannot be impervious to.

THE ADVENTURE OF THE BLUE CARBUNCLE:

A CHRISTMAS MYSTERY

I had called upon my friend Sherlock Holmes upon the second morning after Christmas, with the intention of wishing him the compliments of the season. He was lounging upon the sofa in a purple dressing-gown, a pipe-rack within his reach upon the right, and a pile of crumpled morning papers, evidently newly studied, near at hand. Beside the couch was a wooden chair, and on the angle of the back hung a very seedy and disreputable hard-felt hat, much the worse for wear, and cracked in several places. A lens and a forceps lying upon the seat of the chair suggested that the hat had been suspended in this manner for the purpose of examination.

"You are engaged," said I; "perhaps I interrupt you."

"Not at all. I am glad to have a friend with whom I can discuss my results. The matter is a perfectly trivial one"—he jerked his thumb in the direction of the old hat—"but there are points in connection with it which are not entirely devoid of interest and even of instruction."

I seated myself in his armchair and warmed my hands before his crackling fire, for a sharp frost had set in, and the windows were thick with the ice crystals. "I suppose," I remarked, "that, homely as it looks, this thing has some deadly story linked on to it—that it is the clue which will guide you in the solution of some mystery and the punishment of some crime."

"No, no. No crime," said Sherlock Holmes, laughing. "Only one of those whimsical little incidents which will happen when you have four million human beings all jostling each other within the space of a few square miles. Amid the action and reaction of so dense a swarm of humanity, every possible combination of events may be expected to take place, and many a little problem will be presented which may be striking and bizarre without being criminal. We have already had experience of such."

"So much so," I remarked, "that of the last six cases which I have added to my notes, three have been entirely free of any legal crime."

"Precisely. You allude to my attempt to recover the Irene Adler papers, to the singular case of Miss Mary Sutherland, and to the adventure of the man with the twisted lip. Well, I have no doubt that this small matter will fall into the same innocent category. You know Peterson, the commissionaire?"

"Yes."

"It is to him that this trophy belongs."

"It is his hat."

"No, no, he found it. Its owner is unknown. I beg that you will look upon it not as a battered billycock but as an intellectual problem. And, first, as to how it came here. It arrived upon Christmas morning, in company with a good fat goose, which is, I have no doubt, roasting at this moment in front of Peterson's fire.

The facts are these: about four o'clock on Christmas morning, Peterson, who, as you know, is a very honest fellow, was returning from some small jollification and was making his way homeward down Tottenham Court Road. In front of him he saw, in the gaslight, a tallish man, walking with a slight stagger, and carrying a white goose slung over his shoulder. As he reached the corner of Goodge Street, a row broke out between this stranger and a little knot of roughs. One of the latter knocked off the man's hat, on which he raised his stick to defend himself and, swinging it over his head, smashed the shop window behind him.

Peterson had rushed forward to protect the stranger from his assailants; but the man, shocked at having broken the window, and seeing an official-looking person in uniform rushing towards him, dropped his goose, took to his heels, and vanished amid the labyrinth of small streets which lie at the back of Tottenham Court Road. The roughs had also fled at the appearance of Peterson, so that he was left in possession of the field of battle, and also of the spoils of victory in the shape of this battered hat and a most unimpeachable Christmas goose."

"Which surely he restored to their owner?"

"My dear fellow, there lies the problem. It is true that 'For Mrs. Henry Baker' was printed upon a small card which was tied to the bird's left leg, and it is also true that the initials 'H. B.' are legible upon the lining of this hat, but as there are some thousands of Bakers, and some hundreds of Henry Bakers in this city of ours, it is not easy to restore lost property to any one of them."

"What, then, did Peterson do?"

"He brought round both hat and goose to me on Christmas morning, knowing that even the smallest problems are of interest to me. The goose we retained until this morning, when there were signs that, in spite of the slight frost, it would be well that it should be eaten without unnecessary delay. Its finder has carried it off, therefore, to fulfil the ultimate destiny of a goose, while I continue to retain the hat of the unknown gentleman who lost his Christmas dinner."

"Did he not advertise?"

"No."

"Then, what clue could you have as to his identity?"

"Only as much as we can deduce."

"From his hat?"

"Precisely."

"But you are joking. What can you gather from this old battered felt?"

"Here is my lens. You know my methods. What can you gather yourself as to the individuality of the man who has worn this article?"

I took the tattered object in my hands and turned it over rather ruefully. It was a very ordinary black hat of the usual round shape, hard and much the worse for wear. The lining had been of red silk, but was a good deal discoloured. There was no maker's name; but, as Holmes had remarked, the initials "H. B." were scrawled upon one side. It was pierced in the brim for a hat-securer, but the elastic was missing. For the rest, it was cracked, exceedingly dusty, and spotted in several places, although there seemed to have been some attempt to hide the discoloured patches by smearing them with ink.

"I can see nothing," said I, handing it back to my friend.

"On the contrary, Watson, you can see everything. You fail, however, to reason from what you see. You are too timid in drawing your inferences."

"Then, pray tell me what it is that you can infer from this hat?"

He picked it up and gazed at it in the peculiar introspective fashion which was characteristic of him. "It is perhaps less suggestive than it might have been," he remarked, "and yet there are a few inferences which are very distinct, and a few others which represent at least a strong balance of probability. That the man was highly intellectual is of course obvious upon the face of it, and also that he was fairly well-to-do within the last three years, although he has now fallen upon evil days. He had foresight, but has less now than formerly, pointing to a moral retrogression, which, when taken with the decline of his fortunes, seems to indicate some evil influence, probably drink, at work upon him. This may account also for the obvious fact that his wife has ceased to love him."

"My dear Holmes!"

"He has, however, retained some degree of self-respect," he continued, disregarding my remonstrance. "He is a man who leads a sedentary life, goes out little, is out of training entirely, is middle-aged, has grizzled hair which he has had cut within the last few days, and which he anoints with lime-cream. These are the more patent facts which are to be deduced from his hat. Also, by the way, that it is extremely improbable that he has gas laid on in his house."

"You are certainly joking, Holmes."

"Not in the least. Is it possible that even now, when I give you these results, you are unable to see how they are attained?"

"I have no doubt that I am very stupid, but I must confess that I am unable to follow you. For example, how did you deduce that this man was intellectual?"

For answer Holmes clapped the hat upon his head. It came right over the forehead and settled upon the bridge of his nose. "It is a question of cubic capacity," said he; "a man with so large a brain must have something in it."

"The decline of his fortunes, then?"

"This hat is three years old. These flat brims curled at the edge came in then. It is a hat of the very best quality. Look at the band of ribbed silk and the excellent lining. If this man could afford to buy so expensive a hat three years ago, and has had no hat since, then he has assuredly gone down in the world."

"Well, that is clear enough, certainly. But how about the foresight and the moral retrogression?"

Sherlock Holmes laughed. "Here is the foresight," said he putting his finger upon the little disc and loop of the hat-securer. "They are never sold upon hats. If this man ordered one, it is a sign of a certain amount of foresight, since he went out of his way to take this precaution against the wind. But since we see that he has broken the elastic and has not troubled to replace it, it is obvious that he has less foresight now than formerly, which is a distinct proof of a weakening nature. On the other hand, he has endeavoured to conceal some of these stains upon the felt by daubing them with ink, which is a sign that he has not entirely lost his self-respect."

"Your reasoning is certainly plausible."

"The further points, that he is middle-aged, that his hair is grizzled, that it has been recently cut, and that he uses lime-cream, are all to be gathered from a close examination of the lower part of the lining. The lens discloses a large number of hair-ends, clean cut by the scissors of the barber. They all appear to be adhesive, and there is a distinct odour of lime-cream. This dust, you will observe, is not the gritty, grey dust of the street but the fluffy brown dust of the house, showing that it has been hung up indoors most of the time, while the marks of moisture upon the inside are proof positive that the wearer perspired very freely, and could therefore, hardly be in the best of training."

"But his wife—you said that she had ceased to love him."

"This hat has not been brushed for weeks. When I see you, my dear Watson, with a week's accumulation of dust upon your hat, and when your wife allows you to go out in such a state, I shall fear that you also have been unfortunate enough to lose your wife's affection."

"But he might be a bachelor."

"Nay, he was bringing home the goose as a peace-offering to his wife. Remember the card upon the bird's leg."

"You have an answer to everything. But how on earth do you deduce that the gas is not laid on in his house?"

"One tallow stain, or even two, might come by chance; but when I see no less than five, I think that there can be little doubt that the individual must be brought into frequent contact with burning tallow—walks upstairs at night probably with his hat in one hand and a guttering candle in the other. Anyhow, he never got tallow-stains from a gas-jet. Are you satisfied?"

"Well, it is very ingenious," said I, laughing; "but since, as you said just now, there has been no crime committed, and no harm done save the loss of a goose, all this seems to be rather a waste of energy."

Sherlock Holmes had opened his mouth to reply, when the door flew open, and Peterson, the commissionaire, rushed into the apartment with flushed cheeks and the face of a man who is dazed with astonishment.

"The goose, Mr. Holmes! The goose, sir!" he gasped.

"Eh? What of it, then? Has it returned to life and flapped off through the kitchen window?" Holmes twisted himself round upon the sofa to get a fairer view of the man's excited face.

"See here, sir! See what my wife found in its crop!" He held out his hand and displayed upon the centre of the palm a brilliantly scintillating blue stone, rather smaller than a bean in size, but of such purity and radiance that it twinkled like an electric point in the dark hollow of his hand.

Sherlock Holmes sat up with a whistle. "By Jove, Peterson!" said he, "this is treasure trove indeed. I suppose you know what you have got?"

"A diamond, sir? A precious stone. It cuts into glass as though it were putty."

"It's more than a precious stone. It is *the* precious stone."

"Not the Countess of Morcar's blue carbuncle!" I ejaculated.

"Precisely so. I ought to know its size and shape, seeing that I have read the advertisement about it in *The Times* every day lately. It is absolutely unique, and its value can only be conjectured, but the reward offered of £ 1000 is certainly not within a twentieth part of the market price."

"A thousand pounds! Great Lord of mercy!" The commissionaire plumped down into a chair and stared from one to the other of us.

"That is the reward, and I have reason to know that there are sentimental considerations in the background which would induce the Countess to part with half her fortune if she could but recover the gem."

"It was lost, if I remember aright, at the Hotel Cosmopolitan," I remarked.

"Precisely so, on December 22nd, just five days ago. John Horner, a plumber, was accused of having abstracted it from the lady's jewel-case. The evidence against him was so strong that the case has been referred to the Assizes. I have some account of the matter here, I believe." He rummaged amid his newspapers, glancing over the dates, until at last he smoothed one out, doubled it over, and read the following paragraph:

"Hotel Cosmopolitan Jewel Robbery. John Horner, 26, plumber, was brought up upon the charge of having upon the 22nd inst., abstracted from the jewel-case of the Countess of Morcar the valuable gem known as the blue carbuncle. James Ryder, upper-attendant at the hotel, gave his evidence to the effect that he had shown Horner up to the dressing-room of the Countess of Morcar upon the day of the robbery in order that he might solder the second bar of the grate, which was loose. He had remained with Horner some little time, but had finally been called away.

On returning, he found that Horner had disappeared, that the bureau had been forced open, and that the small morocco casket in which, as it afterwards transpired, the Countess was accustomed to keep her jewel, was lying empty upon the dressing-table. Ryder instantly gave the alarm, and Horner was arrested the same evening; but the stone could not be found either upon his person or in his rooms. Catherine Cusack, maid to the Countess, deposed to having heard Ryder's cry of dismay on discovering the robbery, and to having rushed into the room, where she found matters as described by the last witness. Inspector Bradstreet, B division, gave evidence as to the arrest of Horner, who struggled frantically, and protested his innocence in the strongest terms.

Evidence of a previous conviction for robbery having been given against the prisoner, the magistrate refused to deal summarily with the offence, but referred it to the Assizes. Horner, who had shown signs of intense emotion during the proceedings, fainted away at the conclusion and was carried out of court."

"Hum! So much for the police-court," said Holmes thoughtfully, tossing aside the paper. "The question for us now to solve is the sequence of events leading from a rifled jewel-case at one end to the crop of a goose in Tottenham Court Road at the other. You see, Watson, our little deductions have suddenly assumed a much more important and less innocent aspect. Here is the stone; the stone came from the goose, and the goose came from Mr. Henry Baker, the gentleman with the bad hat and all the other characteristics with which I have bored you. So now we must set ourselves very seriously to finding this gentleman and ascertaining what part he has played in this little mystery. To do this, we must try the simplest means first, and these lie undoubtedly in an advertisement in all the evening papers. If this fail, I shall have recourse to other methods."

"What will you say?"

"Give me a pencil and that slip of paper. Now, then: 'Found at the corner of Goodge Street, a goose and a black felt hat. Mr. Henry Baker can have the same by applying at 6:30 this evening at 221B, Baker Street.' That is clear and concise."

"Very. But will he see it?"

"Well, he is sure to keep an eye on the papers, since, to a poor man, the loss was a heavy one. He was clearly so scared by his mischance in breaking the window and by the approach of Peterson that he thought of nothing but flight, but since then he must have bitterly regretted the impulse which caused him to drop his bird. Then, again, the introduction of his name will cause him to see it, for everyone who knows him will direct his attention to it. Here you are, Peterson, run down to the advertising agency and have this put in the evening papers."

"In which, sir?"

"Oh, in the *Globe, Star, Pall Mall, St. James's Gazette, Evening News, Standard, Echo,* and any others that occur to you."

"Very well, sir. And this stone?"

"Ah, yes, I shall keep the stone. Thank you. And, I say, Peterson, just buy a goose on your way back and leave it here with me, for we must have one to give to this gentleman in place of the one which your family is now devouring."

When the commissionaire had gone, Holmes took up the stone and held it against the light. "It's a bonny thing," said he. "Just see how it glints and sparkles. Of course it is a nucleus and focus of crime. Every good stone is. They are the devil's pet baits. In the larger and older jewels every facet may stand for a bloody deed. This stone is not yet twenty years old. It was found in the banks of the Amoy River in southern China and is remarkable in having every characteristic of the carbuncle, save that it is blue in shade instead of ruby red. In spite of its youth, it has already a sinister history. There have been two murders, a vitriol-throwing, a suicide, and several robberies brought about for the sake of this forty-grain weight of crystallised charcoal. Who would think that so pretty a toy would be a purveyor to the gallows and the prison? I'll lock it up in my strong box now and drop a line to the Countess to say that we have it."

"Do you think that this man Horner is innocent?"

"I cannot tell."

"Well, then, do you imagine that this other one, Henry Baker, had anything to do with the matter?"

"It is, I think, much more likely that Henry Baker is an absolutely innocent man, who had no idea that the bird which he was carrying was of considerably more value than if it were made of solid gold. That, however, I shall determine by a very simple test if we have an answer to our advertisement."

"And you can do nothing until then?"

"Nothing."

"In that case I shall continue my professional round. But I shall come back in the evening at the hour you have mentioned, for I should like to see the solution of so tangled a business."

"Very glad to see you. I dine at seven. There is a woodcock, I believe. By the way, in view of recent occurrences, perhaps I ought to ask Mrs. Hudson to examine its crop."

I had been delayed at a case, and it was a little after half-past six when I found myself in Baker Street once more. As I approached the house I saw a tall man in a Scotch bonnet with a coat which was buttoned up to his chin waiting outside in the bright semicircle which was thrown from the fanlight. Just as I arrived the door was opened, and we were shown up together to Holmes' room.

"Mr. Henry Baker, I believe," said he, rising from his armchair and greeting his visitor with the easy air of geniality which he could so readily assume. "Pray take this chair by the fire, Mr. Baker. It is a cold night, and I observe that your circulation is more adapted for summer than for winter. Ah, Watson, you have just come at the right time. Is that your hat, Mr. Baker?"

"Yes, sir, that is undoubtedly my hat."

He was a large man with rounded shoulders, a massive head, and a broad, intelligent face, sloping down to a pointed beard of grizzled brown. A touch of red in nose and cheeks, with a slight tremor of his extended hand, recalled Holmes' surmise as to his habits. His rusty black frock-coat was buttoned right up in front, with the collar turned up, and his lank wrists protruded from his sleeves without a sign of cuff or shirt. He spoke in a slow staccato fashion, choosing his words with care, and gave the impression generally of a man of learning and letters who had had ill-usage at the hands of fortune.

"We have retained these things for some days," said Holmes, "because we expected to see an advertisement from you giving your address. I am at a loss to know now why you did not advertise."

Our visitor gave a rather shamefaced laugh. "Shillings have not been so plentiful with me as they once were," he remarked. "I had no doubt that the gang of roughs who assaulted me had carried off both my hat and the bird. I did not care to spend more money in a hopeless attempt at recovering them."

"Very naturally. By the way, about the bird, we were compelled to eat it."

"To eat it!" Our visitor half rose from his chair in his excitement.

"Yes, it would have been of no use to anyone had we not done so. But I presume that this other goose upon the sideboard, which is about the same weight and perfectly fresh, will answer your purpose equally well?"

"Oh, certainly, certainly," answered Mr. Baker with a sigh of relief.

"Of course, we still have the feathers, legs, crop, and so on of your own bird, so if you wish—"

The man burst into a hearty laugh. "They might be useful to me as relics of my adventure," said he, "but beyond that I can hardly see what use the *disjecta membra* of my late acquaintance are going to be to me. No, sir, I think that, with your permission, I will confine my attentions to the excellent bird which I perceive upon the sideboard."

Sherlock Holmes glanced sharply across at me with a slight shrug of his shoulders.

"There is your hat, then, and there your bird," said he. "By the way, would it bore you to tell me where you got the other one from? I am somewhat of a fowl fancier, and I have seldom seen a better grown goose."

"Certainly, sir," said Baker, who had risen and tucked his newly gained property under his arm. "There are a few of us who frequent the Alpha Inn, near the Museum—we are to be found in the Museum itself during the day, you understand. This year our good host, Windigate by name, instituted a goose club, by which, on consideration of some few pence every week, we were each to receive a bird at Christmas. My pence were duly paid, and the rest is familiar to you. I am much indebted to you, sir, for a Scotch bonnet is fitted neither to my years nor my gravity." With a comical pomposity of manner he bowed solemnly to both of us and strode off upon his way.

"So much for Mr. Henry Baker," said Holmes when he had closed the door behind him. "It is quite certain that he knows nothing whatever about the matter. Are you hungry, Watson?"

"Not particularly."

"Then I suggest that we turn our dinner into a supper and follow up this clue while it is still hot."

"By all means."

It was a bitter night, so we drew on our ulsters[1] and wrapped cravats about our throats. Outside, the stars were shining coldly in a cloudless sky, and the breath of the passers-by blew out into smoke like so many pistol shots. Our footfalls rang out crisply and loudly as we swung through the doctors' quarter, Wimpole Street, Harley Street, and so through Wigmore Street into Oxford Street. In a quarter of an hour we were in Bloomsbury at the Alpha Inn, which is a small public-house at the corner of one of the streets which runs down into Holborn. Holmes pushed open the door of the private bar and ordered two glasses of beer from the ruddy-faced, white-aproned landlord.

"Your beer should be excellent if it is as good as your geese," said he.

"My geese!" The man seemed surprised.

"Yes. I was speaking only half an hour ago to Mr. Henry Baker, who was a member of your goose club."

"Ah! yes, I see. But you see, sir, them's not *our* geese."

"Indeed! Whose, then?"

"Well, I got the two dozen from a salesman in Covent Garden."

"Indeed? I know some of them. Which was it?"

"Breckinridge is his name."

"Ah! I don't know him. Well, here's your good health landlord, and prosperity to your house. Good-night."

"Now for Mr. Breckinridge," he continued, buttoning up his coat as we came out into the frosty air. "Remember, Watson that though we have so homely a thing as a goose at one end of this chain, we have at the other a man who will certainly get seven years' penal servitude unless we can establish his innocence. It is possible that our inquiry may but confirm his guilt; but, in any case, we have a line of investigation which has been missed by the police, and which a singular chance has placed in our hands. Let us follow it out to the bitter end. Faces to the south, then, and quick march!"

We passed across Holborn, down Endell Street, and so through a zigzag of slums to Covent Garden Market. One of the largest stalls bore the name of Breckinridge upon it, and the proprietor a horsey-looking man, with a sharp face and trim side-whiskers was helping a boy to put up the shutters.

"Good-evening. It's a cold night," said Holmes.

The salesman nodded and shot a questioning glance at my companion.

"Sold out of geese, I see," continued Holmes, pointing at the bare slabs of marble.

"Let you have five hundred to-morrow morning."

"That's no good."

"Well, there are some on the stall with the gas-flare."

"Ah, but I was recommended to you."

"Who by?"

"The landlord of the Alpha."

"Oh, yes; I sent him a couple of dozen."

"Fine birds they were, too. Now where did you get them from?"

To my surprise the question provoked a burst of anger from the salesman.

"Now, then, mister," said he, with his head cocked and his arms akimbo, "what are you driving at? Let's have it straight, now."

"It is straight enough. I should like to know who sold you the geese which you supplied to the Alpha."

"Well then, I shan't tell you. So now!"

"Oh, it is a matter of no importance; but I don't know why you should be so warm over such a trifle."

"Warm! You'd be as warm, maybe, if you were as pestered as I am. When I pay good money for a good article there should be an end of the business; but it's 'Where are the geese?' and 'Who did you sell the geese to?' and 'What will you take for the geese?' One would think they were the only geese in the world, to hear the fuss that is made over them."

"Well, I have no connection with any other people who have been making inquiries," said Holmes carelessly. "If you won't tell us the bet is off, that is all. But I'm always ready to back my opinion on a matter of fowls, and I have a fiver on it that the bird I ate is country bred."

"Well, then, you've lost your fiver, for it's town bred," snapped the salesman.

"It's nothing of the kind."

"I say it is."

"I don't believe it."

"D'you think you know more about fowls than I, who have handled them ever since I was a nipper? I tell you, all those birds that went to the Alpha were town bred."

"You'll never persuade me to believe that."

"Will you bet, then?"

"It's merely taking your money, for I know that I am right. But I'll have a sovereign on with you, just to teach you not to be obstinate."

The salesman chuckled grimly. "Bring me the books, Bill," said he.

The small boy brought round a small thin volume and a great greasy-backed one, laying them out together beneath the hanging lamp.

"Now then, Mr. Cocksure," said the salesman, "I thought that I was out of geese, but before I finish you'll find that there is still one left in my shop. You see this little book?"

"Well?"

"That's the list of the folk from whom I buy. D'you see? Well, then, here on this page are the country folk, and the numbers after their names are where their accounts are in the big ledger. Now, then! You see this other page in red ink? Well, that is a list of my town suppliers. Now, look at that third name. Just read it out to me."

"Mrs. Oakshott, 117, Brixton Road—249," read Holmes.

"Quite so. Now turn that up in the ledger."

Holmes turned to the page indicated. "Here you are, 'Mrs. Oakshott, 117, Brixton Road, egg and poultry supplier.'"

"Now, then, what's the last entry?"

"'December 22nd. Twenty-four geese at 7s. 6d.'"

"Quite so. There you are. And underneath?"

"'Sold to Mr. Windigate of the Alpha, at 12s.'"

"What have you to say now?"

Sherlock Holmes looked deeply chagrined. He drew a sovereign from his pocket and threw it down upon the slab, turning away with the air of a man whose disgust is too deep for words. A few yards off he stopped under a lamp-post and laughed in the hearty, noiseless fashion which was peculiar to him.

"When you see a man with whiskers of that cut and the 'Pink 'un' protruding out of his pocket, you can always draw him by a bet," said he. "I daresay that if I had put £ 100 down in front of him, that man would not have given me such complete information as was drawn from him by the idea that he was doing me on a wager. Well, Watson, we are, I fancy, nearing the end of our quest, and the only point which remains to be determined is whether we should go on to this Mrs. Oakshott to-night, or whether we should reserve it for to-morrow. It is clear from what that surly fellow said that there are others besides ourselves who are anxious about the matter, and I should—"

His remarks were suddenly cut short by a loud hubbub which broke out from the stall which we had just left. Turning round we saw a little rat-faced fellow standing in the centre of the circle of yellow light which was thrown by the swinging lamp, while Breckinridge, the salesman, framed in the door of his stall, was shaking his fists fiercely at the cringing figure.

"I've had enough of you and your geese," he shouted. "I wish you were all at the devil together. If you come pestering me any more with your silly talk I'll set the dog at you. You bring Mrs. Oakshott here and I'll answer her, but what have you to do with it? Did I buy the geese off you?"

"No; but one of them was mine all the same," whined the little man.

"Well, then, ask Mrs. Oakshott for it."

"She told me to ask you."

"Well, you can ask the King of Proosia, for all I care. I've had enough of it. Get out of this!" He rushed fiercely forward, and the inquirer flitted away into the darkness.

"Ha! this may save us a visit to Brixton Road," whispered Holmes. "Come with me, and we will see what is to be made of this fellow." Striding through the scattered knots of people who lounged round the flaring stalls, my companion speedily overtook the little man and touched him upon the shoulder. He sprang round, and I could see in the gas-light that every vestige of colour had been driven from his face.

"Who are you, then? What do you want?" he asked in a quavering voice.

"You will excuse me," said Holmes blandly, "but I could not help overhearing the questions which you put to the salesman just now. I think that I could be of assistance to you."

"You? Who are you? How could you know anything of the matter?"

"My name is Sherlock Holmes. It is my business to know what other people don't know."

"But you can know nothing of this?"

"Excuse me, I know everything of it. You are endeavouring to trace some geese which were sold by Mrs. Oakshott, of Brixton Road, to a salesman named Breckinridge, by him in turn to Mr. Windigate, of the Alpha, and by him to his club, of which Mr. Henry Baker is a member."

"Oh, sir, you are the very man whom I have longed to meet," cried the little fellow with outstretched hands and quivering fingers. "I can hardly explain to you how interested I am in this matter."

Sherlock Holmes hailed a four-wheeler which was passing. "In that case we had better discuss it in a cosy room rather than in this wind-swept market-place," said he. "But pray tell me, before we go farther, who it is that I have the pleasure of assisting."

The man hesitated for an instant. "My name is John Robinson," he answered with a sidelong glance.

"No, no; the real name," said Holmes sweetly. "It is always awkward doing business with an alias."

A flush sprang to the white cheeks of the stranger. "Well then," said he, "my real name is James Ryder."

"Precisely so. Head attendant at the Hotel Cosmopolitan. Pray step into the cab, and I shall soon be able to tell you everything which you would wish to know."

The little man stood glancing from one to the other of us with half-frightened, half-hopeful eyes, as one who is not sure whether he is on the verge of a windfall or of a catastrophe. Then he stepped into the cab, and in half an hour we were back in the sitting-room at Baker Street. Nothing had been said during our drive, but the high, thin breathing of our new companion, and the claspings and unclaspings of his hands, spoke of the nervous tension within him.

"Here we are!" said Holmes cheerily as we filed into the room. "The fire looks very seasonable in this weather. You look cold, Mr. Ryder. Pray take the basket-chair. I will just put on my slippers before we settle this little matter of yours. Now, then! You want to know what became of those geese?"

"Yes, sir."

"Or rather, I fancy, of that goose. It was one bird, I imagine in which you were interested—white, with a black bar across the tail."

Ryder quivered with emotion. "Oh, sir," he cried, "can you tell me where it went to?"

"It came here."

"Here?"

"Yes, and a most remarkable bird it proved. I don't wonder that you should take an interest in it. It laid an egg after it was dead—the bonniest, brightest little blue egg that ever was seen. I have it here in my museum."

Our visitor staggered to his feet and clutched the mantelpiece with his right hand. Holmes unlocked his strong-box and held up the blue carbuncle, which shone out like a star, with a cold, brilliant, many-pointed radiance. Ryder stood glaring with a drawn face, uncertain whether to claim or to disown it.

"The game's up, Ryder," said Holmes quietly. "Hold up, man, or you'll be into the fire! Give him an arm back into his chair, Watson. He's not got blood enough to go in for felony with impunity. Give him a dash of brandy. So! Now he looks a little more human. What a shrimp it is, to be sure!"

For a moment he had staggered and nearly fallen, but the brandy brought a tinge of colour into his cheeks, and he sat staring with frightened eyes at his accuser.

"I have almost every link in my hands, and all the proofs which I could possibly need, so there is little which you need tell me. Still, that little may as well be cleared up to make the case complete. You had heard, Ryder, of this blue stone of the Countess of Morcar's?"

"It was Catherine Cusack who told me of it," said he in a crackling voice.

"I see—her ladyship's waiting-maid. Well, the temptation of sudden wealth so easily acquired was too much for you, as it has been for better men before you; but you were not very scrupulous in the means you used. It seems to me, Ryder, that there is the making of a very pretty villain in you. You knew that this man Horner, the plumber, had been concerned in some such matter before, and that suspicion would rest the more readily upon him. What did you do, then? You made some small job in my lady's room—you and your confederate Cusack—and you managed that he should be the man sent for. Then, when he had left, you rifled the jewel-case, raised the alarm, and had this unfortunate man arrested. You then—"

Ryder threw himself down suddenly upon the rug and clutched at my companion's knees. "For God's sake, have mercy!" he shrieked. "Think of my father! Of my mother! It would break their hearts. I never went wrong before! I never will again. I swear it. I'll swear it on a Bible. Oh, don't bring it into court! For Christ's sake, don't!"

"Get back into your chair!" said Holmes sternly. "It is very well to cringe and crawl now, but you thought little enough of this poor Horner in the dock for a crime of which he knew nothing."

"I will fly, Mr. Holmes. I will leave the country, sir. Then the charge against him will break down."

"Hum! We will talk about that. And now let us hear a true account of the next act. How came the stone into the goose, and how came the goose into the open market? Tell us the truth, for there lies your only hope of safety."

Ryder passed his tongue over his parched lips. "I will tell you it just as it happened, sir," said he. "When Horner had been arrested, it seemed to me that it would be best for me to get away with the stone at once, for I did not know at what moment the police might not take it into their heads to search me and my room. There was no place about the hotel where it would be safe. I went out, as if on some commission, and I made for my sister's house. She had married a man named Oakshott, and lived in Brixton Road, where she fattened fowls for the market. All the way there every man I met seemed to me to be a policeman or a detective; and, for all that it was a cold night, the sweat was pouring down my face before I came to the Brixton Road. My sister asked me what was the matter, and why I was so pale; but I told her that I had been upset by the jewel robbery at the hotel. Then I went into the back yard and smoked a pipe and wondered what it would be best to do.

"I had a friend once called Maudsley, who went to the bad, and has just been serving his time in Pentonville. One day he had met me, and fell into talk about the ways of thieves, and how they could get rid of what they stole. I knew that he would be true to me, for I knew one or two things about him; so I made up my mind to go right on to Kilburn, where he lived, and take him into my confidence. He would show me how to turn the stone into money. But how to get to him in safety? I thought of the agonies I had gone through in coming from the hotel. I might at any moment be seized and searched, and there would be the stone in my waistcoat pocket. I was leaning against the wall at the time and looking at the geese which were waddling about round my feet, and suddenly an idea came into my head which showed me how I could beat the best detective that ever lived.

"My sister had told me some weeks before that I might have the pick of her geese for a Christmas present, and I knew that she was always as good as her word. I would take my goose now, and in it I would carry my stone to Kilburn. There was a little shed in the yard, and behind this I drove one of the birds—a fine big one, white, with a barred tail. I caught it, and prying its bill open, I thrust the stone down its throat as far as my finger could reach. The bird gave a gulp, and I felt the stone pass along its gullet and down into its crop. But the creature flapped and struggled, and out came my sister to know what was the matter. As I turned to speak to her the brute broke loose and fluttered off among the others.

"'Whatever were you doing with that bird, Jem?' says she.

"'Well,' said I, 'you said you'd give me one for Christmas, and I was feeling which was the fattest.'

"'Oh,' says she, 'we've set yours aside for you—Jem's bird, we call it. It's the big white one over yonder. There's twenty-six of them, which makes one for you, and one for us, and two dozen for the market.'

"'Thank you, Maggie,' says I; 'but if it is all the same to you, I'd rather have that one I was handling just now.'

"'The other is a good three pound heavier,' said she, 'and we fattened it expressly for you.'

"'Never mind. I'll have the other, and I'll take it now,' said I.

"'Oh, just as you like,' said she, a little huffed. 'Which is it you want, then?'

"'That white one with the barred tail, right in the middle of the flock.'

"'Oh, very well. Kill it and take it with you.'

"Well, I did what she said, Mr. Holmes, and I carried the bird all the way to Kilburn. I told my pal what I had done, for he was a man that it was easy to tell a thing like that to. He laughed until he choked, and we got a knife and opened the goose. My heart turned to water, for there was no sign of the stone, and I knew that some terrible mistake had occurred. I left the bird, rushed back to my sister's, and hurried into the back yard. There was not a bird to be seen there.

"'Where are they all, Maggie?' I cried.

"'Gone to the dealer's, Jem.'

"'Which dealer's?'

"'Breckinridge, of Covent Garden.'

"'But was there another with a barred tail?' I asked, 'the same as the one I chose?'

"'Yes, Jem; there were two barred-tailed ones, and I could never tell them apart.'

"Well, then, of course I saw it all, and I ran off as hard as my feet would carry me to this man Breckinridge; but he had sold the lot at once, and not one word would he tell me as to where they had gone. You heard him yourselves to-night. Well, he has always answered me like that. My sister thinks that I am going mad. Sometimes I think that I am myself. And now—and now I am myself a branded thief, without ever having touched the wealth for which I sold my character. God help me! God help me!" He burst into convulsive sobbing, with his face buried in his hands.

There was a long silence, broken only by his heavy breathing and by the measured tapping of Sherlock Holmes' finger-tips upon the edge of the table. Then my friend rose and threw open the door.

"Get out!" said he.

"What, sir! Oh, Heaven bless you!"

"No more words. Get out!"

And no more words were needed. There was a rush, a clatter upon the stairs, the bang of a door, and the crisp rattle of running footfalls from the street.

"After all, Watson," said Holmes, reaching up his hand for his clay pipe, "I am not retained by the police to supply their deficiencies. If Horner were in danger it would be another thing; but this fellow will not appear against him, and the case must collapse. I suppose that I am commuting a felony, but it is just possible that I am saving a soul. This fellow will not go wrong again; he is too terribly frightened. Send him to gaol now, and you make him a gaol-bird for life. Besides, it is the season of forgiveness. Chance has put in our way a most singular and whimsical problem, and its solution is its own reward. If you will have the goodness to touch the bell, Doctor, we will begin another investigation, in which, also a bird will be the chief feature."

<hr>

[1] *Ulster—a long, loose overcoat of Irish origin made of heavy material. (Merriam-Webster Dictionary)*

The Philanthropist's Christmas

JAMES WEBER LINN

James Weber Linn, 1876 – 1939

American educator, writer and politician

Not a prolific writer, Linn nevertheless authored this sweet tale where even an acknowledged philanthropist learns what charity means in a new way.

THE PHILANTHROPIST'S CHRISTMAS

"Did you see this committee yesterday, Mr. Mathews?" asked the philanthropist. His secretary looked up.

"Yes, sir."

"You recommend them then?"

"Yes, sir."

"For fifty thousand?"

"For fifty thousand—yes, sir."

"Their corresponding subscriptions are guaranteed?"

"I w'ent over the list carefully, Mr. Carter. The money is promised, and by responsible people."

"Very well," said the philanthropist. "You may notify them, Mr. Mathews, that my fifty thousand will be available as the bills come in."

"Yes, sir."

Old Mr. Carter laid down the letter he had been reading, and took up another. As he perused it his white eyebrows rose in irritation.

"Mr. Mathews!" he snapped.

"Yes, sir?"

"You are careless, sir!"

"I beg your pardon, Mr. Carter?" questioned the secretary, his face flushing.

The old gentleman tapped impatiently the letter he held in his hand. "Do you pay no attention, Mr. Mathews, to my rule that NO personal letters containing appeals for aid are to reach me? How do you account for this, may I ask?"

"I beg your pardon," said the secretary again. "You will see, Mr. Carter, that that letter is dated three weeks ago. I have had the woman's case carefully investigated. She is undoubtedly of good reputation, and undoubtedly in need; and as she speaks of her father as having associated with you, I thought perhaps you would care to see her letter."

"A thousand worthless fellows associated with me," said the old man, harshly. "In a great factory, Mr. Mathews, a boy works alongside of the men he is put with; he does not pick and choose. I dare say this woman is telling the truth. What of it? You know that I regard my money as a public trust. Were my energy, my concentration, to be wasted by innumerable individual assaults, what would become of them? My fortune would slip through my fingers as unprofitably as sand. You understand, Mr. Mathews? Let me see no more individual letters. You know that Mr. Whittemore has full authority to deal with them. May I trouble you to ring? I am going out."

A man appeared very promptly in answer to the bell.

"Sniffen, my overcoat," said the philanthropist.

"It is 'ere, sir," answered Sniffen, helping the thin old man into the great fur folds.

"There is no word of the dog, I suppose, Sniffen?"

"None, sir. The police was here again yesterday sir, but they said as 'ow—"

"The police!" The words were fierce with scorn. "Eight thousand incompetents!" He turned abruptly and went toward the door, where he halted a moment.

"Mr. Mathews, since that woman's letter did reach me, I suppose I must pay for my carelessness—or yours. Send her—what does she say—four children?—send her a hundred dollars. But, for my sake, send it anonymously. Write her that I pay no attention to such claims." He went out, and Sniffen closed the door behind him.

"Takes losin' the little dog 'ard, don't he?" remarked Sniffen, sadly, to the secretary. "I'm afraid there ain't a chance of findin' 'im now. 'E ain't been stole, nor 'e ain't been found, or they'd 'ave brung him back for the reward. 'E's been knocked on the 'ead, like as not. 'E wasn't much of a dog to look at, you see—just a pup, I'd call 'im. An' after 'e learned that trick of slippin' 'is collar off—well, I fancy Mr. Carter's seen the last of 'im. I do, indeed."

Mr. Carter meanwhile was making his way slowly down the snowy avenue, upon his accustomed walk. The walk, however, was dull to-day, for Skiddles, his little terrier, was not with him to add interest and excitement. Mr. Carter had found Skiddles in the country a year and a half before. Skiddles, then a puppy, was at the time in a most undignified and undesirable position, stuck in a drain tile, and unable either to advance or to retreat. Mr. Carter had shoved him forward, after a heroic struggle, whereupon Skiddles had licked his hand. Something in the little dog's eye, or his action, had induced the rich philanthropist to bargain for him and buy him at a cost of half a dollar. Thereafter Skiddles became his daily companion, his chief distraction, and finally the apple of his eye.

Skiddles was of no known parentage, hardly of any known breed, but he suited Mr. Carter. What, the millionaire reflected with a proud cynicism, were his own antecedents, if it came to that? But now Skiddles had disappeared.

As Sniffen said, he had learned the trick of slipping free from his collar. One morning the great front doors had been left open for two minutes while the hallway was aired. Skiddles must have slipped down the marble steps unseen, and dodged round the corner. At all events, he had vanished, and although the whole police force of the city had been roused to secure his return, it was aroused in vain. And for three weeks, therefore, a small, straight, white bearded man in a fur overcoat had walked in mournful irritation alone.

He stood upon a corner uncertainly. One way led to the park, and this he usually took; but to-day he did not want to go to the park—it was too reminiscent of Skiddles. He looked the other way. Down there, if one went far enough, lay "slums," and Mr. Carter hated the sight of slums; they always made him miserable and discontented. With all his money and his philanthropy, was there still necessity for such misery in the world? Worse still came the intrusive question at times: Had all his money anything to do with the creation of this misery? He owned no tenements; he paid good wages in every factory; he had given sums such as few men have given in the history of philanthropy. Still—there were the slums. However, the worst slums lay some distance off, and he finally turned his back on the park and walked on.

It was the day before Christmas. You saw it in people's faces; you saw it in the holly wreaths that hung in windows; you saw it, even as you passed the splendid, forbidding houses on the avenue, in the green that here and there banked massive doors; but most of all, you saw it in the shops. Up here the shops were smallish, and chiefly of the provision variety, so there was no bewildering display of gifts; but there were Christmas-trees everywhere, of all sizes. It was astonishing how many people in that neighbourhood seemed to favour the old-fashioned idea of a tree.

Mr. Carter looked at them with his irritation softening. If they made him feel a trifle more lonely, they allowed him to feel also a trifle less responsible—for, after all, it was a fairly happy world.

At this moment he perceived a curious phenomenon a short distance before him—another Christmas-tree, but one which moved, apparently of its own volition, along the sidewalk. As Mr. Carter overtook it, he saw that it was borne, or dragged, rather by a small boy who wore a bright red flannel cap and mittens of the same peculiar material. As Mr. Carter looked down at him, he looked up at Mr. Carter, and spoke cheerfully:

"Goin' my way, mister?"

"Why," said the philanthropist, somewhat taken back, "I WAS!"

"Mind draggin' this a little way?" asked the boy, confidently, "my hands is cold."

"Won't you enjoy it more if you manage to take it home by yourself?"

"Oh, it ain't for me!" said the boy.

"Your employer," said the philanthropist, severely, "is certainly careless if he allows his trees to be delivered in this fashion."

"I ain't deliverin' it, either," said the boy. "This is Bill's tree."

"Who is Bill?"

"He's a feller with a back that's no good."

"Is he your brother?"

"No. Take the tree a little way, will you, while I warm myself?"

The philanthropist accepted the burden—he did not know why. The boy, released, ran forward, jumped up and down, slapped his red flannel mittens on his legs, and then ran back again. After repeating these manoeuvres two or three times, he returned to where the old gentleman stood holding the tree.

"Thanks," he said. "Say, mister, you look like Santa Claus yourself, standin' by the tree, with your fur cap and your coat. I bet you don't have to run to keep warm, hey?" There was high admiration in his look. Suddenly his eyes sparkled with an inspiration.

"Say, mister," he cried, "will you do something for me? Come in to Bill's—he lives only a block from here—and just let him see you. He's only a kid, and he'll think he's seen Santa Claus, sure. We can tell him you're so busy to-morrow you have to go to lots of places to-day. You won't have to give him anything. We're looking out for all that. Bill got hurt in the summer, and he's been in bed ever since. So we are giving him a Christmas—tree and all. He gets a bunch of things—an air gun, and a train that goes around when you wind her up. They're great!"

"You boys are doing this?"

"Well, it's our club at the settlement, and of course Miss Gray thought of it, and she's givin' Bill the train. Come along, mister."

But Mr. Carter declined.

"All right," said the boy. "I guess, what with Pete and all, Bill will have Christmas enough."

"Who is Pete?"

"Bill's dog. He's had him three weeks now—best little pup you ever saw!"

A dog which Bill had had three weeks—and in a neighbourhood not a quarter of a mile from the avenue. It was three weeks since Skiddles had disappeared. That this dog was Skiddles was of course most improbable, and yet the philanthropist was ready to grasp at any clue which might lead to the lost terrier.

"How did Bill get this dog?" he demanded.

"I found him myself. Some kids had tin-canned him, and he came into our entry. He licked my hand, and then sat up on his hind legs. Somebody'd taught him that, you know. I thought right away, 'Here's a dog for Bill!' And I took him over there and fed him, and they kept him in Bill's room two or three days, so he shouldn't get scared again and run off; and now he wouldn't leave Bill for anybody. Of course, he ain't much of a dog, Pete ain't," he added "he's just a pup, but he's mighty friendly!"

"Boy," said Mr. Carter, "I guess I'll just go round and"—he was about to add, "have a look at that dog," but fearful of raising suspicion, he ended—"and see Bill."

The tenements to which the boy led him were of brick, and reasonably clean. Nearly every window showed some sign of Christmas.

The tree-bearer led the way into a dark hall, up one flight—Mr. Carter assisting with the tree—and down another dark hall, to a door, on which he knocked. A woman opened it.

"Here's the tree!" said the boy, in a loud whisper. "Is Bill's door shut?"

Mr. Carter stepped forward out of the darkness. "I beg your pardon, madam," he said. "I met this young man in the street, and he asked me to come here and see a playmate of his who is, I understand, an invalid. But if I am intruding—"

"Come in," said the woman, heartily, throwing the door open. "Bill will be glad to see you, sir."

The philanthropist stepped inside.

The room was decently furnished and clean. There was a sewing machine in the corner, and in both the windows hung wreaths of holly. Between the windows was a cleared space, where evidently the tree, when decorated, was to stand.

"Are all the things here?" eagerly demanded the tree-bearer.

"They're all here, Jimmy," answered Mrs. Bailey. "The candy just came."

"Say," cried the boy, pulling off his red flannel mittens to blow on his fingers, "won't it be great? But now Bill's got to see Santa Claus. I'll just go in and tell him, an' then, when I holler, mister, you come on, and pretend you're Santa Claus." And with incredible celerity the boy opened the door at the opposite end of the room and disappeared.

"Madam," said Mr. Carter, in considerable embarrassment, "I must say one word. I am Mr. Carter, Mr. Allan Carter. You may have heard my name?"

She shook her head. "No, sir."

"I live not far from here on the avenue. Three weeks ago I lost a little dog that I valued very much I have had all the city searched since then, in vain. To-day I met the boy who has just left us. He informed me that three weeks ago he found a dog, which is at present in the possession of your son. I wonder—is it not just possible that this dog may be mine?"

Mrs. Bailey smiled. "I guess not, Mr. Carter. The dog Jimmy found hadn't come off the avenue—not from the look of him. You know there's hundreds and hundreds of dogs without homes, sir. But I will say for this one, he has a kind of a way with him."

"Hark!" said Mr. Carter.

There was a rustling and a snuffing at the door at the far end of the room, a quick scratching of feet. Then:

"Woof! woof! woof!" sharp and clear came happy impatient little barks. The philanthropist's eyes brightened. "Yes," he said, "that is the dog."

"I doubt if it can be, sir," said Mrs. Bailey, deprecatingly.

"Open the door, please," commanded the philanthropist, "and let us see." Mrs. Bailey complied. There was a quick jump, a tumbling rush, and Skiddles, the lost Skiddles, was in the philanthropist's arms. Mrs. Bailey shut the door with a troubled face.

"I see it's your dog, sir," she said, "but I hope you won't be thinking that Jimmy or I—"

"Madam," interrupted Mr. Carter, "I could not be so foolish. On the contrary, I owe you a thousand thanks."

Mrs. Bailey looked more cheerful. "Poor little Billy!" she said. "It'll come hard on him, losing Pete just at Christmas time. But the boys are so good to him, I dare say he'll forget it."

"Who are these boys?" inquired the philanthropist. "Isn't their action—somewhat unusual?"

"It's Miss Gray's club at the settlement, sir," explained Mrs. Bailey. "Every Christmas they do this for somebody. It's not charity; Billy and I don't need charity, or take it. It's just friendliness. They're good boys."

"I see," said the philanthropist. He was still wondering about it, though, when the door opened again, and Jimmy thrust out a face shining with anticipation.

"All ready, mister!" he said. "Bill's waitin' for you!"

"Jimmy," began Mrs. Bailey, about to explain, "the gentleman—"

But the philanthropist held up his hand, interrupting her. "You'll let me see your son, Mrs. Bailey?" he asked, gently.

"Why, certainly, sir."

Mr. Carter put Skiddles down and walked slowly into the inner room. The bed stood with its side toward him. On it lay a small boy of seven, rigid of body, but with his arms free and his face lighted with joy. "Hello, Santa Claus!" he piped, in a voice shrill with excitement.

"Hello, Bill!" answered the philanthropist, sedately.

The boy turned his eyes on Jimmy.

"He knows my name," he said, with glee.

"He knows everybody's name," said Jimmy. "Now you tell him what you want, Bill, and he'll bring it to-morrow.

"How would you like," said the philanthropist, reflectively, "an—an—" he hesitated, it seemed so incongruous with that stiff figure on the bed—"an airgun?"

"I guess yes," said Bill, happily.

"And a train of cars," broke in the impatient Jimmy, "that goes like sixty when you wind her?"

"Hi!" said Bill.

The philanthropist solemnly made notes of this.

"How about," he remarked, inquiringly, "a tree?"

"Honest?" said Bill.

"I think it can be managed," said Santa Claus. He advanced to the bedside.

"I'm glad to have seen you, Bill. You know how busy I am, but I hope—I hope to see you again."

"Not till next year, of course," warned Jimmy.

"Not till then, of course," assented Santa Claus. "And now, good-bye."

"You forgot to ask him if he'd been a good boy," suggested Jimmy.

"I have," said Bill. "I've been fine. You ask mother."

"She gives you—she gives you both a high character," said Santa Claus. "Good-bye again," and so saying he withdrew. Skiddles followed him out. The philanthropist closed the door of the bedroom, and then turned to Mrs. Bailey.

She was regarding him with awestruck eyes.

"Oh, sir," she said, "I know now who you are—the Mr. Carter that gives so much away to people!"

The philanthropist nodded, deprecatingly.

"Just so, Mrs. Bailey," he said. "And there is one gift—or loan rather—which I should like to make to you. I should like to leave the little dog with you till after the holidays. I'm afraid I'll have to claim him then; but if you'll keep him till after Christmas—and let me find, perhaps, another dog for Billy—I shall be much obliged."

Again the door of the bedroom opened, and Jimmy emerged quietly.

"Bill wants the pup," he explained.

"Pete! Pete!" came the piping but happy voice from the inner room.

Skiddles hesitated. Mr. Carter made no sign.

"Pete! Pete!" shrilled the voice again.

Slowly, very slowly, Skiddles turned and went back into the bedroom.

"You see," said Mr. Carter, smiling, "he won't be too unhappy away from me, Mrs. Bailey."

On his way home the philanthropist saw even more evidences of Christmas gaiety along the streets than before. He stepped out briskly, in spite of his sixty-eight years; he even hummed a little tune.

When he reached the house on the avenue he found his secretary still at work.

"Oh, by the way, Mr. Mathews," he said, "did you send that letter to the woman, saying I never paid attention to personal appeals? No? Then write her, please, enclosing my check for two hundred dollars, and wish her a very Merry Christmas in my name, will you? And hereafter will you always let me see such letters as that one—of course after careful investigation? I fancy perhaps I may have been too rigid in the past."

"Certainly, sir," answered the bewildered secretary. He began fumbling excitedly for his note-book.

"I found the little dog," continued the philanthropist. "You will be glad to know that."

"You have found him?" cried the secretary. "Have you got him back, Mr. Carter? Where was he?"

"He was—detained—on Oak Street, I believe," said the philanthropist. "No, I have not got him back yet. I have left him with a young boy till after the holidays."

He settled himself to his papers, for philanthropists must toil even on the twenty-fourth of December, but the secretary shook his head in a daze. "I wonder what's happened?" he said to himself.

A Hymn on the Nativity of My Saviour

BEN JONSON

Ben Jonson, 1572 – 1637
Poet, Essayist, and Playwright

Jonson is considered a major dramatist of the seventeenth century. Among his friends were William Shakespeare, John Donne, and Robert Herrick. In 1616, Shakespeare acted a leading role in one of Jonson's plays. The following poem was written ca.1600.

A HYMN ON THE NATIVITY OF MY SAVIOUR

I sing the birth was born tonight,
The Author both of life and light;
The angels so did sound it,
And like the ravished shepherds said,
Who saw the light, and were afraid,
Yet searched, and true they found it.

The Son of God, the eternal King,
That did us all salvation bring,
And freed the soul from danger;

He whom the whole world could not take,
The Word, which heaven and earth did make,
Was now laid in a manger.

The Father's wisdom willed it so,
The Son's obedience knew no "No,"
Both wills were in one stature;
And as that wisdom had decreed,
The Word was now made Flesh indeed,
And took on Him our nature.

What comfort by Him do we win?
Who made Himself the Prince of sin,
To make us heirs of glory?
To see this Babe, all innocence,
A Martyr born in our defense,
Can man forget this story?

The Thin Santa Claus

ELLIS PARKER BUTLER

Ellis Parker Butler, 1869 – 1937

Novelist and short story writer
Original Illustrations by May Wilson Preston

A story about Santa Claus in this collection? I'll leave it to the reader to decide whether it is, indeed, about the sleigh-riding do-gooder, or is Mrs. Gratz wiser than she lets on?

In either case, this doesn't make it a reverent story, but it's comical and fun, and here for sheer reading pleasure.

THE THIN SANTA CLAUS

Mrs. Gratz opened her eyes and looked out at the drizzle that made the Christmas morning gray. Her bed stood against the window, and it was easy for her to look out; all she had to do was to roll over and pull the shade aside. Having looked at the weather she rolled again on to the broad flat of her back and made herself comfortable for awhile, for there was no reason why she should get up until she felt like it.

"Such a Christmas!" she said good-naturedly to herself. "I guess such weathers is bad for Santy Claus. Mebby it is because of such weathers he don't come by my house. I don't blame him. So muddy!"

She let her eyes close indolently. Not yet was she hungry enough to imagine the tempting odour of fried bacon and eggs, and she idly slipped into sleep again. She was in no hurry. She was never in a hurry. What is the use of being in a hurry when you own a good little house and have money in the bank and are a widow? What is the use of being in a hurry, anyway? Mrs. Gratz was always placid and fat, and she always had been. What is the use of having money in the bank and a good little house if you are not placid and fat? Mrs. Gratz lay on her back and slept, placidly and fatly, with her mouth open, as if she expected Santa Claus to pass by and drop a present into it. Her dreams were pleasant.

It was no disappointment to Mrs. Gratz that Santa Claus had not come to her house. She had not expected him. She did not even believe in him.

"Yes," she had told Mrs. Flannery, next door, as she handed a little parcel of toys over the fence for the little Flannerys, "once I believes in such a Santy Claus myself, yet. I make me purty good times then. But now I'm too old. I don't believe in such things. But I make purty good times, still. I have a good little house, and money in the bank—"

Suddenly Mrs. Gratz closed her mouth and opened her eyes. She smelled imaginary bacon frying. She felt real hunger. She slid out of bed and began to dress herself, and she had just buttoned her red flannel petticoat around her wide waist when she heard a silence, and paused. For a full minute she stood, trying to realize what the silence meant. The English sparrows were chirping as usual and making enough noise, but through their bickerings the silence still annoyed Mrs. Gratz, and then, quite suddenly again, she knew. Her chickens were not making their usual morning racket.

"I bet you I know what it is, sure," she said, and continued to dress as placidly as before. When she went down she found that she had won the bet.

A week before two chickens had been stolen from her coop, and she had had a strong padlock put on the chicken house. Now the padlock was pried open, and the chicken house was empty, and nine hens and a rooster were gone. Mrs. Gratz stooped and entered the low gate and surveyed the vacant chicken yard placidly. If they were gone, they were gone.

"Such a Santy Claus!" she said good-naturedly. "I don't like such a Santy Claus—taking away and not bringing! Purty soon he don't have such a good name any more if he keeps up doing like this. People likes the bringing Santy Claus. I guess they don't think much of the taking-away business. He gets a bad name quick enough if he does this much."

She turned to bend her head to look into the vacant chicken house and stood still. She put out her foot and touched something her eyes had lighted upon, and the thing moved. It was a purse of worn, black leather, soaked by the drizzle, but still holding the bend that comes to men's purses when worn long in a back trouser pocket. One end of the purse was muddy and pressed deep into the soft soil where a heel had tramped on it. Mrs. Gratz bent and picked it up.

There was nine hundred dollars in bills in the purse. Mrs. Gratz stood still while she counted the bills, and as she counted her hands began to tremble, and her knees shook, and she sank on the doorsill of the chicken house and laughed until the tears rolled down her face. Occasionally she stopped to wipe her eyes, and the flood of laughter gradually died away into ripples of intermittent giggles that were like sobs after sorrow. Mrs. Gratz had no great sense of humour, but she could see the fun of finding nine hundred dollars. It was enough to make her laugh, so she laughed.

"Goodness, such a Santy Claus!" she exclaimed with a final sigh of pleasure. "Such a Christmas present from Santy Claus! No wonder he is so fat, yet when he eats ten chickens in one night already. But I don't kick. I like me that Santy Claus all right. I believes in him purty good after this, I bet!"

She went at once to tell Mrs. Flannery, and Mrs. Flannery was far more excited about it than Mrs. Gratz had been. She said it was the Hand of Retribution paying back the chicken thief, and the Hand of Justice repaying Mrs. Gratz for sending toys to the little Flannerys, and Pure Luck giving Mrs. Gratz what she always got, and a number of other things.

"'Tis the luck of ye, Mrs. Gratz, ma'am," she said, "and often I do be sayin' it is the Dutch for luck, meanin' no disrespect to ye, and the fatter the luckier, as I often told me old man, rest his soul, and him so thin! And Christmas mornin' at that, ma'am, which is nothin' at all but th' judgment of hivin on th' dirty chicken thief, pickin' such a day for his thievin', when there's plenty other days in th' year for him. Keep th' money, ma'am, for 't is yours by good rights, and I knew there would some good come till ye th' minute ye handed me th' prisints for the kids. The good folks sure all gits ther reward in this world, only some don't, an' I'm only sorry mine is a pig instid of chickens, but not wishin' ye hadn't th' money yersilf, at all, but who would come to steal a pig, and them such loud squealers? And who do you suspicion it was, Mrs. Gratz, ma'am?"

"I think mebby I got me a present from Santy Claus, yes?" said Mrs. Gratz.

"And hear th' woman!" said Mrs. Flannery. "Do ye hear that now? Well, true for ye, ma'am, and stick to it, for there's no tellin' who'll be claimin' th' money, and if ever Santy Claus brought a thing to a mortal soul 't was him brought ye that. And 't was only yesterday ye was sayin' ye had no belief in him!"

"Yesterday I don't have no beliefs in him," said Mrs. Gratz. "To-day I have plenty of beliefs in him. I like him plenty. I don't care if he comes every year."

"Sure not," said Mrs. Flannery, "and you with th' nine hundred dollars in yer pocket. I'd be glad of the chanst. I'd believe in him, mesilf, for four hundred and fifty."

That afternoon Mrs. Flannery, whose excitement had not abated in the least, went over to Mrs. Gratz's to spend the afternoon talking to her about the money. She felt that it was good to be that near it, at any rate, and when one can make a whole afternoon's conversation out of what Mrs. Casey said to Mrs. O'Reilly about Mrs. McNally, it is a shame to miss a chance to talk about nine hundred dollars. Mrs. Flannery was rocking violently and talking rapidly, and Mrs. Gratz was slowly moving her rocker and answering in monosyllables, when someone knocked at the door. Mrs. Gratz answered the knock.

Her visitor was a tall, thin man, and he had a slouch hat, which he held in his hands as he talked. He seemed nervous, and his face wore a worried look—extremely worried. He looked like a man who had lost nine hundred dollars, but he did not look like Santa Claus. He was thinner and not so jolly-looking. At first Mrs. Gratz had no idea that Santa Claus was standing before her, for he did not have a sleigh-bell about him, and he had left his red cotton coat with the white batting trimming at home. He stood in the door playing with his hat, unable to speak. He seemed to have some delicacy about beginning.

"Well, what it is?" said Mrs. Gratz.

Her visitor pulled himself together with an effort.

"Well, ma'am, I'll tell you," he said frankly. "I'm a chicken buyer. I buy chickens. That's my business—dealin' in poultry—so I came out to-day to buy some chickens—"

"On Christmas Day?" asked Mrs. Gratz.

"Well," said the man, moving uneasily from one foot to the other, "I did come on Christmas Day, didn't I? I don't deny that, ma'am. I did come on Christmas Day. I'd like to go out and have a look at your chickens—"

"It ain't so usual for buyers to come buying chickens on Christmas Day, is it?" interposed Mrs. Gratz, good-naturedly.

He looked like a man who had lost nine hundred dollars, but he did not look like Santa Claus

"Well, no, it ain't, and that's a fact," said the man uneasily. "But I always do. The people I buy chickens for is just as apt to want to eat chicken one day as another day—and more so. Turkey on Christmas Day, and chicken the next, for a change—that's what they always tell me. So I have to buy chickens every day. I hate to, but I have to, and if I could just go out and look around your chicken yard—"

It was right there that Mrs. Gratz had a suspicion that Santa Claus stood before her.

"But I don't sell such a chicken yard, yet," she said. The man wiped his forehead.

"Sure not," he said nervously. "I was goin' to say look around your chicken yard and see the chickens. I can't buy chickens without I see them, can I? Some folks might, but I can't with the kind of customers I've got. I've got mighty particular customers, and I pay extra prices so as to get the best for them, and when I go out and look around the chicken yard—"

"How much you pay for such nice, big, fat chickens, mebby?" asked Mrs. Gratz.

"Well, I'll tell you," said the man. "Seven cents a pound is regular, ain't it? Well, I pay twelve. I'll give you twelve cents, and pay you right now, and take all the chickens you've got. That's my rule. But, if you want to let me go out and see the chickens first, and pick out the kind my regular customers like, I pay twenty cents a pound. But I won't pay twenty cents without I can see the chickens first."

"Sure," said Mrs. Gratz. "I wouldn't do it, too. Mebby I go out and bring in a couple such chickens for you to look at? Yes?"

"No, don't!" said the man impulsively. "Don't do it! It wouldn't be no good. I've got to see the chickens on the hoof, as I might say."

"On the hoofs?" said Mrs. Gratz. "Such poultry don't have no hoofs."

"Runnin' around," explained the visitor. "Runnin' around in the coop. I can tell if a chicken has got any disease that my trade wouldn't like, if I see it runnin' around in the coop. There's a lot in the way a chicken runs. In the way it h'ists up its leg, for instance. That's what the trade calls 'on the hoof.' So I'll just go out and have a look around the coop—"

"For twenty cents a pound anybody could let buyers see their chickens on the hoof, I guess," said Mrs. Gratz.

"Now, that's the way to talk!" exclaimed the man.

"Only but I ain't got any such chickens," said Mrs. Gratz. "So it ain't of use to look how they walk. So good-bye."

"Now, say—" said the man, but Mrs. Gratz closed the door in his face.

"I guess such a Santy Claus came back yet," said Mrs. Gratz when she went into the room where Mrs. Flannery was sitting. "But it ain't any use. He don't leave many more such presents."

"Th' impidince of him!" exclaimed Mrs. Flannery.

"For nine hundred dollars I could be impudent, too," said Mrs. Gratz calmly. "But I don't like such nowadays Santy Clauses, coming back all the time. Once, when I believes in Santy Clauses, they don't come back so much."

The thin Santa Claus had not gone far. He had crossed the street and stood gazing at Mrs. Gratz's door, and now he crossed again and knocked. Mrs. Gratz arose and went to the door.

"I believe he comes back once yet," she said to Mrs. Flannery, and opened the door. He had, indeed, come back.

"Now see here," he said briskly, "ain't your name Mrs. Gratz? Well, I knowed it was, and I knowed you was a widow lady, and that's why I said I was a chicken buyer. I didn't want to frighten you. But I ain't no chicken buyer."

"No?" asked Mrs. Gratz.

"No, I ain't. I just said that so I could get a look at your chicken yard. I've got to see it. What I am is chicken-house inspector for the Ninth Ward, and the Mayor sent me up here to inspect your chicken house, and I've got to do it before I go away, or lose my job. I'll go right out now, and it'll be all over in a minute—"

"I guess it ain't some use," said Mrs. Gratz. "I guess I don't keep any more chickens. They go too easy. Yesterday I have plenty, and to-day I haven't any."

"That's it!" said the thin Santa Claus. "That's just it! That's the way toober-chlosis bugs act—quick like that. They're a bad epidemic—toober-chlosis bugs is. You see how they act—yesterday you have chickens, and last night the toober-chlosis bugs gets at them, and this morning they've eat them all up."

"Goodness!" exclaimed Mrs. Gratz without emotion. "With the fedders and the bones, too?"

"Sure," said the thin Santa Claus. "Why, them toober-chlosis bugs is perfectly ravenous. Once they git started they eat feathers and bones and feet and all—a chicken hasn't no chance at all. That's why the Mayor sent me up here. He heard all your chickens was gone, and gone quick, and he says to me, 'Toober-chlosis bugs!' That's what he says, and he says, 'You ain't doing your duty. You ain't inspected Mrs. Gratz's chicken coop. You go and do it, or you're fired, see?' He says that, and he says, 'You inspect Mrs. Gratz's coop, and you kill off them bugs before they git into her house and eat her all up—bones and all.'"

"And fedders?" asked Mrs. Gratz calmly.

"No, he didn't say feathers. This ain't nothing to fool about. It's serious. So I'll go right out and have a look—"

"I guess such bugs ain't been in *my* coop last night," said Mrs. Gratz carelessly. "I aint afraid of such bugs in winter time."

"Well, that's where you make your mistake," said the thin Santa Claus. "Winter is just the bad time for them bugs. The more a toober-chlosis bug freezes up the more dangerous it is. In summer they ain't so bad—they're soft like and squash up when a chicken gits them, but in winter they freeze up hard and git brittle. Then a chicken comes along and grabs one, and it busts into a thousand pieces, and each piece turns into a new toober-chlosis bug and busts into a thousand pieces, and so on, and the chicken gits all filled full of toober-chlosis bugs before it knows it. When a chicken snaps up one toober-chlosis bug it has a million in it inside of half an hour and that chicken don't last long, and when the bugs make for the house—What's that on your dress there now?"

Mrs. Gratz looked at her arm indifferently.

"Nothing," she said.

"I thought mebby it was a toober-chlosis bug had got on you already," said the thin Santa Claus. "If it was you would be all eat up inside of half an hour. Them bugs is awful rapacious."

"Yes?" inquired Mrs. Gratz with interest. "Such strong bugs, too, is it not?"

"You bet they are strong—" began the stranger.

"I should think so," interrupted Mrs. Gratz, "to smash up padlocks on such chicken houses. You make me afraid of such bugs. I don't dare let you go out there to get your bones and feet all eat up by them. I guess not!"

"Well, you see—you see—" said the thin Santa Claus, puzzled, and then he cheered up. "You see, I ain't afraid of them. I've been fumigated against them. Fumigated and antiskep—antiskepticized. I've been vaccinated against them by the Board of Health. I'll show you the mark on my arm, if you want to see it."

"No, don't," said Mrs. Gratz. "I let you go and look in that chicken coop if you want to, but it ain't no use. There ain't nothing there."

The thin Santa Claus paused and looked at Mrs. Gratz with suspicion.

"Why? Did you find it?" he asked.

"Find what?" asked Mrs. Gratz innocently, and the thin Santa Claus sighed and walked around to the back of the house. Mrs. Gratz went with him.

As Mrs. Gratz watched the thin man search the chicken yard for toober-chlosis bugs all doubt that he was her Santa Claus left her mind. He made a most minute investigation, but he did it more as a man might search for a lost purse than as a health officer would search for germs. He even got down on his hands and knees and poked under the chicken house with a stick, and, when he had combed the chicken yard thoroughly and had looked all through the chicken house, he even searched the denuded vegetable garden in the back yard, and looked over the fence into Mrs. Flannery's yard. Evidently he was not pleased with his investigation, for he did not even say good-bye to Mrs. Gratz, but went away looking mad and cross.

"Mrs. Gratz watched the thin man search the chicken yard for toober-chlosis bugs"

When Mrs. Gratz went into her house she took her seat in her rocking-chair and began rocking herself calmly and slowly.

"'T was him done it, sure," said Mrs. Flannery.

"I don't like such come-agains, much," said Mrs. Gratz placidly. "I try me to believe in such a Santy Claus, but I like not such come-agains. In Germany did not Santy Claus come back so much. I don't like a Santy Claus should be so anxious. Still I believes in him, but, if he has too many such come-agains, I don't believe in him much."

"I would be settin' th' police on him, Santy Claus or no Santy Claus," said Mrs. Flannery vindictively; "th' mean chicken thief!"

"Oh," said Mrs. Gratz easily, "I guess I don't care much should a nine-hundred-dollar Santy Claus steal some chickens. I ain't mad."

But she was a little provoked when another knock came at the door a few minutes later, and when, on opening it, she saw the thin Santa Claus before her again.

"So!" she said, "Santy Claus is back yet once!"

"What's that?" asked the man suspiciously.

"I say, what it is you want?" said Mrs. Gratz.

"Oh!" said the man. "Well, I ain't a-goin' to fool with you no longer, Mrs. Gratz. I'm a-goin' to tell you right out what I am and who I am. I'm a detective of the police, and I'm looking up a mighty bad character."

"I guess I know right where you find one," said Mrs. Gratz politely.

"Now, don't be funny," said the thin Santa Claus peevishly. "Mebby you noticed I didn't say nothing when you spoke about that padlock being busted? Mebby you noticed how careful I looked over your chicken coop, and how I looked over the fence into the next yard? Well, I won't fool you. I ain't no chicken-yard inspector, and I ain't no chicken buyer—them was just my detective disguises. I'm out detecting a chicken thief—just a plain, ordinary chicken thief—and what I come for is clues."

"Yes?" said Mrs. Gratz. "And what is it, such cloos? I haven't any clooses."

The thin Santa Claus seemed provoked.

"Now, look here!" he said. "You may think this is funny, but it isn't. I have got to catch that chicken thief or I'll lose my job, and I can't catch him unless I have some clues to catch him with. Now, didn't you have some chickens stolen last night?"

"Chickens?" asked Mrs. Gratz. "No, I didn't have chickens stolen. Such toober-chlosis bugs eat them. With fedders, too. And bones. Right off the hoofs, ain't it a pity?"

It may have been a blush of shame, but it was more like a flush of anger, that overspread the face of the thin Santa Claus. He stared hard at the placid German face of Mrs. Gratz, and decided she was too stupid to mean it—that she was not teasing him.

"You don't catch on," he said. "You see, there ain't any such things as toober-chlosis bugs. I just made that up as a sort of detective disguise. Them chickens wasn't eat by no bugs at all—they was stole. See? A chicken thief come right into the coop and stole them. Do you think any kind of a bug could pry off a padlock?"

Mrs. Gratz seemed to let this sink into her mind and to revolve there, and get to feeling at home, before she answered.

"No," she said at length, "I guess not. But Santy Claus could do it. Such a big, fat man. Sure he could do it."

"Why, you—" began the thin man crossly, and then changed his tone. "There ain't no such thing as Santy Claus," he said as one might speak to a child—but even a chicken thief would not tell a child such a thing, I hope.

"No?" queried Mrs. Gratz sadly. "No Santy Claus? And I was scared of it, myself, with such toober-chlosis bugs around. He should not to have gone into such a chicken coop with so many bugs busting up all over. He had a right to have fumigated himself, once.

And now he ain't. He's all eat up, on the hoof, bones, and feet and all. And such a kind man, too."

The thin Santa Claus frowned. He had half an idea that Mrs. Gratz was fooling with him, and when he spoke it was crisply.

"Now, see here," he said, "last night somebody broke into your chicken coop and stole all your chickens. I know that. And he's been stealing chickens all around this town, and all around this part of the country, too, and I know that. And this stealing has got to stop. I've got to catch that thief. And to catch him I've got to have a clue. A clue is something he has left around, or dropped, where he was stealing. Now, did that chicken thief drop any clues in your chicken yard? That's what I want to know—did he drop any clues?"

"Mebby, if he dropped some cloos, those toober-chlosis bugs eat them up," suggested Mrs. Gratz. "They eats bones and fedders; mebby they eats cloos, too."

"Now, ain't that smart?" sneered the thin Santa Claus. "Don't you think you're funny? But I'll tell you the clue I'm looking for. Did that thief drop a pocketbook, or anything like that?"

"Oh, a pocketbook!" said Mrs. Gratz. "How much should be in such a pocketbook, mebby?"

"Nine hundred dollars," said the thin Santa Claus promptly.

"Goodness!" exclaimed Mrs. Gratz. "So much money all in one cloos! Come out to the chicken yard once; I'll help hunt for cloos, too."

The thin Santa Claus stood a minute looking doubtfully at Mrs. Gratz. Her face was large and placid and unemotional.

"Well," he said with a sigh, "it ain't much use, but I'll try it again."

When he had gone, after another close search of the chicken yard and coop, Mrs. Gratz returned to her friend, Mrs. Flannery.

"Purty soon I don't belief any more in Santy Claus at all," she said. "Purty soon I have more beliefs in chicken thiefs than in Santy Claus. Yet a while I beliefs in him, but, one more of those come-agains, and I don't."

"He'll not be comin' back any more," said Mrs. Flannery positively. "I'm wonderin' he came at all, and the jail so handy. All ye have t' do is t' call a cop."

"Sure!" said Mrs. Gratz. "But it is not nice I should put Santy Claus in jail. Such a liberal Santy Claus, too."

"Have it yer own way, ma'am," said Mrs. Flannery. "I'll own 'tis some different whin chickens is stole. 'Tis hard to expind th' affections on a bunch of chickens, but, if any one was t' steal my pig, t' jail he would go, Santy Claus or no Santy Claus. Not but what ye have a kind heart anyway, ma'am, not wantin' t' put th' poor fellow in jail whin he has already lost nine hundred dollars, which, goodness knows, ye might have t' hand back, was th' law t' take a hand in it."

"So!" said Mrs. Gratz. "Such is the law, yet? All right, I don't belief in chicken thiefs, no matter how much he comes again. I stick me to Santy Claus. Always will I belief in Santy Claus. Chicken thiefs gives, and wants to take away again, but Santy Claus is always giving and never taking."

"Ye 're fergettin' th' chickens that was took," suggested Mrs. Flannery.

"Took?" said Mrs. Gratz.

"Tooken," Mrs. Flannery corrected.

"Tooked?" said Mrs. Gratz. "I beliefs me not in Santy Claus that way. I beliefs he is a good old man. For givings I beliefs in Santy Claus, but for takings I beliefs in toober-chlo-sis bugs."

"An' th' busted padlock, then?" asked Mrs. Flannery.

"Ach!" exclaimed Mrs. Gratz. "Them reindeers is so frisky, yet. They have a right to kick up and bust it, mebby."

Mrs. Flannery sighed.

"'T is a grand thing t' have faith, ma'am," she said.

"Y-e-s," said Mrs. Gratz indolently, "that's nice. And it is nice to have nine hundred dollars more in the bank, ain't it?"

Thoughts on Modern Christmas, and, The House of Christmas

G.K. CHESTERTON

G. K. Chesterton, 1874– 1936

English writer, philosopher, Christian apologist, poet, literary and art critic.

When considering all he accomplished as a writer and critic, it's safe to say that Chesterton was quite brilliant, in fact, one of the greatest thinkers and authors of the twentieth century. Among his better-known creations is the Father Brown character of BBC fame. This hard-hitting and yet playful essay is a defense of Christmas but even more, of eating turkey at Christmas! One can 'hear' the accusations and arguments Chesterton encountered by how he responds to them.

THOUGHTS ON MODERN CHRISTMAS

Let us be consistent, therefore, about Christmas, and either keep customs or not keep them. If you do not like sentiment and symbolism, you do not like Christmas; go away and celebrate something else; I should suggest the birthday of Mr. M'Cabe. No doubt you could have a sort of scientific Christmas with a hygienic pudding and highly instructive presents stuffed into a Jaeger stocking; go and have it then.

If you like those things, doubtless you are a good sort of fellow, and your intentions are excellent. I have no doubt that you are really interested inhumanity; but I cannot think that humanity will ever be much interested in you. Humanity is unhygienic from its very nature and beginning. It is so much an exception in Nature that the laws of Nature really mean nothing to it. Now Christmas is attacked also on the humanitarian ground. Ouida called it a feast of slaughter and gluttony. Mr. Shaw suggested that it was invented by poulterers. That should be considered before it becomes more considerable.

I do not know whether an animal killed at Christmas has had a better or a worse time than it would have had if there had been no Christmas or no Christmas dinners. But I do know that the fighting and suffering brotherhood to which I belong and owe everything, Mankind, would have a much worse time if there were no such thing as Christmas or Christmas dinners.

Whether the turkey which Scrooge gave to Bob Cratchit had experienced a lovelier or more melancholy career than that of less attractive turkeys is a subject upon which I cannot even conjecture. But that Scrooge was better for giving the turkey and Cratchit happier for getting it I know as two facts, as I know that I have two feet. What life and death may be to a turkey is not my business; but the soul of Scrooge and the body of Cratchit are my business. Nothing shall induce me to darken human homes, to destroy human festivities, to insult human gifts and human benefactions for the sake of some hypothetical knowledge which Nature curtained from our eyes.

We men and women are all in the same boat, upon a stormy sea. We owe to each other a terrible and tragic loyalty. If we catch sharks for food, let them be killed most mercifully; let any one who likes love the sharks, and pet the sharks, and tie ribbons round their necks and give them sugar and teach them to dance. But if once a man suggests that a shark is to be valued against a sailor, or that the poor shark might be permitted to bite off a leg occasionally; then I would court-martial the man—he is a traitor to the ship.

And while I take this view of humanitarianism of the anti-Christmas kind, it is cogent to say that I am a strong anti-vivisectionist. That is, if there is any vivisection, I am against it. I am against the cutting-up of conscious dogs for the same reason that I am in favour of the eating of dead turkeys. The connection may not be obvious; but that is because of the strangely unhealthy condition of modern thought. I am against cruel vivisection as I am against a cruel anti-Christmas asceticism, because they both involve the upsetting of existing fellowships and the shocking of normal good feelings for the sake of something that is intellectual, fanciful, and remote.

...Meanwhile, it remains true that I shall eat a great deal of turkey this Christmas; and it is not in the least true (as the vegetarians say) that I shall do it because I do not realise what I am doing, or because I do what I know is wrong, or that I do it with shame or doubt or a fundamental unrest of conscience.

In one sense I know quite well what I am doing; in another sense I know quite well that I know not what I do. Scrooge and the Cratchits and I are, as I have said, all in one boat; the turkey and I are, to say the most of it, ships that pass in the night, and greet each other in passing. I wish him well; but it is really practically impossible to discover whether I treat him well. I can avoid, and I do avoid with horror, all special and artificial tormenting of him, sticking pins in him for fun or sticking knives in him for scientific investigation. But whether by feeding him slowly and killing him quickly for the needs of my brethren, I have improved in his own solemn eyes his own strange and separate destiny,—that is far more removed from my possibilities of knowledge than the most abstruse intricacies of mysticism or theology.

A turkey is more occult [1] and awful than all the angels and archangels. In so far as God has partly revealed to us an angelic world, he has partly told us what an angel means. But God has never told us what a turkey means. And if you go and stare at a live turkey for an hour or two, you will find by the end of it that the enigma has rather increased than diminished.

---

[1] *'Occult' here means not revealed, not easily apprehended or understood.*

THE HOUSE OF CHRISTMAS

Chesterton's tone is quite different here than in most of his lighter-hearted works. I couldn't say it better, so here, from Poetry.com: "'The House of Christmas' presents a unique perspective on the true meaning of home, juxtaposing the physical structures of human dwellings with the spiritual home found in the heart. Chesterton suggests that despite the comforts of home, humanity is inherently restless and disconnected. True belonging is only found in the humble and unexpected place where Christ was born: the stable."

There fared a mother driven forth
Out of an inn to roam;
In the place where she was homeless
All men are at home.
The crazy stable close at hand,
With shaking timber and shifting sand,
Grew a stronger thing to abide and stand
Than the square stones of Rome.

For men are homesick in their homes,
And strangers under the sun,
And they lay on their heads in a foreign land
Whenever the day is done.
Here we have battle and blazing eyes,
And chance and honour and high surprise,
But our homes are under miraculous skies
Where the yule tale was begun.

A Child in a foul stable,
Where the beasts feed and foam;
Only where He was homeless
Are you and I at home;
We have hands that fashion and heads that know,
But our hearts we lost – how long ago!
In a place no chart nor ship can show
Under the sky's dome.

This world is wild as an old wives' tale,
And strange the plain things are,
The earth is enough and the air is enough
For our wonder and our war;
But our rest is as far as the fire-drake swings
And our peace is put in impossible things
Where clashed and thundered unthinkable wings
Round an incredible star.

To an open house in the evening
Home shall men come,
To an older place than Eden
And a taller town than Rome.
To the end of the way of the wandering star,
To the things that cannot be and that are,
To the place where God was homeless
And all men are at home.

GOING FURTHER

For a fuller analysis of the poem, (which is quite good) see the notes from https://allpo
etry.com/The-House-of-Christmas

Carol of the Brown King

LANGSTON HUGHES

Langston Hughes, 1901 – 1967
American poet, novelist, playwright, and columnist

Langston Hughes (James Mercer Langston Hughes) began writing in high school and published works in many different genres over the next forty years for adults and children. His writing is rich with the experience of black America in the twentieth century, especially its early decades. The following is a small taste of a huge, wonderful talent.

CAROL OF THE BROWN KING

Of the three Wise Men
Who came to thy King,
One was a brown man,
So they sing.

Of the three Wise Men
Who followed the Star,
One was a brown king
From afar.

They brought fine gifts
Of spices and gold

In jeweled boxes
Of beauty untold.

Unto his humble
Manger they came,
And bowed their heads
In Jesus' name.

Three Wise Men,
One dark like me –
Part of his
Nativity.

The Trapper's Christmas Tale

RUTH SAWYER

Ruth Sawyer, 1880 – 1970

American Writer and Story teller

Sawyer was an award-winning writer for children and adults. The following folk tale is an excerpt from her children's book, This Way to Christmas.

THE TRAPPER'S CHRISTMAS TALE

"Tell me," said David, suddenly, "do your people have any stories—stories of Christmas?"

"Christmas!"

The trapper repeated it—almost as if it were a strange word to him. "Wait a minute—keep very still. I will see can I think back a story of Christmas."

David sat without stirring, almost without breathing, as the trapper puffed silently at his pipe. He puffed the bowl quite empty, then knocking the ashes clean out of his pipe he put it back in his pocket again and looked up at David with the old grave look.

"There is a people in our country who are called wanderers; some say they have been wanderers for two thousand years. You call them gipsies or Egyptians; we call them 'Tzigan.' Now, they are vagabonds, for the most part, dirty, thieving rascals, ready to tell a fortune or pick a pocket, as the fancy takes them; but—it was not always so.

Some say that they have been cursed because they feared to give shelter to Mary and Joseph and the Child when the King of Judea forced them to flee into Egypt. But the gipsies themselves say that this is not true; and this is the story the Tzigan mothers tell their children on the night of Christmas, as they sit around the fire that is always burning in the heart of a Romany camp."

It was winter—and twelve months since the gipsies had driven their flocks of mountain-sheep over the dark, gloomy Balkans, and had settled in the southlands near to the Ægean. It was twelve months since they had seen a wonderful star appear in the sky and heard the singing of angelic voices afar off.

They had marveled much concerning the star until a runner had passed them from the South bringing them news that the star had marked the birth of a Child whom the wise men had hailed as "King of Israel" and "Prince of Peace." This had made Herod of Judea both afraid and angry and he had sent soldiers secretly to kill the Child; but in the night they had miraculously disappeared—the Child with Mary and Joseph—and no one knew whither they had gone.

Therefore Herod had sent runners all over the lands that bordered the Mediterranean with a message forbidding every one giving food or shelter or warmth to the child, under penalty of death. For Herod's anger was far-reaching and where his anger fell there fell his sword likewise. Having given his warning, the runner passed on, leaving the gipsies to marvel much over the tale they had heard and the meaning of the star.

Now on that day that marked the end of the twelve months since the star had shone the gipsies said among themselves: "Dost thou think that the star will shine again to-night? If it were true, what the runner said, that when it shone twelve months ago it marked the place where the Child lay it may even mark His hiding-place this night. Then Herod would know where to find Him, and send his soldiers again to slay Him. That would be a cruel thing to happen!"

The air was chill with the winter frost, even there in the southland, close to the Ægean; and the gipsies built high their fire and hung their kettle full of millet, fish, and bitter herbs for their supper. The king lay on his couch of tiger-skins and on his arms were amulets of heavy gold, while rings of gold were on his fingers and in his ears. His tunic was of heavy silk covered with a leopard cloak, and on his feet were shoes of goat-skin trimmed with fur. Now, as they feasted around the fire a voice came to them through the darkness, calling. It was a man's voice, climbing the mountains from the south.

"Ohe! Ohe!" he shouted. And then nearer, "O—he!"

The gipsies were still disputing among themselves whence the voice came when there walked into the circle about the fire a tall, shaggy man, grizzled with age, and a sweet-faced young mother carrying a child.

"We are outcasts," said the man, hoarsely. "Ye must know that whosoever succors us will bring Herod's vengeance like a sword about his head. For a year we have wandered homeless and cursed over the world. Only the wild creatures have not feared to share their food and give us shelter in their lairs. But to-night we can go no farther; and we beg the warmth of your fire and food enough to stay us until the morrow."

The king looked at them long before he made reply. He saw the weariness in their eyes and the famine in their cheeks; he saw, as well, the holy light that hung about the child, and he said at last to his men:

"It is the Child of Bethlehem, the one they call the 'Prince of Peace.' As yon man says, who shelters them shelters the wrath of Herod as well. Shall we let them tarry?"

One of their number sprang to his feet, crying: "It is a sin to turn strangers from the fire, a greater sin if they be poor and friendless. And what is a king's wrath to us? I say bid them welcome. What say the rest?"

And with one accord the gipsies shouted, "Yea, let them tarry!"

They brought fresh skins and threw them down beside the fire for the man and woman to rest on. They brought them food and wine, and goat's milk for the Child; and when they had seen that all was made comfortable for them they gathered round the Child—these black gipsy men—to touch His small white hands and feel His golden hair. They brought Him a chain of gold to play with and another for His neck and tiny arm.

"See, these shall be Thy gifts, little one," said they, "the gifts for Thy first birthday."

And long after all had fallen asleep the Child lay on His bed of skins beside the blazing fire and watched the light dance on the beads of gold. He laughed and clapped His hands together to see the pretty sight they made; and then a bird called out of the thicket close by.

"Child of Bethlehem," it called, "I, too, have a birth gift for Thee. I will sing Thy cradle song this night." And softly, like the tinkling of a silver bell and like clear water running over mossy places, the nightingale sang and sang, filling the air with melodies.

And then another voice called to him:

"Little Child of Bethlehem, I am only a tree with boughs all bare, for the winter has stolen my green cloak, but I also can give Thee a birth gift. I can give Thee shelter from the biting north wind that blows." And the tree bent low its branches and twined a rooftree and a wall about the Child.

Soon the Child was fast asleep, and while He slept a small brown bird hopped out of the thicket. Cocking his little head, he said:

"What can I be giving the Child of Bethlehem? I could fetch Him a fat worm to eat or catch Him the beetle that crawls on yonder bush, but He would not like that! And I could tell Him a story of the lands of the north, but He is asleep and would not hear." And the brown bird shook its head quite sorrowfully. Then it saw that the wind was bringing the sparks from the fire nearer and nearer to the sleeping Child.

"I know what I can do," said the bird, joyously. "I can catch the hot sparks on my breast, for if one should fall upon the Child it would burn Him grievously."

So the small brown bird spread wide his wings and caught the sparks on his own brown breast. So many fell that the feathers were burned; and burned was the flesh beneath until the breast was no longer brown, but red.

Next morning, when the gipsies awoke, they found Mary and Joseph and the Child gone. For Herod had died, and an angel had come in the night and carried them back to the land of Judea. But the good God blessed those who had cared that night for the Child.

To the nightingale He said: "Your song shall be the sweetest in all the world, for ever and ever; and only you shall sing the long night through."

To the tree He said: "Little fir-tree, never more shall your branches be bare. Winter and summer you and your seedlings shall stay green, ever green."

Last of all He blessed the brown bird: "Faithful little watcher, from this night forth you and your children shall have red breasts, that the world may never forget your gift to the Child of Bethlehem."

A Christmas Matinee

Mrs. M. A. L. Lane

MRS. M.A.L. LANE

No biographical record for Mrs. Lane could be found, but this story was first published in the Youth's Companion, volume 74, and then the Children's Book of Christmas Stories, 1913.

A CHRISTMAS MATINEE

It was the day before Christmas in the year 189-. Snow was falling heavily in the streets of Boston, but the crowd of shoppers seemed undiminished. As the storm increased, groups gathered at the corners and in sheltering doorways to wait for belated cars; but the holiday cheer was in the air, and there was no grumbling. Mothers dragging tired children through the slush of the streets; pretty girls hurrying home for the holidays; here and there a harassed-looking man with perhaps a single package which he had taken a whole morning to select—all had the same spirit of tolerant good-humor.

"School Street! School Street!" called the conductor of an electric car. A group of young people at the farther end of the car started to their feet. One of them, a young man wearing a heavy fur-trimmed coat, addressed the conductor angrily.

"I said, 'Music Hall,' didn't I?" he demanded. "Now we've got to walk back in the snow because of your stupidity!"

"Oh, never mind, Frank!" one of the girls interposed. "We ought to have been looking out ourselves! Six of us, and we went by without a thought! It is all Mrs. Tirrell's fault! She shouldn't have been so entertaining!"

The young matron dimpled and blushed. "That's charming of you, Maidie," she said, gathering up her silk skirts as she prepared to step down into the pond before her. "The compliment makes up for the blame. But how it snows!"

"It doesn't matter. We all have gaiters on[1]," returned Maidie Williams, undisturbed.

"Fares, please!" said the conductor stolidly.

Frank Armstrong thrust his gloved hand deep into his pocket with angry vehemence. "There's your money," he said, "and be quick about the change, will you? We've lost time enough!"

The man counted out the change with stiff, red fingers, closed his lips firmly as if to keep back an obvious rejoinder, rang up the six fares with careful accuracy, and gave the signal to go ahead. The car went on into the drifting storm.

Armstrong laughed shortly as he rapidly counted the bits of silver lying in his open palm. He turned instinctively, but two or three cars were already between him and the one he was looking for.

"The fellow must be an imbecile," he said, rejoining the group on the crossing. "He's given me back a dollar and twenty cents, and I handed him a dollar bill."

"Oh, can't you stop him?" cried Maidie Williams, with a backward step into the wet street.

The Harvard junior, who was carrying her umbrella, protested: "What's the use. Miss Williams? He'll make it up before he gets to Scollay Square, you may be sure. Those chaps don't lose anything. Why, the other day, I gave one a quarter and he went off as cool as you please. 'Where's my change?' said I. 'You gave me a nickel,' said he. And there wasn't anybody to swear that I didn't except myself, and I didn't count."

"But that doesn't make any difference," insisted the girl warmly. "Because one conductor was dishonest, we needn't be. I beg your pardon, Frank, but it does seem to me just stealing."

"Oh, come along!" said her cousin, with an easy laugh. "I guess the West End Corporation won't go without their dinners to-morrow. Here, Maidie, here's the ill-gotten fifty cents. *I* think you ought to treat us all after the concert; still, I won't urge you. I wash my hands of all responsibility. But I do wish you hadn't such an unpleasant conscience."

Maidie flushed under the sting of his cousinly rudeness, but she went on quietly with the rest. It was evident that any attempt to overtake the car was out of the question.

"Did you notice his number, Frank?" she asked, suddenly.

"No, I never thought of it" said Frank, stopping short. "However, I probably shouldn't make any complaint if I had. I shall forget all about it tomorrow. I find it's never safe to let the sun go down on my wrath.[2] It's very likely not to be there the next day."

"I wasn't thinking of making a complaint," said Maidie; but the two young men were enjoying the small joke too much to notice what she said.

The great doorway of Music Hall was just ahead. In a moment the party were within its friendly shelter, stamping off the snow. The girls were adjusting veils and hats with adroit feminine touches; the pretty chaperon was beaming approval upon them, and the young men were taking off their wet overcoats, when Maidie turned again in sudden desperation.

"Mr. Harris," she said, rather faintly, for she did not like to make herself disagreeable, "do you suppose that car comes right back from Scollay Square?"

"What car?" asked Walter Harris, blankly. "Oh, the one we came in? Yes, I suppose it does. They're running all the time, anyway. Why, you are not sick, are you, Miss Williams?"

There was genuine concern in his tone. This girl, with her sweet, vibrant voice, her clear gray eyes, seemed very charming to him. She wasn't beautiful, perhaps, but she was the kind of girl he liked. There was a steady earnestness in the gray eyes that made him think of his mother.

"No," said Maidie, slowly. "I'm all right, thank you. But I wish I could find that man again. I know sometimes they have to make it up if their accounts are wrong, and I couldn't—we couldn't feel very comfortable—"

Frank Armstrong interrupted her. "Maidie," he said, with the studied calmness with which one speaks to an unreasonable child, "you are perfectly absurd. Here it is within five minutes of the time for the concert to begin. It is impossible to tell when that car is coming back. You are making us all very uncomfortable. Mrs. Tirrell, won't you please tell her not to spoil our afternoon?"

"I think he's right, Maidie," said Mrs. Tirrell. "It's very nice of you to feel so sorry for the poor man, but he really was very careless. It was all his own fault. And just think how far he made us walk! My feet are quite damp. We ought to go in directly or we shall all take cold, and I'm sure you wouldn't like that, my dear."

She led the way as she spoke, the two girls and young Armstrong following. Maidie hesitated. It was so easy to go in, to forget everything in the light and warmth and excitement.

"No," said she, very firmly, and as much to herself as to the young man who stood waiting for her. "I must go back and try to make it right. I'm so sorry, Mr. Harris, but if you will tell them—"

"Why, I'm going with you, of course" said the young fellow, impulsively. "If I'd only looked once at the man I'd go alone, but I shouldn't know him from Adam."

Maidie laughed. "Oh, I don't want to lose the whole concert, Mr. Harris, and Frank has all the tickets. You must go after them and try to make my peace. I'll come just as soon as I can. Don't wait for me, please. If you'll come and look for me here the first number, and not let them scold me too much—" She ended with an imploring little catch in her breath that was almost a sob.

"They sha'n't say a word, Miss Williams!" cried Walter Harris, with honest admiration in his eyes.

But she was gone already, and conscious that further delay was only making matters worse, he went on into the hall.

Meanwhile, the car swung heavily along the wet rails on its way to the turning-point. It was nearly empty now. An old gentleman and his nurse were the only occupants. Jim Stevens, the conductor, had stepped inside the car.

"Too bad I forgot those young people wanted to get off at Music Hall," he was thinking to himself. "I don't see how I came to do it. That chap looked as if he wanted to complain of me, and I don't know as I blame him. I'd have said I was sorry if he hadn't been so sharp with his tongue. I hope he won't complain just now. 'Twould be a pretty bad time for me to get into trouble, with Mary and the baby both sick. I'm too sleepy to be good for much, that's a fact. Sitting up three nights running takes hold of a fellow somehow when he's at work all day. The rent's paid, that's one thing, if it hasn't left me but half a dollar to my name. Hullo!" He was struck by a sudden distinct recollection of the coins he had returned. "Why, I gave him fifty cents too much!"

He glanced up at the dial which indicated the fares and began to count the change in his pocket. He knew exactly how much money he had had at the beginning of the trip. He counted carefully. Then he plunged his hand into the heavy canvas pocket of his coat. Perhaps he had half a dollar there. No, it was empty!

He faced the fact reluctantly. Fifty cents short, ten fares! Gone into the pocket of the young gentleman with the fur collar! The conductor's hand shook as he put the money back in his pocket. It meant—what did it mean? He drew a long breath.

Christmas Eve! A dark dreary little room upstairs in a noisy tenement house. A pale, thin woman on a shabby lounge vainly trying to quiet a fretful child. The child is thin and pale, too, with a hard, racking cough. There is a small fire in the stove, a very small fire; coal is so high. The medicine stands on the shelf. "Medicine won't do much good," the doctor had said; "he needs beef and cream."

Jim's heart sank at the thought. He could almost hear the baby asking; "Isn't papa coming soon? Isn't he, mamma?"

"Poor little kid!" Jim said, softly, under his breath. "And I shan't have a thing to take home to him; nor Mary's violets, either. It'll be the first Christmas *that* ever happened. I suppose that chap would think it was ridiculous for me to be buying violets. He wouldn't understand what the flowers mean to Mary. Perhaps he didn't notice I gave him too much. That kind don't know how much they have. They just pull it out as if it was newspaper."

The conductor went out into the snow to help the nurse who was assisting the old gentleman to the ground. Then the car swung on again. Jim turned up the collar of his coat about his ears and stamped his feet. There was the florist's shop where he had meant to buy the violets, and the toy-shop was just around the corner.

A thought flashed across his tired brain. "Plenty of men would do it; they do it every day. Nobody ever would be the poorer for it. This car will be crowded going home. I needn't ring in every fare; nobody could tell. But Mary! She wouldn't touch those violets if she knew. And she'd know. I'd have to tell her. I couldn't keep it from her, she's that quick."

He jumped off to adjust the trolley with a curious sense of unreality. It couldn't be that he was really going home this Christmas Eve with empty hands. Well, they must all suffer together for his carelessness. It was his own fault, but it was hard. And he was so tired!

To his amazement he found his eyes were blurred as he watched the people crowding into the car. What? Was he going to cry like a baby—he, a great burly man of thirty years?

"It's no use," he thought. "I couldn't do it. The first time I gave Mary violets was the night she said she'd marry me. I told her then I'd do my best to make her proud of me. I guess she wouldn't be very proud of a man who could cheat. She'd rather starve than have a ribbon she couldn't pay for."

He rang up a dozen fares with a steady hand. The temptation was over. Six more strokes—then nine without a falter. He even imagined the bell rang more distinctly than usual, even encouragingly. The car stopped. Jim flung the door open with a triumphant sweep of his arm. He felt ready to face the world. But the baby—his arm dropped. It was hard.

He turned to help the young girl who was waiting at the step. Through the whirling snow he saw her eager face, with a quick recognition lighting the steady eyes, and wondered dimly, as he stood with his hand on the signal-strap, where he could have seen her before.

He knew immediately.

"There was a mistake," she said, with a shy tremor in her voice. "You gave us too much change and here it is." She held out to Jim the piece of silver which had given him such an unhappy quarter of an hour.

He took it like one dazed. Would the young lady think he was crazy to care so much about so small a coin? He must say something. "Thank you, miss," he stammered as well as he could. "You see, I thought it was gone—and there's the baby—and it's Christmas Eve—and my wife's sick—and you can't understand—"

It certainly was not remarkable that she couldn't.

"But I do," she said, simply. "I was afraid of that. And I thought perhaps there was a baby, so I brought my Christmas present for her," and something else dropped into Jim's cold hand.

"What you waiting for?" shouted the motorman from the front platform. The girl had disappeared in the snow.

Jim rang the bell to go ahead, and gazed again at the two shining half dollars in his hand.

"I didn't have a chance to tell her," he explained to his wife late in the evening, as he sat in a tiny rocking-chair several sizes too small for him, "that the baby wasn't a her at all, though if I thought he'd grow up into such a lovely one as she is, I don't know but I almost wish he was."

"Poor Jim!" said Mary, with a little laugh as she put up her hand to stroke his rough cheek. "I guess you're tired."

"And I should say," he added, stretching out his long legs toward the few red sparks in the bottom of the grate, "I should say she had tears in her eyes, too, but I was that near crying myself I couldn't be sure."

The little room was sweet with the odour of English violets. Asleep in the bed lay the boy, a toy horse clasped close to his breast.

"Bless her heart!" said Mary, softly.

"Well, Miss Williams," said Walter Harris, as he sprang to meet a snow-covered figure coming swiftly along the sidewalk. "I can see that you found him. You've lost the first number, but they won't scold you—not this time."

The girl turned a radiant face upon him. "Thank you," she said, shaking the snowy crystals from her skirt. "I don't care now if they do. I should have lost more than that if I had stayed."

[1]*Gaiters are coverings worn over the lower pants leg and the shoe to protect the feet from debris, snow, weather, and water.*

[2] *The reference is to Ephesians 4: 26.*

Mr. Bluff's Experience of the Holidays

OLIVER BELL BUNCE

Oliver Bell Bunce, 1828 – 1890

American author, editor, and playwright

Possibly intended for children, this surprise-ending short story supports the idea that even the most cynical can learn what love means at Christmas.

MR. BLUFF'S EXPERIENCE OF THE HOLIDAYS

"I hate holidays," said Bachelor Bluff to me, with some little irritation, on a Christmas a few years ago. Then he paused an instant, after which he resumed: "I don't mean to say that I hate to see people enjoying themselves. But I hate holidays, nevertheless, because to me they are always the saddest and dreariest days of the year. I shudder at the name of holiday. I dread the approach of one, and thank heaven when it is over. I pass through, on a holiday, the most horrible sensations, the bitterest feelings, the most oppressive melancholy; in fact, I am not myself at holiday-times."

"Very strange," I ventured to interpose.

"A plague on it!" said he, almost with violence. "I'm not inhuman. I don't wish anybody harm. I'm glad people can enjoy themselves. But I hate holidays all the same. You see, this is the reason: I am a bachelor; I am without kin; I am in a place that did not know me at birth. And so, when holidays come around, there is no place anywhere for me. I have friends, of course; I don't think I've been a very sulky, shut-in, reticent fellow; and there is many a board that has a place for me—but not at Christmastime.

At Christmas, the dinner is a family gathering; and I've no family. There is such a gathering of kindred on this occasion, such a reunion of family folk, that there is no place for a friend, even if the friend be liked. Christmas, with all its kindliness and charity and good-will, is, after all, deuced selfish. Each little set gathers within its own circle; and people like me, with no particular circle, are left in the lurch. So you see, on the day of all the days in the year that my heart pines for good cheer, I'm without an invitation.

"Oh, it's because I pine for good cheer," said the bachelor, sharply, interrupting my attempt to speak, "that I hate holidays. If I were an infernally selfish fellow, I wouldn't hate holidays. I'd go off and have some fun all to myself, somewhere or somehow. But, you see, I hate to be in the dark when all the rest of the world is in light. I hate holidays because I ought to be merry and happy on holidays and can't.

"Don't tell me," he cried, stopping the word that was on my lips; "I tell you, I hate holidays. The shops look merry, do they, with their bright toys and their green branches? The pantomime is crowded with merry hearts, is it? The circus and the show are brimful of fun and laughter, are they? Well, they all make me miserable. I haven't any pretty-faced girls or bright-eyed boys to take to the circus or the show, and all the nice girls and fine boys of my acquaintance have their uncles or their grand-dads or their cousins to take them to those places; so, if I go, I must go alone. But I don't go. I can't bear the chill of seeing everybody happy, and knowing myself so lonely and desolate. Confound it, sir, I've too much heart to be happy under such circumstances! I'm too humane, sir! And the result is, I hate holidays. It's miserable to be out, and yet I can't stay at home, for I get thinking of Christmases past. I can't read—the shadow of my heart makes it impossible. I can't walk—for I see nothing but pictures through the bright windows, and happy groups of pleasure-seekers. The fact is, I've nothing to do but to hate holidays. But will you not dine with me?"

Of course, I had to plead engagement with my own family circle, and I couldn't quite invite Mr. Bluff home that day, when Cousin Charles and his wife, and Sister Susan and her daughter, and three of my wife's kin had come in from the country, all to make a merry Christmas with us. I felt sorry, but it was quite impossible, so I wished Mr. Bluff a "Merry Christmas," and hurried homeward through the cold and nipping air.

I did not meet Bachelor Bluff again until a week after Christmas of the next year, when I learned some strange particulars of what occurred to him after our parting on the occasion just described. I will let Bachelor Bluff tell his adventure for himself.

"I went to church," said he, "and was as sad there as everywhere else. Of course, the evergreens were pretty, and the music fine; but all around me were happy groups of people, who could scarcely keep down merry Christmas long enough to do reverence to sacred Christmas. And nobody was alone but me. Every happy paterfamilias in his pew tantalized me, and the whole atmosphere of the place seemed so much better suited to every one else than me that I came away hating holidays worse than ever.

Then I went to the play, and sat down in a box all alone by myself. Everybody seemed on the best of terms with everybody else, and jokes and banter passed from one to another with the most good-natured freedom. Everybody but me was in a little group of friends. I was the only person in the whole theatre that was alone. And then there was such clapping of hands, and roars of laughter, and shouts of delight at all the fun going on upon the stage, all of which was rendered doubly enjoyable by everybody having somebody with whom to share and interchange the pleasure, that my loneliness got simply unbearable, and I hated holidays infinitely worse than ever.

"By five o'clock the holiday became so intolerable that I said I'd go and get a dinner. The best dinner the town could provide. A sumptuous dinner for one. A dinner with many courses, with wines of the finest brands, with bright lights, with a cheerful fire, with every condition of comfort—and I'd see if I couldn't for once extract a little pleasure out of a holiday!

"The handsome dining-room at the club looked bright, but it was empty. Who dines at this club on Christmas but lonely bachelors? There was a flutter of surprise when I ordered a dinner, and the few attendants were, no doubt, glad of something to break the monotony of the hours.

"My dinner was well served. The spacious room looked lonely; but the white, snowy cloths, the rich window hangings, the warm tints of the walls, the sparkle of the fire in the steel grate, gave the room an air of elegance and cheerfulness; and then the table at which I dined was close to the window, and through the partly drawn curtains were visible centres of lonely, cold streets, with bright lights from many a window, it is true, but there was a storm, and snow began whirling through the street. I let my imagination paint the streets as cold and dreary as it would, just to extract a little pleasure by way of contrast from the brilliant room of which I was apparently sole master.

"I dined well, and recalled in fancy old, youthful Christmases, and pledged mentally many an old friend, and my melancholy was mellowing into a low, sad undertone, when, just as I was raising a glass of wine to my lips, I was startled by a picture at the windowpane. It was a pale, wild, haggard face, in a great cloud of black hair, pressed against the glass. As I looked it vanished.

With a strange thrill at my heart, which my lips mocked with a derisive sneer, I finished the wine and set down the glass. It was, of course, only a beggar-girl that had crept up to the window and stole a glance at the bright scene within; but still the pale face troubled me a little, and threw a fresh shadow on my heart. I filled my glass once more with wine, and was again about to drink, when the face reappeared at the window. It was so white, so thin, with eyes so large, wild, and hungry-looking, and the black, unkempt hair, into which the snow had drifted, formed so strange and weird a frame to the picture, that I was fairly startled.

Replacing, untasted, the liquor on the table, I rose and went close to the pane. The face had vanished, and I could see no object within many feet of the window. The storm had increased, and the snow was driving in wild gusts through the streets, which were empty, save here and there a hurrying wayfarer. The whole scene was cold, wild, and desolate, and I could not repress a keen thrill of sympathy for the child, whoever it was, whose only Christmas was to watch, in cold and storm, the rich banquet ungratefully enjoyed by the lonely bachelor.

I resumed my place at the table; but the dinner was finished, and the wine had no further relish. I was haunted by the vision at the window, and began, with an unreasonable irritation at the interruption, to repeat with fresh warmth my detestation of holidays. One couldn't even dine alone on a holiday with any sort of comfort, I declared. On holidays one was tormented by too much pleasure on one side, and too much misery on the other. And then, I said, hunting for justification of my dislike of the day, 'How many other people are, like me, made miserable by seeing the fullness of enjoyment others possess!'

"Oh, yes, I know," sarcastically replied the bachelor to a comment of mine; "of course, all magnanimous, generous, and noble-souled people delight in seeing other people made happy, and are quite content to accept this vicarious felicity. But I, you see, and this dear little girl—"

"Dear little girl?"

"Oh, I forgot," said Bachelor Bluff, blushing a little, in spite of a desperate effort not to do so. "I didn't tell you. Well, it was so absurd! I kept thinking, thinking of the pale, haggard, lonely little girl on the cold and desolate side of the window-pane, and the over-fed, discontented, lonely old bachelor on the splendid side of the window-pane, and I didn't get much happier thinking about it, I can assure you. I drank glass after glass of the wine—not that I enjoyed its flavour any more, but mechanically, as it were, and with a sort of hope thereby to drown unpleasant reminders.

"I tried to attribute my annoyance in the matter to holidays, and so denounced them more vehemently than ever. I rose once in a while and went to the window, but could see no one to whom the pale face could have belonged.

"At last, in no very amiable mood, I got up, put on my wrappers, and went out; and the first thing I did was to run against a small figure crouching in the doorway. A face looked up quickly at the rough encounter, and I saw the pale features of the window-pane. I was very irritated and angry, and spoke harshly; and then, all at once, I am sure I don't know how it happened, but it flashed upon me that I, of all men, had no right to utter a harsh word to one oppressed with so wretched a Christmas as this poor creature was.

"I couldn't say another word, but began feeling in my pocket for some money, and then I asked a question or two, and then I don't quite know how it came about—isn't it very warm here?" exclaimed Bachelor Bluff, rising and walking about, and wiping the perspiration from his brow.

"Well, you see," he resumed nervously, "it was very absurd, but I did believe the girl's story—the old story, you know, of privation and suffering, and just thought I'd go home with the brat and see if what she said was all true. And then I remembered that all the shops were closed, and not a purchase could be made. I went back and persuaded the steward to put up for me a hamper of provisions, which the half-wild little youngster helped me carry through the snow, dancing with delight all the way. And isn't this enough?"

"Not a bit, Mr. Bluff. I must have the whole story."

"I declare," said Bachelor Bluff, "there's no whole story to tell. A widow with children in great need, that was what I found; and they had a feast that night, and a little money to buy them a load of wood and a garment or two the next day; and they were all so bright, and so merry, and so thankful, and so good, that, when I got home that night, I was mightily amazed that, instead of going to bed sour at holidays, I was in a state of great contentment in regard to holidays. In fact, I was really merry. I whistled. I sang. I do believe

I cut a caper. The poor wretches I had left had been so merry over their unlooked-for Christmas banquet that their spirits infected mine.

"And then I got thinking again. Of course, holidays had been miserable to me, I said. What right had a well-to-do, lonely old bachelor hovering wistfully in the vicinity of happy circles, when all about there were so many people as lonely as he, and yet oppressed with want? 'Good gracious!' I exclaimed, 'to think of a man complaining of loneliness with thousands of wretches yearning for his help and comfort, with endless opportunities for work and company, with hundreds of pleasant and delightful things to do.

"Just to think of it! It put me in a great fury at myself to think of it. I tried pretty hard to escape from myself and began inventing excuses and all that sort of thing, but I rigidly forced myself to look squarely at my own conduct. And then I reconciled my confidence by declaring that, if ever after that day I hated a holiday again, might my holidays end at once and forever!

"Did I go and see my proteges again? What a question! Why—well, no matter. If the widow is comfortable now, it is because she has found a way to earn without difficulty enough for her few wants. That's no fault of mine. I would have done more for her, but she wouldn't let me. But just let me tell you about New Year's—the New-Year's day that followed the Christmas I've been describing.

"It was lucky for me there was another holiday only a week off. Bless you! I had so much to do that day I was completely bewildered, and the hours weren't half long enough. I did make a few social calls, but then I hurried them over; and then hastened to my little girl, whose face had already caught a touch of colour; and she, looking quite handsome in her new frock and her ribbons, took me to other poor folk, and,—well, that's about the whole story.

"Oh, as to the next Christmas. Well, I didn't dine alone, as you may guess. It was up three stairs, that's true, and there was none of that elegance that marked the dinner of the year before; but it was merry, and happy, and bright; it was a generous, honest, hearty Christmas dinner, that it was, although I do wish the widow hadn't talked so much about the mysterious way a turkey had been left at her door the night before.

"And Molly—that's the little girl—and I had a rousing appetite. We went to church early; then we had been down to the Five Points to carry the poor outcasts there something for their Christmas dinner; in fact, we had done wonders of work, and Molly was in high spirits, and so the Christmas dinner was a great success.

"Dear me, sir, no! Just as you say. Holidays are not in the least wearisome any more.

Plague on it! When a man tells me now that he hates holidays, I find myself getting very wroth. I pin him by the buttonhole at once, and tell him my experience. The fact is, if I were at dinner on a holiday, and anybody should ask me for a sentiment, I should say, 'God bless all holidays!'"

A Christmas Mystery: The Story of the Three Wise Men

WILLIAM J. LOCKE

William J. Locke, 1863 – 1930

Original Illustrations by Blendon Campbell

Though there are some harsh elements in this story—this isn't one to read to the young-sters—it is nevertheless a beautiful tale of Christmas wonder when all is said and done. Three old curmudgeons who have missed out on the best that life offers (unbeknownst to them at the outset) become soft-hearted beings with new eyes after the events of this special Christmas Eve unfold. It reminds us that no heart is too hard for the hand of providence to touch, no tragedy without its divine uses.

There are touches of irony, beginning with the title: Is this a story of three wise men or of three who become wiser? And what of the ominous motifs and imagery that the sharp reader will note? They lose their power in the face of tender redemption at Christmas.

A CHRISTMAS MYSTERY: THE STORY OF THREE WISE MEN

I cannot tell how the truth may be: I say the tale as 'twas said to me."

Three men who had gained great fame and honour throughout the world met unexpectedly in front of the bookstall at Paddington Station. Like most of the great ones of the earth they were personally acquainted, and they exchanged surprised greetings. Sir Angus McCurdie, the eminent physicist, scowled at the two others beneath his heavy black eyebrows.

"I'm going to a God-forsaken place in Cornwall called Trehenna," said he.

"That's odd; so am I," croaked Professor Biggleswade. He was a little, untidy man with round spectacles, a fringe of greyish beard and a weak, rasping voice, and he knew more of Assyriology than any man, living or dead. A flippant pupil once remarked that the Professor's face was furnished with a Babylonic cuneiform in lieu of features.

"People called Deverill, at Foulis Castle?" asked Sir Angus. "Yes," replied Professor Biggleswade.

"How curious! I am going to the Deverills, too," said the third man. This man was the Right Honourable Viscount Doyne, the renowned Empire Builder and Administrator, around whose solitary and remote life popular imagination had woven many legends. He looked at the world through tired grey eyes, and the heavy, drooping, blonde moustache seemed tired, too, and had dragged down the tired face into deep furrows. He was smoking a long black cigar.

"I suppose we may as well travel down together," said Sir Angus, not very cordially. Lord Doyne said courteously, "I have a reserved carriage. The railway company is always good enough to place one at my disposal. It would give me great pleasure if you would share it." The invitation was accepted, and the three men crossed the busy, crowded platform to take their seats in the great express train. A porter, laden with an incredible load of paraphernalia, trying to make his way through the press, happened to jostle Sir Angus McCurdie. He rubbed his shoulder fretfully.

"Why the whole land should be turned into a bear garden on account of this exploded superstition of Christmas is one of the anomalies of modern civilization. Look at this insensate welter of fools travelling in wild herds to disgusting places merely because it's Christmas!"

"You seem to be travelling yourself, McCurdie," said Lord Doyne.

"Yes—and why the devil I'm doing it, I've not the faintest notion," replied Sir Angus. "It's going to be a beast of a journey," he remarked some moments later, as the train carried them slowly out of the station. "The whole country is under snow—and as far as I can understand we have to change twice and wind up with a twenty-mile motor drive." He was an iron-faced, beetle-browed, stern man, and this morning he did not seem to be in the best of tempers. Finding his companions inclined to be sympathetic, he continued his lamentation. "And merely because it's Christmas I've had to shut up my laboratory and give my young fools a holiday—just when I was in the midst of a most important series of experiments."

Professor Biggleswade, who had heard vaguely of and rather looked down upon such new-fangled toys as radium and thorium and helium and argon—for the latest astonishing developments in the theory of radio-activity had brought Sir Angus McCurdie his worldwide fame—said somewhat ironically: "If the experiments were so important, why didn't you lock yourself up with your test tubes and electric batteries and finish them alone?"

"Man!" said McCurdie, bending across the carriage, and speaking with a curious intensity of voice, "d'ye know I'd give a hundred pounds to be able to answer that question?"

"What do you mean?" asked the Professor, startled. "I should like to know why I'm sitting in this damned train and going to visit a couple of addle-headed society people whom I'm scarcely acquainted with, when I might be at home in my own good company furthering the progress of science."

"I myself," said the Professor, "am not acquainted with them at all."

It was Sir Angus McCurdie's turn to look surprised. "Then why are you spending Christmas with them?"

"I reviewed a ridiculous blank-verse tragedy written by Deverill on the Death of Sennacherib. Historically it was puerile. I said so in no measured terms. He wrote a letter claiming to be a poet and not an archaeologist. I replied that the day had passed when poets could with impunity commit the abominable crime of distorting history. He retorted with some futile argument, and we went on exchanging letters, until his invitation and my acceptance concluded the correspondence."

McCurdie, still bending his black brows on him, asked him why he had not declined. The Professor screwed up his face till it looked more like a cuneiform than ever. He, too, found the question difficult to answer, but he showed a bold front. "I felt it my duty," said he, "to teach that preposterous ignoramus something worth knowing about Sennacherib. Besides I am a bachelor and would sooner spend Christmas, as to whose irritating and meaningless annoyance I cordially agree with you, among strangers than among my married sisters' numerous and nerve-racking families."

Sir Angus McCurdie, the hard, metallic apostle of radio-activity, glanced for a moment out of the window at the grey, frost-bitten fields. Then he said: "I'm a widower. My wife died many years ago and, thank God, we had no children. I generally spend Christmas alone." He looked out of the window again. Professor Biggleswade suddenly remembered the popular story of the great scientist's antecedents, and reflected that as McCurdie had once run, a barefoot urchin, through the Glasgow mud, he was likely to have little kith or kin. He himself envied McCurdie. He was always praying to be delivered from his sisters and nephews and nieces, whose embarrassing demands no calculated coldness could repress.

"Children are the root of all evil," said he. "Happy the man who has his quiver empty." Sir Angus McCurdie did not reply at once; when he spoke again it was with reference to their prospective host. "I met Deverill," said he, "at the Royal Society's Soiree this year. One of my assistants was demonstrating a peculiar property of thorium and Deverill seemed interested. I asked him to come to my laboratory the next day, and found he didn't know a d------- thing about anything. That's all the acquaintance I have with him."

Lord Doyne, the great administrator, who had been wearily turning over the pages of an illustrated weekly chiefly filled with flamboyant photographs of obscure actresses, took his gold glasses from his nose and the black cigar from his lips, and addressed his companions. "I've been considerably interested in your conversation," said he, "and as you've been frank, I'll be frank too. I knew Mrs. Deverill's mother, Lady Carstairs, very well years ago, and of course Mrs. Deverill when she was a child. Deverill I came across once in Egypt—he had been sent on a diplomatic mission to Teheran. As for our being invited on such slight acquaintance, little Mrs. Deverill has the reputation of being the only really successful celebrity hunter in England. She inherited the faculty from her mother, who entertained the whole world. We're sure to find archbishops, and eminent actors, and illustrious divorcees asked to meet us. That's one thing. But why I, who loathe country house parties and children and Christmas as much as Biggleswade, am going down there to-day, I can no more explain than you can. It's a devilish odd coincidence."

The three men looked at one another. Suddenly McCurdie shivered and drew his fur coat around him. "I'll thank you," said he, "to shut that window."

"It is shut," said Doyne.

"It's just uncanny," said McCurdie, looking from one to the other.

"What?" asked Doyne.

"Nothing, if you didn't feel it."

"There did seem to be a sudden draught," said Professor Biggleswade. "But as both window and door are shut, it could only be imaginary."

"It wasn't imaginary," muttered McCurdie. Then he laughed harshly. "My father and mother came from Cromarty," he said with apparent irrelevance.

"That's the Highlands," said the Professor.

"Ay," said McCurdie. Lord Doyne said nothing, but tugged at his moustache and looked out of the window as the frozen meadows and bits of river and willows raced past. A dead silence fell on them. McCurdie broke it with another laugh and took a whiskey flask from his hand-bag. "Have a nip?"

"Thanks, no," said the Professor. "I have to keep to a strict dietary, and I only drink hot milk and water—and of that sparingly. I have some in a thermos bottle." Lord Doyne also declining the whiskey, McCurdie swallowed a dram and declared himself to be better. The Professor took from his bag a foreign review in which a German sciolist had dared to question his interpretation of a Hittite inscription. Over the man's ineptitude he fell asleep and snored loudly. To escape from his immediate neighbourhood McCurdie went to the other end of the seat and faced Lord Doyne, who had resumed his gold glasses and his listless contemplation of obscure actresses. McCurdie lit a pipe, Doyne another black cigar. The train thundered on.

Presently they all lunched together in the restaurant car. The windows steamed, but here and there through a wiped patch of pane a white world was revealed. The snow was falling. As they passed through Westbury, McCurdie looked mechanically for the famous white horse carved into the chalk of the down; but it was not visible beneath the thick covering of snow. "It'll be just like this all the way to Gehenna—Trehenna, I mean," said McCurdie.

Doyne nodded. He had done his life's work amid all extreme fiercenesses of heat and cold, in burning droughts, in simoons and in icy wildernesses, and a ray or two more of the pale sun or a flake or two more of the gentle snow of England mattered to him but little. But Biggleswade rubbed the pane with his table-napkin and gazed apprehensively at the prospect.

"If only this wretched train would stop," said he, "I would go back again." And he thought how comfortable it would be to sneak home again to his books and thus elude not only the Deverills, but the Christmas jollities of his sisters' families, who would think him miles away. But the train was timed not to stop till Plymouth, two hundred and thirty-five miles from London, and thither was he being relentlessly carried. Then he quarrelled with his food, which brought a certain consolation.

The train did stop, however, before Plymouth—indeed, before Exeter. An accident on the line had dislocated the traffic. The express was held up for an hour, and when it was permitted to proceed, instead of thundering on, it went cautiously, subject to continual stoppings. It arrived at Plymouth two hours late. The travellers learned that they had missed the connection on which they had counted and that they could not reach Trehenna till nearly ten o'clock. After weary waiting at Plymouth they took their seats in the little, cold local train that was to carry them another stage on their journey. Hot-water cans put in at Plymouth mitigated to some extent the iciness of the compartment. But that only lasted a comparatively short time, for soon they were set down at a desolate, shelterless wayside junction, dumped in the midst of a hilly snow-covered waste, where they went through another weary wait for another dismal local train that was to carry them to Trehenna. And in this train there were no hot-water cans, so that the compartment was as cold as death.

McCurdie fretted and shook his fist in the direction of Trehenna. "And when we get there we have still a twenty miles' motor drive to Foullis Castle. It's a fool name and we're fools to be going there."

"I shall die of bronchitis," wailed Professor Biggleswade.

"A man dies when it is appointed for him to die," said Lord Doyne, in his tired way; and he went on smoking long black cigars. "It's not the dying that worries me," said McCurdie. "That's a mere mechanical process which every organic being from a king to a cauliflower has to pass through. It's the being forced against my will and my reason to come on this accursed journey, which something tells me will become more and more accursed as we go on, that is driving me to distraction."

"What will be, will be," said Doyne.

"I can't see where the comfort of that reflection comes in," said Biggleswade.

"And yet you've travelled in the East," said Doyne. "I suppose you know the Valley of the Tigris as well as any man living."

"Yes," said the Professor. "I can say I dug my way from Tekrit to Bagdad and left not a stone unexamined."

"Perhaps, after all," Doyne remarked, "that's not quite the way to know the East."

"I never wanted to know the modern East," returned the Professor. "What is there in it of interest compared with the mighty civilizations that have gone before?"

McCurdie took a pull from his flask. "I'm glad I thought of having a refill at Plymouth," said he. At last, after many stops at little lonely stations they arrived at Trehenna. The guard opened the door and they stepped out on to the snow-covered platform. An oil lamp hung from the tiny pent-house roof that, structurally, was Trehenna Station. They looked around at the silent gloom of white undulating moorland, and it seemed a place where no man lived and only ghosts could have a bleak and unsheltered being.

A porter came up and helped the guard with the luggage. Then they realized that the station was built on a small embankment, for, looking over the railing, they saw below the two great lamps of a motor car. A fur-clad chauffeur met them at the bottom of the stairs. He clapped his hands together and informed them cheerily that he had been waiting for four hours. It was the bitterest winter in these parts within the memory of man, said he, and he himself had not seen snow there for five years. Then he settled the three travellers in the great roomy touring car covered with a Cape-cart hood, wrapped them up in many rugs and started. After a few moments, the huddling together of their bodies—for, the Professor being a spare man, there was room for them all on the back seat—the pile of rugs, the serviceable and all but air-tight hood, induced a pleasant warmth and a pleasant drowsiness. Where they were being driven they knew not. The perfectly upholstered seat eased their limbs, the easy swinging motion of the car soothed their spirits. They felt that already they had reached the luxuriously appointed home which, after all, they knew awaited them. McCurdie no longer railed, Professor Biggleswade forgot the dangers of bronchitis, and Lord Doyne twisted the stump of a black cigar between his lips without any desire to relight it.

A tiny electric lamp inside the hood made the darkness of the world to right and left and in front of the talc windows still darker. McCurdie and Biggleswade fell into a doze. Lord Doyne chewed the end of his cigar. The car sped on through an unseen wilderness. Suddenly there was a horrid jolt and a lurch and a leap and a rebound, and then the car stood still, quivering like a ship that has been struck by a heavy sea. The three men were pitched and tossed and thrown sprawling over one another onto the bottom of the car. Biggleswade screamed. McCurdie cursed. Doyne scrambled from the confusion of rugs and limbs and, tearing open the side of the Cape-cart hood, jumped out.

The chauffeur had also just leaped from his seat. It was pitch dark save for the great shaft of light down the snowy road cast by the acetylene lamps. The snow had ceased falling. "What's gone wrong?"

"It sounds like the axle," said the chauffeur ruefully. He unshipped a lamp and examined the car, which had wedged itself against a great drift of snow on the off side. Meanwhile McCurdie and Biggleswade had alighted.

"Yes, it's the axle," said the chauffeur.

"Then we're done," remarked Doyne.

"I'm afraid so, my lord."

"What's the matter? Can't we get on?" asked Biggleswade in his querulous voice.

McCurdie laughed. "How can we get on with a broken axle? The thing's as useless as a man with a broken back. Gad, I was right. I said it was going to be an infernal journey."

The little Professor wrung his hands. "But what's to be done?" he cried.

"Tramp it," said Lord Doyne, lighting a fresh cigar.

"It's ten miles," said the chauffeur.

"It would be the death of me," the Professor wailed.

"I utterly refuse to walk ten miles through a Polar waste with a gouty foot," McCurdie declared wrathfully. The chauffeur offered a solution of the difficulty. He would set out alone for Foullis Castle—five miles farther on was an inn where he could obtain a horse and trap—and would return for the three gentlemen with another car. In the meanwhile they could take shelter in a little house which they had just passed, some half mile up the road. This was agreed to.

The chauffeur went on cheerily enough with a lamp, and the three travellers with another lamp started off in the opposite direction. As far as they could see they were in a long, desolate valley, a sort of No Man's Land, deathly silent. The eastern sky had cleared somewhat, and they faced a loose rack through which one pale star was dimly visible.

"I'm a man of science," said McCurdie as they trudged through the snow, "and I dismiss the supernatural as contrary to reason; but I have Highland blood in my veins that plays me exasperating tricks. My reason tells me that this place is only a commonplace moor, yet it seems like a Valley of Bones haunted by malignant spirits who have lured us here to our destruction. There's something guiding us now. It's just uncanny."

"Why on earth did we ever come?" croaked Biggleswade.

Lord Doyne answered: "The Koran says, 'Nothing can befall us but what God hath destined for us.' So why worry?"

"Because I'm not a Mohammedan," retorted Biggleswade.

"You might be worse," said Doyne. Presently the dim outline of the little house grew perceptible. A faint light shone from the window. It stood unfenced by any kind of hedge or railing a few feet away from the road in a little hollow beneath some rising ground.

As far as they could discern in the darkness when they drew near, the house was a mean, dilapidated hovel. A guttering candle stood on the inner sill of the small window and afforded a vague view into a mean interior. Doyne held up the lamp so that its rays fell full on the door.

"I TOLD YOU THE PLACE WAS UNCANNY."

"I told you the place was uncanny."

As he did so, an exclamation broke from his lips and he hurried forward, followed by the others. A man's body lay huddled together on the snow by the threshold. He was dressed like a peasant, in old corduroy trousers and rough coat, and a handkerchief was knotted round his neck. In his hand he grasped the neck of a broken bottle. Doyne set the lamp on the ground and the three bent down together over the man.

Close by the neck lay the rest of the broken bottle, whose contents had evidently run out into the snow.

"Drunk?" asked Biggleswade. Doyne felt the man and laid his hand on his heart. "No," said he, "dead."

McCurdie leaped to his full height. "I told you the place was uncanny!" he cried. "It's fey." Then he hammered wildly at the door. There was no response. He hammered again till it rattled. This time a faint prolonged sound like the wailing of a strange sea-creature was heard from within the house. McCurdie turned round, his teeth chattering. "Did ye hear that, Doyne?"

"Perhaps it's a dog," said the Professor. Lord Doyne, the man of action, pushed them aside and tried the door-handle. It yielded, the door stood open, and the gust of cold wind entering the house extinguished the candle within. They entered and found themselves in a miserable stone-paved kitchen, furnished with poverty-stricken meagreness—a wooden chair or two, a dirty table, some broken crockery, old cooking utensils, a fly-blown missionary society almanac, and a fireless grate. Doyne set the lamp on the table. "We must bring him in," said he. They returned to the threshold, and as they were bending over to grip the dead man the same sound filled the air, but this time louder, more intense, a cry of great agony. The sweat dripped from McCurdie's forehead. They lifted the dead man and brought him into the room, and after laying him on a dirty strip of carpet they did their best to straighten the stiff limbs. Biggleswade put on the table a bundle which he had picked up outside. It contained some poor provisions—a loaf, a piece of fat bacon, and a paper of tea.

As far as they could guess (and as they learned later they guessed rightly) the man was the master of the house, who, coming home blind drunk from some distant inn, had fallen at his own threshold and got frozen to death. As they could not unclasp his fingers from the broken bottleneck they had to let him clutch it as a dead warrior clutches the hilt of his broken sword.

"I HEARD IT. I FELT IT. IT WAS LIKE THE BEATING
OF WINGS."

Then suddenly the whole place was rent with another and yet another long, soul-piercing moan of anguish. "There's a second room," said Doyne, pointing to a door. "The sound comes from there." He opened the door, peeped in, and then, returning for the lamp, disappeared, leaving McCurdie and Biggleswade in the pitch darkness, with the dead man on the floor.

"For heaven's sake, give me a drop of whiskey," said the Professor, "or I shall faint." Presently the door opened and Lord Doyne appeared in the shaft of light. He beckoned to his companions. "It is a woman in childbirth," he said in his even, tired voice. "We must aid her. She appears unconscious. Does either of you know anything about such things?"

They shook their heads, and the three looked at each other in dismay. Masters of knowledge that had won them world-wide fame and honour, they stood helpless, abashed before this, the commonest phenomenon of nature. "My wife had no child," said Mc-Curdie.

"I've avoided women all my life," said Biggleswade.

"And I've been too busy to think of them. God forgive me," said Doyne. The history of the next two hours was one that none of the three men ever cared to touch upon. They did things blindly, instinctively, as men do when they come face to face with the elemental. A fire was made, they knew not how, water drawn they knew not whence, and a kettle boiled. Doyne accustomed to command, directed. The others obeyed. At his suggestion they hastened to the wreck of the car and came staggering back beneath rugs and travelling bags which could supply clean linen and needful things, for amid the poverty of the house they could find nothing fit for human touch or use.

Early they saw that the woman's strength was failing, and that she could not live. And there, in that nameless hovel, with death on the hearthstone and death and life hovering over the pitiful bed, the three great men went through the pain and the horror and squalor of birth, and they knew that they had never yet stood before so great a mystery. With the first wail of the newly born infant a last convulsive shudder passed through the frame of the unconscious mother. Then three or four short gasps for breath, and the spirit passed away. She was dead.

Professor Biggleswade threw a corner of the sheet over her face, for he could not bear to see it. They washed and dried the child as any crone of a midwife would have done, and dipped a small sponge which had always remained unused in a cut-glass bottle in Doyne's dressing-bag in the hot milk and water of Biggleswade's thermos bottle, and put it to his lips; and then they wrapped him up warm in some of their own woollen undergarments, and took him into the kitchen and placed him on a bed made of their fur coats in front of the fire.

As the last piece of fuel was exhausted they took one of the wooden chairs and broke it up and cast it into the blaze. And then they raised the dead man from the strip of carpet and carried him into the bedroom and laid him reverently by the side of his dead wife, after which they left the dead in darkness and returned to the living. And the three grave men stood over the wisp of flesh that had been born a male into the world. Then, their task being accomplished, reaction came, and even Doyne, who had seen death in many lands, turned faint. But the others, losing control of their nerves, shook like men stricken with palsy.

Suddenly McCurdie cried in a high pitched voice, "My God! Don't you feel it?" and clutched Doyne by the arm. An expression of terror appeared on his iron features. "There! It's here with us."

Little Professor Biggleswade sat on a corner of the table and wiped his forehead. "I heard it. I felt it. It was like the beating of wings."

"It's the fourth time," said McCurdie. "The first time was just before I accepted the Deverills' invitation. The second in the railway carriage this afternoon. The third on the way here. This is the fourth." Biggleswade plucked nervously at the fringe of whisker under his jaws and said faintly, "It's the fourth time up to now. I thought it was fancy."

"I have felt it, too," said Doyne. "It is the Angel of Death." And he pointed to the room where the dead man and woman lay.

"For God's sake let us get away from this," cried Biggleswade. "And leave the child to die, like the others?" said Doyne. "We must see it through," said McCurdie.

A silence fell upon them as they sat round in the blaze with the new-born babe wrapped in its odd swaddling clothes asleep on the pile of fur coats, and it lasted until Sir Angus McCurdie looked at his watch.

"Good Lord," said he, "it's twelve o'clock."

"Christmas morning," said Biggleswade. "A strange Christmas," mused Doyne.

McCurdie put up his hand. "There it is again! The beating of wings." And they listened like men spellbound.

McCurdie kept his hand uplifted, and gazed over their heads at the wall, and his gaze was that of a man in a trance, and he spoke: "Unto us a child is born, unto us a son is given—"

Doyne sprang from his chair, which fell behind him with a crash. "Man—what the devil are you saying?"

INSTINCTIVELY THEY ALL KNELT DOWN.

Then McCurdie rose and met Biggleswade's eyes staring at him through the great round spectacles, and Biggleswade turned and met the eyes of Doyne. A pulsation like the beating of wings stirred the air. The three wise men shivered with a queer exaltation.

Something strange, mystical, dynamic had happened. It was as if scales had fallen from their eyes and they saw with a new vision. They stood together humbly, divested of all their greatness, touching one another in the instinctive fashion of children, as if seeking mutual protection, and they looked, with one accord, irresistibly compelled, at the child.

At last McCurdie unbent his black brows and said hoarsely: "It was not the Angel of Death, Doyne, but another Messenger that drew us here." The tiredness seemed to pass away from the great administrator's face, and he nodded his head with the calm of a man who has come to the quiet heart of a perplexing mystery. "It's true," he murmured. "Unto us a child is born, unto us a son is given. Unto the three of us."

Biggleswade took off his great round spectacles and wiped them. "Gaspar, Melchior, Balthazar. But where are the gold, frankincense and myrrh?"

"In our hearts, man," said McCurdie. The babe cried and stretched its tiny limbs. Instinctively they all knelt down together to discover, if possible, and administer ignorantly to, its wants. The scene had the appearance of an adoration. Then these three wise, lonely, childless men who, in furtherance of their own greatness, had cut themselves adrift from the sweet and simple things of life and from the kindly ways of their brethren, and had grown old in unhappy and profitless wisdom, knew that an inscrutable Providence had led them, as it had led three Wise Men of old, on a Christmas morning long ago, to a nativity which should give them a new wisdom, a new link with humanity, a new spiritual outlook, a new hope. And, when their watch was ended, they wrapped up the babe with precious care, and carried him with them, an inalienable joy and possession, into the great world.

CARRIED WITH THEM AN INALIENABLE JOY
AND POSSESSION INTO THE GREAT WORLD.

Going Further : A Christmas Mystery

1. The host's name is "Deverill"and one of the guests makes a slip of the tongue, saying they're headed to "Gehenna"instead of "Trehenna." In the Old Testament, Gehenna refers to the place of the dead. Why do you think the writer used these words?

2. On a later stage of their journey in a desolate location, a little comfortless train compartment is described as being "as cold as death." Their destination is "Foullis Castle." Does the author want you to think something foul could be going on there?

3. One guest fears he shall die of bronchitis before ever reaching their destination, and Lord Doyne, the only of the three who seems to have a regard for Christmas, children, and good things, says, "A man dies when it is appointed for him to die." What do you think of this statement? Do you know that it comes from the Bible? (See Hebrews9:27)

4.   More than once the men hear "the beating of wings." What do you think is the source of this? Note the direction of the man's gaze in the illustration (the man without a hat)-where is he looking? (What might they be hearing?)

Even Further

1. Why is it that the author never shows the travelers reaching Deverill's Castle?

2. Is the journey of these three "wise men" similar to the journey of the wise men in the Bible? How?

3. What do you think the imagery of death is meant to suggest for these men?

4. If you were to read the return trip to their homes after this experience, would the imagery change? How?

5. Without being preachy or "in your face," how does the author bring out the joy of Christmas?

The Gift of the Magi

O. HENRY

O. Henry, 1862 – 1910

American writer and poet.

In this, perhaps his most famous short story, O. Henry (the pen name of William Sidney Porter) demonstrates by the sacrificial giving of Della and Jim that the best and wisest gift of all is love. Though the story seems dated, its message is timeless. (A Christmas collection could hardly be respectable without it.)

THE GIFT OF THE MAGI

One dollar and eighty-seven cents. That was all. And sixty cents of it was in pennies. Pennies saved one and two at a time by bulldozing the grocer and the vegetable man and the butcher until one's cheeks burned with the silent imputation of parsimony that such close dealing implied. Three times Della counted it. One dollar and eighty-seven cents. And the next day would be Christmas.

There was clearly nothing to do but flop down on the shabby little couch and howl. So Della did it. Which instigates the moral reflection that life is made up of sobs, sniffles, and smiles, with sniffles predominating.

While the mistress of the home is gradually subsiding from the first stage to the second, take a look at the home. A furnished flat at $8 per week. It did not exactly beggar description, but it certainly had that word on the lookout for the mendicancy squad.

In the vestibule below was a letter-box into which no letter would go, and an electric button from which no mortal finger could coax a ring. Also appertaining thereunto was a card bearing the name "Mr. James Dillingham Young."

The "Dillingham" had been flung to the breeze during a former period of prosperity when its possessor was being paid $30 per week. Now, when the income was shrunk to $20, though, they were thinking seriously of contracting to a modest and unassuming D. But whenever Mr. James Dillingham Young came home and reached his flat above he was called "Jim" and greatly hugged by Mrs. James Dillingham Young, already introduced to you as Della. Which is all very good.

Della finished her cry and attended to her cheeks with the powder rag. She stood by the window and looked out dully at a gray cat walking a gray fence in a gray backyard. Tomorrow would be Christmas Day, and she had only $1.87 with which to buy Jim a present. She had been saving every penny she could for months, with this result. Twenty dollars a week doesn't go far. Expenses had been greater than she had calculated. They always are. Only $1.87 to buy a present for Jim. Her Jim. Many a happy hour she had spent planning for something nice for him. Something fine and rare and sterling—something just a little bit near to being worthy of the honor of being owned by Jim.

There was a pier glass between the windows of the room. Perhaps you have seen a pier glass in an $8 flat. A very thin and very agile person may, by observing his reflection in a rapid sequence of longitudinal strips, obtain a fairly accurate conception of his looks. Della, being slender, had mastered the art.

Suddenly she whirled from the window and stood before the glass. Her eyes were shining brilliantly, but her face had lost its color within twenty seconds. Rapidly she pulled down her hair and let it fall to its full length.

Now, there were two possessions of the James Dillingham Youngs in which they both took a mighty pride. One was Jim's gold watch that had been his father's and his grandfather's. The other was Della's hair. Had the queen of Sheba lived in the flat across the airshaft, Della would have let her hair hang out the window some day to dry just to depreciate Her Majesty's jewels and gifts. Had King Solomon been the janitor, with all his treasures piled up in the basement, Jim would have pulled out his watch every time he passed, just to see him pluck at his beard from envy.

So now Della's beautiful hair fell about her rippling and shining like a cascade of brown waters. It reached below her knee and made itself almost a garment for her. And then she did it up again nervously and quickly. Once she faltered for a minute and stood still while a tear or two splashed on the worn red carpet.

On went her old brown jacket; on went her old brown hat. With a whirl of skirts and with the brilliant sparkle still in her eyes, she fluttered out the door and down the stairs to the street.

Where she stopped the sign read: "Mme. Sofronie. Hair Goods of All Kinds." One flight up Della ran, and collected herself, panting. Madame, large, too white, chilly, hardly looked the "Sofronie."

"Will you buy my hair?" asked Della.

"I buy hair," said Madame. "Take yer hat off and let's have a sight at the looks of it." Down rippled the brown cascade.

"Twenty dollars," said Madame, lifting the mass with a practised hand.

"Give it to me quick," said Della.

Oh, and the next two hours tripped by on rosy wings. Forget the hashed metaphor. She was ransacking the stores for Jim's present.

She found it at last. It surely had been made for Jim and no one else. There was no other like it in any of the stores, and she had turned all of them inside out. It was a platinum fob chain simple and chaste in design, properly proclaiming its value by substance alone and not by meretricious ornamentation—as all good things should do. It was even worthy of The Watch. As soon as she saw it she knew that it must be Jim's. It was like him. Quietness and value—the description applied to both. Twenty-one dollars they took from her for it, and she hurried home with the 87 cents. With that chain on his watch Jim might be properly anxious about the time in any company. Grand as the watch was, he sometimes looked at it on the sly on account of the old leather strap that he used in place of a chain.

When Della reached home her intoxication gave way a little to prudence and reason. She got out her curling irons and lighted the gas and went to work repairing the ravages made by generosity added to love. Which is always a tremendous task, dear friends—a mammoth task.

Within forty minutes her head was covered with tiny, close-lying curls that made her look wonderfully like a truant schoolboy. She looked at her reflection in the mirror long, carefully, and critically.

"If Jim doesn't kill me," she said to herself, "before he takes a second look at me, he'll say I look like a Coney Island chorus girl. But what could I do—oh! what could I do with a dollar and eighty-seven cents?"

At 7 o'clock the coffee was made and the frying-pan was on the back of the stove hot and ready to cook the chops.

Jim was never late. Della doubled the fob chain in her hand and sat on the corner of the table near the door that he always entered. Then she heard his step on the stair away down on the first flight, and she turned white for just a moment. She had a habit of saying a little silent prayer about the simplest everyday things, and now she whispered: "Please God, make him think I am still pretty."

The door opened and Jim stepped in and closed it. He looked thin and very serious. Poor fellow, he was only twenty-two—and to be burdened with a family! He needed a new overcoat and he was without gloves.

Jim stopped inside the door, as immovable as a setter at the scent of quail. His eyes were fixed upon Della, and there was an expression in them that she could not read, and it terrified her. It was not anger, nor surprise, nor disapproval, nor horror, nor any of the sentiments that she had been prepared for. He simply stared at her fixedly with that peculiar expression on his face.

Della wriggled off the table and went for him.

"Jim, darling," she cried, "don't look at me that way. I had my hair cut off and sold because I couldn't have lived through Christmas without giving you a present. It'll grow out again—you won't mind, will you? I just had to do it. My hair grows awfully fast. Say 'Merry Christmas!' Jim, and let's be happy. You don't know what a nice—what a beautiful, nice gift I've got for you."

"You've cut off your hair?" asked Jim, laboriously, as if he had not arrived at that patent fact yet even after the hardest mental labor.

"Cut it off and sold it," said Della. "Don't you like me just as well, anyhow? I'm me without my hair, ain't I?"

Jim looked about the room curiously.

"You say your hair is gone?" he said, with an air almost of idiocy.

"You needn't look for it," said Della. "It's sold, I tell you—sold and gone, too. It's Christmas Eve, boy. Be good to me, for it went for you. Maybe the hairs of my head were numbered," she went on with sudden serious sweetness, "but nobody could ever count my love for you. Shall I put the chops on, Jim?"

Out of his trance Jim seemed quickly to wake. He enfolded his Della. For ten seconds let us regard with discreet scrutiny some inconsequential object in the other direction. Eight dollars a week or a million a year—what is the difference? A mathematician or a wit would give you the wrong answer. The magi brought valuable gifts, but that was not among them. This dark assertion will be illuminated later on.

Jim drew a package from his overcoat pocket and threw it upon the table.

"Don't make any mistake, Dell," he said, "about me. I don't think there's anything in the way of a haircut or a shave or a shampoo that could make me like my girl any less. But if you'll unwrap that package you may see why you had me going a while at first."

White fingers and nimble tore at the string and paper. And then an ecstatic scream of joy; and then, alas! a quick feminine change to hysterical tears and wails, necessitating the immediate employment of all the comforting powers of the lord of the flat.

For there lay The Combs—the set of combs, side and back, that Della had worshipped long in a Broadway window. Beautiful combs, pure tortoise shell, with jewelled rims—just the shade to wear in the beautiful vanished hair. They were expensive combs, she knew, and her heart had simply craved and yearned over them without the least hope of possession. And now, they were hers, but the tresses that should have adorned the coveted adornments were gone. But she hugged them to her bosom, and at length she was able to look up with dim eyes and a smile and say: "My hair grows so fast, Jim!"

And then Della leaped up like a little singed cat and cried, "Oh, oh!"

Jim had not yet seen his beautiful present. She held it out to him eagerly upon her open palm. The dull precious metal seemed to flash with a reflection of her bright and ardent spirit.

"Isn't it a dandy, Jim? I hunted all over town to find it. You'll have to look at the time a hundred times a day now. Give me your watch. I want to see how it looks on it."

Instead of obeying, Jim tumbled down on the couch and put his hands under the back of his head and smiled.

"Dell," said he, "let's put our Christmas presents away and keep 'em a while. They're too nice to use just at present. I sold the watch to get the money to buy your combs. And now suppose you put the chops on."

The magi, as you know, were wise men—wonderfully wise men—who brought gifts to the Babe in the manger. They invented the art of giving Christmas presents. Being wise, their gifts were no doubt wise ones, possibly bearing the privilege of exchange in case of duplication.

And here I have lamely related to you the uneventful chronicle of two foolish children in a flat who most unwisely sacrificed for each other the greatest treasures of their house. But in a last word to the wise of these days let it be said that of all who give gifts these two were the wisest. Of all who give and receive gifts, such as they are wisest. Everywhere they are wisest. They are the magi.

This is the Month and This the Happy Morn

JOHN MILTON

John Milton, 1608 – 1674

Poet, Polemicist, and Statesman

Milton is regarded as one of the greatest English poets of all time, second only to Shakespeare. Most famous for his epic poem, "Paradise Lost," he also wrote many others. Biographers call him a polemicist as well. What is a polemicist? One who levels "an aggressive attack on or refutation of the opinions or principles of another."[1] In today's jargon, we might say he was a social activist.

Following are stanzas from his poem, "Ode: On the Morning of Christ's Nativity."

ODE: ON THE MORNING OF CHRIST'S NATIVITY

This is the month and this the happy morn
Wherein the Son of Heaven's eternal King,
Of wedded Maid, and Virgin Mother born,
Our great redemption from above did bring;
For so the holy sages once did sing,

That he our deadly forfeit should release,
And with his Father work us a perpetual peace.

That glorious form, that light unsufferable,
And that far-beaming blaze of majesty,
Wherewith he wont at Heaven's high council-table,
To sit the midst of Trinal Unity,
He laid aside; and here with us to be,
Forsook the courts of everlasting day,
And chose with us a darksome house of mortal clay.

The star-led wizards[2] haste with odors sweet:
O run, prevent them with thy humble ode,
And lay it lowly at his blessed feet;
Have thou the honor first, they Lord to greet,
And join they voice unto the angel choir,
From out his secret altar touched with hallowed fire.

1. Merriam-Webster.com
2. "star-led wizards" – the wise men

Christmas at Cedar Hill

Lucy Ellen Guernsey

By Lucy Ellen Guernsey, 1826 – 1899

American author and strong proponent of moral education in children.

This short excerpt from the book by the same title, published in 1869, is a sweet snapshot of an old-fashioned Christmas. Its publication was sponsored by the Sunday School of Christ Church, Bay Ridge, Brooklyn, NY.

CHRISTMAS AT CEDAR HILL

Early the next morning the whole household was astir at Cedar Hill. The children were up and dressed before daylight, wishing everybody "Merry Christmas," and running all over the house, except into the dining room, where the old lady allowed no one to set foot but herself. By-and-by they had prayers in the parlor and the children sung two or three Christmas carols, accompanied by Miss Hope on the piano.

Then the dining room door was opened and they marched in procession to the table. It was set out in great state, and there, before every one's place, was a mysterious pile, carefully covered by a white napkin. Grace was said, and then the piles were all uncovered.

What wonders were disclosed! Books and toys for the children, all sorts of pretty and useful things for everybody. Not one of the strangers was forgotten, but each received a nice present, all the nicer from being wholly unexpected. Abundance of presents had been provided for the grandchildren of the family, besides those which the doctor had in his trunk for his own little flock; and Harry, May and Annie were only too glad to divide with their new friends.

A man had been sent over to the railroad station early in the morning. He returned with the news that no train could possibly get through before next morning. So it was decided that the big lumber sleigh should be got out once more to take the whole party to church in the village, about a mile off. Before church time, there were several private conversations held in the house. Agatha, with Herbert and her brother, sat in a corner of the parlor talking of their family affairs. Miss Hope was closeted with the old lady in her room, and Frank, with some embarrassment, requested to speak with the doctor in the library.

"I wanted to ask you, sir," said he, looking down, "if you thought it would be wrong for me to go to the communion this morning? I am to be confirmed at Easter, at any rate, and—I am so thankful for the way everything has turned out—and—I know I am not good enough, doctor, but I want to be a better boy, and I do love Him!"

"You know, Frank, what is said in the Prayer-book," said the doctor, kindly. "I say nothing of the Rubric, because you have just told me that you are 'ready and desirous to be confirmed;' but here is the invitation. Examine yourself by it. Do you truly and earnestly repent you of your sins?"

"Yes sir, I hope so."

"And are you in love and charity with your neighbors?"

"I believe so," said Frank. "I hav'n't any enemies that I know of, so I hav'n't anything to forgive, and I should be very wicked indeed if I did not feel kindly towards every one this morning, after God has been so good to me."

"And do you intend to lead a new life, following the commandments of God, and walking from henceforth in His holy ways? Think well before you speak."

"I have been trying to do so this long time, doctor," said Frank. "I get discouraged a great many times, but I have not left off trying."

The doctor asked Frank a good many more questions, tending to test his knowledge of Christian doctrine and of his own heart. Frank had been carefully instructed, especially since his residence with Doctor Bower, and the doctor, who was accustomed to dealing with young people, was quite satisfied with his answers.

"Well, my son," said he, at last, "from all that you tell me I can see no reason why you should not draw near with faith and take your part in the feast of love. In the sense of sin-lessness no one is worthy, but any one who repents and believes, placing all his hopes of salvation upon the great atoning sacrifice of Christ our Lord, may safely take this holy sacrament, to his comfort. But how is it with your companions?"

"Oh, Herbert has been a communicant these two years, and Agatha since last Easter. She was so little and looked so young that the bishop was in doubt about her; but he examined her himself and was quite satisfied."

"I am glad to hear it," said the doctor. "I advise you, Frank, to spend the hour between this and church time in prayer and rending."

The doctor marked certain chapters for him, and Frank remained alone in the library till all were called to go to church.

"Isn't it nice?" said Annie to Agatha, as they sat together in the sleigh, coming home. "Grandmamma has been talking with Miss Hope, and she is to stay and be my governess! You see, it is too far for me to go to school in the village, especially in winter, and there is no one to teach me music or French. But grandmamma has found out that she used to know Miss Hope's mother at school, and—oh, I can't tell you all about it, only Miss Hope has no home now, and no money, and she was going to try for a place in a public school. But now she is going to live with us. That will be a great deal nicer for her, won't it?"

"Yes, indeed!" said Agatha, hastily; "and nicer for you, too. Miss Hope seems such a pleasant young lady. I liked her the very first minute I saw her."

"And she will be company for grandmamma too, you know," continued Annie. "Oh, how glad I am you got snowed up and came to our house!"

"And so am I," replied Agatha, smiling.

In the evening the sleigh was again put in requisition, and all the young party went down to the village to attend the Sunday-school festival.

The Lone Scout's Christmas

CYRUS TOWNSEND BRADY

> **Cyrus Townsend Brady, 1861 – 1920**
>
> An American Episcopalian priest, journalist, historian and adventure writer

Brady wrote numerous books, at least three of which are Christmas-themed. In *A Little Book for Christmas*, from which the following story came, were also essays, "personal adventures, meditations, good wishes, advice," and even a carol, all centered on the season. He explained his love of Christmas like this: "*Christmas is one of the great days of obligation and observance in the Church of which I am a Priest; but it is much more than that, it is one of the great days of obligation and observance in the world. [As a priest and missionary...]it is natural that Christmas should have engaged a large part of my attention.*"[1] Let us say, we are glad it did.

THE LONE SCOUT'S CHRISTMAS

Wherein is Set Forth the Courage and Resourcefulness of Youth
A Story for Boys

Every boy likes snow on Christmas Day, but there is such a thing as too much of it. Henry Ives, alone in the long railroad coach, stared out of the clouded windows at the whirling mass of snow with feelings of dismay. It was the day before Christmas, almost Christmas Eve. Henry did not feel any too happy, indeed he had hard work to keep down a sob. His mother had died but a few weeks before and his father, the captain of a freighter on the Great Lakes, had decided, very reluctantly, to send him to his brother who had a big ranch in western Nebraska.

Henry had never seen his uncle or his aunt. He did not know what kind of people they were. The loss of his mother had been a terrible blow to him and to be separated from his father had filled his cup of sorrow to the brim. His father's work did not end with the close of navigation on the lakes, and he could not get away then although he promised to come and see Henry before the ice broke and traffic was resumed in the spring.

The long journey from the little Ohio town on Lake Erie to western Nebraska had been without mishap. His uncle's ranch lay far away from the main line of the railroad on the end of the branch. There was but one train a day upon it, and that was a mixed train. The coach in which Henry sat was attached to the end of a long string of freight cars. Travel was infrequent in that section of the country. On this day Henry was the only passenger.

The train had been going up-grade for many miles and had just about reached the crest of the divide. Bucking the snow had become more and more difficult; several times the train had stopped. Sometimes the engine backed the train some distance to get headway to burst through the drift. So Henry thought nothing of it when the car came to a gentle stop.

The all-day storm blew from the west and the front windows of the car were covered with snow so he could not see ahead. Some time before the conductor and rear brakeman had gone forward to help dig the engine out of the drift and they had not come back.

Henry sat in silence for some time watching the whirling snow. He was sad; even the thought of the gifts of his father and friends in his trunk which stood in the baggage compartment of the car did not cheer him. More than all the Christmas gifts in the world, he wanted at that time his mother and father and friends.

"It doesn't look as though it was going to be a very merry Christmas for me," he said aloud at last, and then feeling a little stiff from having sat still so long he got up and walked to the front of the car.

It was warm and pleasant in the coach. The Baker heater was going at full blast and Henry noticed that there was plenty of coal. He tried to see out from the front door; but as he was too prudent to open it and let in the snow and cold he could make out nothing. The silence rather alarmed him. The train had never waited so long before.

Then, suddenly, came the thought that something very unusual was wrong. He must get a look at the train ahead. He ran back to the rear door, opened it and standing on the leeward side, peered forward. The engine and freight cars were not there! All he saw was the deep cut filled nearly to the height of the car with snow.

Henry was of a mechanical turn of mind and he realized that doubtless the coupling had broken. That was what had happened. The trainmen had not noticed it and the train had gone on and left the coach. The break had occurred at the crest of the divide and the train had gone rapidly down hill on the other side. The amount of snow told the boy that it would not be possible for the train to back up and pick up the car. He was alone in the wilderness of rolling hills in far western Nebraska. And this was Christmas Eve!

It was enough to bring despair to any boy's heart. But Henry Ives was made of good stuff, he was a first-class Boy Scout and on his scout coat in the trunk were four Merit Badges. He had the spirit of his father, who had often bucked the November storms on Lake Superior in his great six-hundred-foot freighter, and danger inspired him.

He went back into the car, closed the door, and sat down to think it over. He had very vague ideas as to how long such a storm would last and how long he might be kept prisoner. He did not even know just where he was or how far it was to the end of the road and the town where his uncle's ranch lay.

It was growing dark so he lighted one of the lamps close to the heater and had plenty of light. In doing so he noticed in the baggage rack a dinner pail. He remembered that the conductor had told him that his wife had packed that dinner pail and although it did not belong to the boy he felt justified in appropriating it in such circumstances. It was full of food—eggs, sandwiches, and a bottle of coffee. He was not very hungry but he ate a sandwich. He was even getting cheerful about the situation because he had something to do. It was an adventure.

While he had been eating, the storm had died away. Now he discovered that it had stopped snowing. All around him the country was a hilly, rolling prairie. The cut ran through a hill which seemed to be higher than others in the neighbourhood. If he could get on top of it he might see where he was. Although day was ending it was not yet dark and Henry decided upon an exploration.

Now he could not walk on foot in that deep and drifted snow without sinking over his head under ordinary conditions, but his troop had done a great deal of winter work, and strapped alongside of his big, telescope grip were a pair of snow-shoes which he himself had made, and with the use of which he was thoroughly familiar.

"I mustn't spoil this new suit," he told himself, so he ran to the baggage-room of the car, opened his trunk, got out his Scout uniform and slipped into it in a jiffy. "Glad I ran in that 'antelope dressing race,'" he muttered, "but I'll beat my former record now." Over his khaki coat he put on his heavy sweater, then donned his wool cap and gloves, and with his snow-shoes under his arm hurried back to the rear platform. The snow was on a level with the platform. It rose higher as the coach reached into the cut. He saw that he would have to go down some distance before he could turn and attempt the hill.

He had used his snow-shoes many times in play but this was the first time they had ever been of real service to him. Thrusting his toes into the straps he struck out boldly.

"Thrusting his toes into the straps he struck out boldly."

To his delight he got along without the slightest difficulty although he strode with great care. He gained the level and in ten minutes found himself on the top of the hill, where he could see miles and miles of rolling prairie. He turned himself slowly about, to get a view of the country.

As his glance swept the horizon, at first it did not fall upon a single, solitary thing except a vast expanse of snow. There was not a tree even. The awful loneliness filled him with dismay. He had about given up when, in the last quarter of the horizon he saw, perhaps a quarter of a mile away, what looked like a fine trickle of blackish smoke that appeared to rise from a shapeless mound that bulged above the monotonous level.

"Smoke means fire, and fire means man," he said, excitedly.

The sky was rapidly clearing. A few stars had already appeared. Remembering what he had learned on camp and trail, he took his bearing by the stars; he did not mean to get lost if he left that hill. Looking back, he could see the car, the lamp of which sent broad beams of light through the windows across the snow.

Then he plunged down the hill, thanking God in his boyish heart for the snow-shoes and his knowledge of them.

It did not take him long to reach the mound whence the smoke rose. It was a sod house, he found, built against a sharp knoll, which no doubt formed its rear wall. The wind had drifted the snow, leaving a half-open way to the door. Noiselessly the boy slipped down to it, drew his feet from the snow-shoes and knocked. There was a burst of sound inside. It made his heart jump, but he was reassured by the fact that the voices were those of children. What they said he could not make out; but, without further ado, he opened the door and entered.

It was a fairly large room. There were two beds in it, a stove, a table, a chest of drawers and a few chairs. From one of the beds three heads stared at him. As each head was covered with a wool cap, drawn down over the ears, like his own, he could not make out who they were. There were dishes on the table, but they were empty. The room was cold, although it was evident that there was still a little fire in the stove.

"Oh!" came from one of the heads in the bed. "I thought you were my father. What is your name?"

"My name," answered the boy, "is Henry Ives. I was left behind alone in the railroad car about a mile back, and saw the smoke from your house and here I am."

"Have you brought us anything to burn?" asked the second head.

"Or anything to eat?" questioned the third.

"My name is Mary Wright," said the first speaker, "and these are my brothers George and Philip. Father went away yesterday morning with the team, to get some coal and some food. He went to Kiowa."

"That's where I am going," interrupted Henry.

"Yes," continued Mary, "I suppose he can't get back because of the snow. It's an awful storm."

"We haven't anything to eat, and I don't know when father will be back," said George.

"And it's Christmas Eve," wailed Philip, who appeared to be about seven.

He set up a howl about this which his brother George, who was about nine, had great difficulty in quieting.

"We put the last shovelful of coal in the stove," said Mary Wright, "and got into bed to keep warm."

"I'll go outside while you get up and dress," said Henry considerately, "and then we will try and get to the car. It is warm there, and there is something to eat."

"You needn't go," said the girl; "we are all dressed." She threw back the covers and sprang out of bed. She was very pretty and about Henry's own age, he discovered, although she was pale and haggard with cold and hunger.

"Goody, goody!" exclaimed little Philip, as his feet landed on the floor. "Maybe we'll have some Christmas, too."

"Maybe we will," said Henry, smiling at him. "At least we will have something to eat."

"Well, let's start right away then," urged George.

This brought Henry face to face with a dilemma. "I have only one pair of snow-shoes," he said at last, "and you probably don't know how to use them anyway, and you can't walk on the snow."

"I have a sled," suggested George.

"That won't do," said Henry. "I've got to have something that won't sink in the snow—that will lie flat, so I can draw you along."

"How about that table?" said the girl.

"Good suggestion," cried Henry.

It was nothing but a common kitchen table. He turned it upside down, took his Scout axe from its sheath, knocked the legs off, fastened a piece of clothesline to the butts of two of them.

"Now if I could have something to turn up along the front, so as not to dig into the snow," he said, "it would be fine." He thought a moment. "Where is that sled of yours, George?"

"Here," said George, dragging it forth. The runners curved upwards. Henry cut them off, in spite of Philip's protests. He nailed these runners to the front of the table and stretched rope tightly across them so that he had four up-curves in front of the table.

"Now I want something to stretch on these things, so as to let the sled ride over the snow, instead of digging into it," he said to the girl.

She brought him her father's old "slicker." Henry cut it into suitable shape and nailed and lashed it securely to the runners and to the table top. Now he had a flat-bottomed sled with a rising front to it that would serve. He smiled as he looked at the queer contrivance and said aloud: "I wish Mr. Lesher could see that!"

"Who is Mr. Lesher?" asked George.

"Oh, he's my Scoutmaster back in Ohio. Now come on!"

He opened the door, drew the sled outside, pushed it up on the snow and stepped on it. It bore his weight perfectly.

"It's all right," he cried. "But it won't take all three of you at once."

"I'll wait," said Mary, "you take the two boys."

"Very well," said Henry.

"You'll surely come back for me?"

"Surely, and I think it's mighty brave of you to stay behind. Now come on, boys," he said.

Leaving Mary filled with pleasure at such praise, he put the two boys carefully into the sled, stepped into his snow-shoes and dragged them rapidly across the prairie. It was quite dark now, but the sky was clear and the stars were bright. The storm had completely stopped. He remembered the bearings he had taken by the stars, and reached the high hill without difficulty. Below him lay the car.

Presently he drew up before the platform. He put the boys in the car, told them to go up to the fire and warm themselves and not to touch anything. Then he went back for the girl.

"Did you think I was not coming?" he asked as he re-entered the cabin.

"I knew you would come back," said the girl and it was Henry's turn to tingle with pride.

He wrapped her up carefully, and fairly ran back to the car. They found the boys warm and comfortable and greatly excited.

"If we just had a Christmas tree and Santa Claus and something to eat and a drink of water and a place to sleep," said the youngest boy, "it would be great fun."

"I am afraid we can't manage the Christmas tree," said Henry, "but we can have everything else."

"Do you mean Santy?"

"Santy too," answered the boy. "First of all, we will get something to eat."

"We haven't had anything since morning," said the girl. Henry divided the sandwiches into three portions. As it happened, there were three hard-boiled eggs. He gave one portion to each of his guests.

"You haven't left any for yourself," said Mary.

"I ate before I looked for you," answered Henry, although the one sandwich had by no means satisfied his hunger.

"My, but this is good!" said George.

"Our mother is dead," said Mary Wright after a pause, "and our father is awful poor. He has taken out a homestead and we are trying to live on it until he gets it proved up. We have had a very hard time since mother died."

"Yes, I know," said Henry, gravely; "my mother died, too."

"I wonder what time it is?" asked the girl at last.

Henry pulled out his watch. "It is after six o'clock," he said.

"Say," broke in George, "that's a funny kind of a uniform you've got on."

"It is a Boy Scout uniform."

"Oh, is it?" exclaimed George. "I never saw one before. I wish I could be a Scout!"

"Maybe you can," answered Henry. "I am going to organize a troop when I get to Kiowa. But now I'm going to fix beds for you. Of course we are all sleepy after such a hard day."

He had seen the trainmen lift up the bottoms of the seats and lay them lengthwise of the car. He did this, and soon made four fairly comfortable beds. The two nearest the stove he gave to the boys. He indicated the next one was for Mary, and the one further down toward the middle of the car was for himself.

"You can all go to bed right away," he said when he had made his preparations. The two boys decided to accept this advice. Mary said she would stay up a little longer and talk with Henry.

"You can't undress," she said to the two boys. "You'll have to sleep as you are." She sat down in one of the car seats; Philip knelt down at one knee and George at the other.

The girl, who was barely fifteen had already taken her mother's place. She laid her hand on each bent head and listened while one after the other the boys said their prayers. She kissed them good-night, saw them comfortably laid out on the big cushions with their overcoats for pillows and turned away.

"Say," began Philip, "you forgot something, Mary."

"What have I forgotten, dear?"

"Why, it's Christmas Eve and we must hang up our stockings."

Mary threw up her hands. "I am afraid this is too far away for Santa Claus. He won't know that we are out here," she said.

"Oh, I don't know," said Henry, thinking rapidly, "let them hang them up."

Mary looked at him in surprise. "They haven't any to hang up," she said. "We can't take those they're wearing."

"You should have thought of that," wailed Philip, "before you brought us here."

"I have some extra ones in my bag," said Henry. "We will hang them up."

He opened the bag and brought out three stockings, one for each of his guests. He fastened them to the baggage racks above the seats and watched the two boys contentedly close their eyes and go to sleep.

"They will be awfully disappointed when they wake up in the morning and do not find anything in them," said Mary.

"They're going to find something in them," said Henry confidently.

He went to the end of the car, opened his trunk and lifted out various packages which had been designed for him. Of course he was going on sixteen, but there were some things that would do for Philip and plenty of things for George and some good books that he had selected himself that would do for Mary. Then there were candy and nuts and cakes and oranges galore. Mary was even more excited than he was as they filled the boys' stockings and arranged things that were too big to go in them.

"These are your own Christmas gifts, I know," said the girl, "and you haven't hung up your stocking."

"I don't need to. I have had my Christmas present."

"And what is that?"

"A chance to make a merry Christmas for you and your little brothers," answered Henry, and his heart was light.

"How long do you suppose we will have to stay here?" asked the girl.

"I don't know. I suppose they will try to dig us out to-morrow. Meanwhile we have nuts, oranges, crackers, and little cakes, to say nothing of the candy, to live on. Now you go to bed and have a good sleep."

"And what will you do?"

"I'll stay up for a while and read one of these books and keep the fire going."

"You are awfully good to us," said Mary, turning away. "You are just like a real Santa Claus."

"We have to help other people—especially people in trouble," answered the boy. "It is one of the first Scout rules. I am really glad I got left behind and found you. Good-night."

The girl, whose experience that day had been hard, soon fell asleep with her brothers. Henry did not feel sleepy at all; he was bright and happy and rejoiced. This certainly *was* an adventure. He wondered what Dick and Joe and Spike and the other fellows of his troop would think when he wrote them about it. He did not realize that he had saved the lives of the children, who would assuredly have frozen to death in the cabin.

When he was satisfied that Mary was sound asleep, he put some things in her stocking and then piled in the rack over her head two books he thought the girl would like. It was late when he went to sleep himself, happier than he had dreamed he could be.

He awoke once in the night to replenish the fire, but he was sleeping soundly at seven o'clock in the morning when the door of the car opened and half a dozen men filed in. They had not made any noise. Even the big snow-plough tearing open the way from Kiowa had not disturbed the four sleepers.

The first man in was the conductor. After the trainmen had discovered that the coach had been left behind they had managed to get into Kiowa and had started back at once with the rotary plough to open the road and to rescue the boy. Henry's uncle had been in town to meet Henry, and of course the trainmen let him go back with them on the plough. The third man was Mr. Wright. He had been caught by the storm and, as he said, the abandoned coach must be near his claim, he asked to be taken along because he was afraid his children would be freezing to death.

The men stopped and surveyed the sleeping boys and girl. Their glances ranged from the children to the bulging stockings and the pile of Christmas presents in the racks.

"Well, can you beat that?" said the conductor.

"By George!" exclaimed Rancher Ives, "a regular Christmas layout!"

"These are my children safe and well, thank God!" cried Mr. Wright.

"Boy," said the conductor, laying his hand on Henry's shoulder, "we came to wish you a Merry Christmas."

"Father!" cried Mary Wright, awakened by the voice, and the next minute she was in his arms, while she told him rapidly what Henry had done for them all.

The boys were awake, too, but humanity had no attraction for them.

"Santa has come!" shouted Philip making a dive for his stocking.

"This is your uncle, Jim Ives," said the conductor to Henry.

"And this is my father," said Mary in turn.

"I am awfully sorry," said Henry to the conductor, "but we had to eat your dinner. And I had to chop up your kitchen table," he added, turning to Mr. Wright.

"I am glad there was something to eat in the pail," said one.

"You could have chopped the cabin down," said the other.

"By George!" said the ranchman proudly. "I wrote to your father to send you out here and we'd make a man of you, but it seems to me you are a man already," he continued as Mary Wright poured forth the story of their rescue.

"No, I am not a man," said Henry to his uncle, as he flushed with pride at the hearty praise of these men. "I am just a—"

"Just a what?" asked the conductor as the boy hesitated.

"Why, just a Boy Scout," answered Henry.

1 From, *A Little Book for Christmas*, Preface, Putnam & Sons, 1917

A Child's Christmas in Wales

DYLAN THOMAS

Dylan Thomas, 1914 – 1953

Welsh poet and writer

Among Thomas's best known poems are "Do not go gentle into that that good night" and "And death shall have no dominion." More than half of his collected poems were written during his late teens.

The following idealized sketch from the viewpoint of a child strives to recreate (in Thomas's poetical fashion) both the wonder of, and traditions pertaining to, Christmas at its best and from his own boyhood. The account is told with affection, humor, and, concerning the characters, exaggeration (for comic effect).

Thomas's style may not be to everyone's taste, but the piece has been adapted for theater, film, television and animation. I like the rollicking pace that mimics the way a young boy would seize such a day, pausing only at bedtime to say a prayer and drop into sleep, the way children do after all the excitement is over.

A CHILD'S CHRISTMAS IN WALES

One Christmas was so much like the other, in those years around the sea-town corner now, out of all sound except the distant speaking of the voices I sometimes hear a moment before sleep, that I can never remember whether it snowed for six days and six nights when I was twelve, or whether it snowed for twelve days and twelve nights when I was six.

All the Christmases roll down towards the two-tongued sea, like a cold and headlong moon bundling down the sky that was our street; and they stop at the rim of the ice-edged, fish-freezing waves, and I plunge my hands in the snow and bring out whatever I can find. In goes my hand into that wool-white bell-tongued ball of holidays resting at the rim of the carol-singing sea, and out come Mrs. Prothero and the firemen.

It was on the afternoon of the day of Christmas Eve, and I was in Mrs. Prothero's garden, waiting for cats, with her son Jim. It was snowing. It was always snowing at Christmas. December, in my memory, is white as Lapland, although there were no reindeers. But there were cats. Patient, cold and callous, our hands wrapped in socks, we waited to snowball the cats. Sleek and long as jaguars and horrible-whiskered, spitting and snarling, they would slide and sidle over the white back-garden walls, and the lynx-eyed hunters, Jim and I, fur-capped and moccasined trappers from Hudson Bay, off Mumbles Road, would hurl our deadly snowballs at the green of their eyes.

The wise cats never appeared. We were so still, Eskimo-footed arctic marksmen in the muffling silence of the eternal snows—eternal, ever since Wednesday—that we never heard Mrs. Prothero's first cry from her igloo at the bottom of the garden. Or, if we heard it at all, it was, to us, like the far-off challenge of our enemy and prey, the neighbor's polar cat. But soon the voice grew louder. "Fire!" cried Mrs. Prothero, and she beat the dinner-gong.

And we ran down the garden, with the snowballs in our arms, towards the house; and smoke, indeed, was pouring out of the dining-room, and the gong was bombilating, and Mrs. Prothero was announcing ruin like a town crier in Pompeii. This was better than all the cats in Wales standing on the wall in a row. We bounded into the house, laden with snowballs, and stopped at the open door of the smoke-filled room.

Something was burning all right; perhaps it was Mr. Prothero, who always slept there after midday dinner with a newspaper over his face. But he was standing in the middle of the room, saying, "A fine Christmas!" and smacking at the smoke with a slipper.

"Call the fire brigade," cried Mrs. Prothero as she beat the gong. "They won't be here," said Mr. Prothero, "it's Christmas."

There was no fire to be seen, only clouds of smoke and Mr. Prothero standing in the middle of them, waving his slipper as though he were conducting.

"Do something," he said.

And we threw all our snowballs into the smoke—I think we missed Mr. Prothero—and ran out of the house to the telephone box.

"Let's call the police as well," Jim said.

"And the ambulance."

"And Ernie Jenkins, he likes fires."

But we only called the fire brigade, and soon the fire engine came and three tall men in helmets brought a hose into the house and Mr. Prothero got out just in time before they turned it on. Nobody could have had a noisier Christmas Eve. And when the firemen turned off the hose and were standing in the wet, smoky room, Jim's Aunt, Miss Prothero, came downstairs and peered in at them. Jim and I waited, very quietly, to hear what she would say to them. She said the right thing, always. She looked at the three tall firemen in their shining helmets, standing among the smoke and cinders and dissolving snowballs, and she said: "Would you like anything to read?"

Years and years ago, when I was a boy, when there were wolves in Wales, and birds the color of red-flannel petticoats whisked past the harp-shaped hills, when we sang and wallowed all night and day in caves that smelt like Sunday afternoons in damp front farmhouse parlors, and we chased, with the jawbones of deacons, the English and the bears, before the motor car, before the wheel, before the duchess-faced horse, when we rode the daft and happy hills bareback, it snowed and it snowed. But here a small boy says: "It snowed last year, too. I made a snowman and my brother knocked it down and I knocked my brother down and then we had tea."

"But that was not the same snow," I say. "Our snow was not only shaken from white-wash buckets down the sky, it came shawling out of the ground and swam and drifted out of the arms and hands and bodies of the trees; snow grew overnight on the roofs of the houses like a pure and grandfather moss, minutely ivied the walls and settled on the postman, opening the gate, like a dumb, numb thunderstorm of white, torn Christmas cards."

"Were there postmen then, too?"

"With sprinkling eyes and wind-cherried noses, on spread, frozen feet they crunched up to the doors and mittened on them manfully. But all that the children could hear was a ringing of bells."

"You mean that the postman went rat-a-tat-tat and the doors rang?"

"I mean that the bells that the children could hear were inside them."

"I only hear thunder sometimes, never bells."

"There were church bells, too."

"Inside them?"

"No, no, no, in the bat-black, snow-white belfries, tugged by bishops and storks. And they rang their tidings over the bandaged town, over the frozen foam of the powder and ice-cream hills, over the crackling sea. It seemed that all the churches boomed for joy under my window; and the weathercocks crew for Christmas, on our fence."

"Get back to the postmen."

"They were just ordinary postmen, fond of walking and dogs and Christmas and the snow. They knocked on the doors with blue knuckles...."

"Ours has got a black knocker...."

"And then they stood on the white Welcome mat in the little, drifted porches and huffed and puffed, making ghosts with their breath, and jogged from foot to foot like small boys wanting to go out."

"And then the presents?"

"And then the Presents, after the Christmas box. And the cold postman, with a rose on his button-nose, tingled down the tea-tray-slithered run of the chilly glinting hill. He went in his ice-bound boots like a man on fishmonger's slabs.

"He wagged his bag like a frozen camel's hump, dizzily turned the corner on one foot, and, by God, he was gone."

"Get back to the Presents."

"There were the Useful Presents: engulfing mufflers of the old coach days, and mittens made for giant sloths; zebra scarfs of a substance like silky gum that could be tug-o'-warred down to the galoshes; blinding tam-o'-shanters like patchwork tea cozies and bunny-suited busbies and balaclavas for victims of head-shrinking tribes; from aunts who always wore wool next to the skin there were mustached and rasping vests that made you wonder why the aunts had any skin left at all; and once I had a little crocheted nose bag from an aunt now, alas, no longer whinnying with us. And pictureless books in which small boys, though warned with quotations not to, *would* skate on Farmer Giles's pond and did and drowned; and books that told me everything about the wasp, except why."

"Go on to the Useless Presents."

"Bags of moist and many-colored jelly babies and a folded flag and a false nose and a tram-conductor's cap and a machine that punched tickets and rang a bell; never a catapult; once, by a mistake that no one could explain, a little hatchet; and a celluloid duck that made, when you pressed it, a most unducklike sound, a mewing moo that an ambitious cat might make who wished to be a cow; and a painting book in which I could make the grass, the trees, the sea and the animals any color I please, and still the dazzling sky-blue sheep are grazing in the red field under the rainbow-billed and pea-green birds.

Hardboileds, toffee, fudge and allsorts, crunches, cracknel, humbugs, glaciers, marzipan, and butterwelsh[1] for the Welsh. And troops of bright tin soldiers who, if they could not fight, could always run. And Snakes-and-Families and Happy Ladders. And Easy Hobbi-Games for Little Engineers, complete with instructions. Oh, easy for Leonardo! And a whistle to make the dogs bark to wake up the old man next door to make him beat on the wall with his stick to shake our picture off the wall. And a packet of cigarettes: you put one in your mouth and you stood at the corner of the street and you waited for hours, in vain, for an old lady to scold you for smoking a cigarette, and then with a smirk you ate it. And then it was breakfast under the balloons."

"Were there Uncles like in our house?"

"There are always Uncles at Christmas. The same Uncles. And on Christmas mornings, with dog-disturbing whistle and sugar fags, I would scour the swathed town for the news of the little world, and find always a dead bird by the Post Office or the white deserted swings; perhaps a robin, all but one of his fires out. Men and women wading, scooping back from chapel, with taproom noses and wind-bussed cheeks, all albinos, huddled their stiff black jarring feathers against the irreligious snow. Mistletoe hung from the gas brackets in all the front parlors; there was sherry and walnuts and bottled beer and crackers by the dessertspoons; and cats in their fur-abouts watched the fires; and the high-heaped fire spat, all ready for the chestnuts and the mulling pokers.

Some few large men sat in the front parlors, without their collars, Uncles almost certainly, trying their new cigars, holding them out judiciously at arms' length, returning them to their mouths, coughing, then holding them out again as though waiting for the explosion; and some few small aunts, not wanted in the kitchen, nor anywhere else for that matter, sat on the very edges of their chairs, poised and brittle, afraid to break, like faded cups and saucers."

Not many those mornings trod the piling streets: an old man always, fawn-bowlered, yellow-gloved and, at this time of year, with spats of snow, would take his constitutional to the white bowling green and back, as he would take it wet or fire on Christmas Day or Doomsday; sometimes two hale young men, with big pipes blazing, no overcoats and wind blown scarfs, would trudge, unspeaking, down to the forlorn sea, to work up an appetite, to blow away the fumes, who knows, to walk into the waves until nothing of them was left but the two curling smoke clouds of their inextinguishable briars. Then I would be slap-dashing home, the gravy smell of the dinners of others, the bird smell, the brandy, the pudding and mince, coiling up to my nostrils, when out of a snow-clogged side lane would come a boy the spit of myself, with a pink-tipped cigarette and the violet past of a black eye, cocky as a bullfinch, leering all to himself.

I hated him on sight and sound, and would be about to put my dog whistle to my lips and blow him off the face of Christmas when suddenly he, with a violet wink, put *his* whistle to *his* lips and blew so stridently, so high, so exquisitely loud, that gobbling faces, their cheek bulged with goose, would press against their tinsled windows, the whole length of the white echoing street.

For dinner we had turkey and blazing pudding, and after dinner the Uncles sat in front of the fire, loosened all buttons, put their large moist hands over their watch chains, groaned a little and slept. Mothers, aunts and sisters scuttled to and fro, bearing tureens. Aunt Bessie, who had already been frightened, twice, by a clock-work mouse, whimpered at the sideboard and had some elderberry wine. The dog was sick. Auntie Dosie had to have three aspirins, but Auntie Hannah, who liked port, stood in the middle of the snowbound back yard, singing like a big-bosomed thrush. I would blow up balloons to see how big they would blow up to; and, then when they burst, which they all did, the Uncles jumped and rumbled.

In the rich and heavy afternoon, the Uncles breathing like dolphins and the snow descending, I would sit among festoons and Chinese lanterns and nibble dates and try to make a model man-o'-war, following the Instructions for Little Engineers, and produce what might be mistaken for a sea-going tramcar.

Or I would go out, my bright new boots squeaking, into the white world, on to the seaward hill, to call on Jim and Dan and Jack and to pad through the still streets, leaving huge deep footprints on the hidden pavements.

"I bet people will think there've been hippos."

"What would you do if you saw a hippo coming down our street?"

"I'd go like this, bang! I'd throw him over the railings and roll him down the hill and then I'd tickle him under the ear and he'd wag his tail."

"What would you do if you saw *two* hippos?"

Iron-flanked and bellowing he-hippos clanked and battered through the scudding snow towards us as we passed Mr. Daniel's house.

"Let's post Mr. Daniel a snowball through his letter box."

"Let's write things in the snow."

"Let's write, 'Mr. Daniel looks like a spaniel' all over his lawn."

Or we walked on the white shore. "Can the fishes see it's snowing?"

The silent one-clouded heavens drifted on to the sea. Now we were snow-blind travelers lost on the north hills, and vast dewlapped dogs, with flasks round their necks, ambled and shambled up to us, baying "Excelsior." We returned home through the poor streets where only a few children fumbled with bare red fingers in the wheel-rutted snow and cat-called after us, their voices fading away, as we trudged uphill, into the cries of the dock birds and the hooting of ships out in the whirling bay. And then, at tea the recovered Uncles would be jolly; and the ice cake loomed in the center of the table like a marble grave. Auntie Hannah laced her tea with rum, because it was only once a year.

Bring out the tall tales now that we told by the fire as the gaslight bubbled like a diver. Ghosts whooed like owls in the long nights when I dared not look over my shoulder; animals lurked in the cubbyhole under the stairs where the gas meter ticked. And I remember that we went singing carols once, when there wasn't the shaving of a moon to light the flying streets. At the end of a long road was a drive that led to a large house, and we stumbled up the darkness of the drive that night, each one of us afraid, each one holding a stone in his hand in case, and all of us too brave to say a word. The wind through the trees made noises as of old and unpleasant and maybe webfooted men wheezing in caves. We reached the black bulk of the house.

"What shall we give them? Hark the Herald?"

"No," Jack said, "Good King Wencelas. I'll count three."

One, two, three, and we began to sing, our voices high and seemingly distant in the snow-felted darkness round the house that was occupied by nobody we knew. We stood close together, near the dark door.

> Good King Wencelas looked out
> On the Feast of Stephen...

And then a small, dry voice, like the voice of someone who has not spoken for a long time, joined our singing: a small, dry, eggshell voice from the other side of the door: a small, dry voice through the keyhole. And when we stopped running we were outside *our* house; the front room was lovely; balloons floated under the hot-water-bottle-gulping gas; everything was good again and shone over the town.

"Perhaps it was a ghost," Jim said.

"Perhaps it was trolls," Dan said, who was always reading.

"Let's go in and see if there's any jelly left," Jack said. And we did that.

Always on Christmas night there was music. An uncle played the fiddle, a cousin sang "Cherry Ripe," and another uncle sang "Drake's Drum." It was very warm in the little house. Auntie Hannah, who had got on to the parsnip wine, sang a song about Bleeding Hearts and Death, and then another in which she said her heart was like a Bird's Nest; and then everybody laughed again; and then I went to bed. Looking through my bedroom window, out into the moonlight and the unending smoke-colored snow, I could see the lights in the windows of all the other houses on our hill and hear the music rising from them up the long, steadily falling night. I turned the gas down, I got into bed. I said some words to the close and holy darkness, and then I slept.

**

[1] *"Hardboileds, toffee, fudge and allsorts, crunches, cracknel, humbugs, glaciers, marzipan, and butterwelsh"—all refer to types of sweets. Butterwelsh is a traditional kind of buttery Welsh toffee.*

I Heard the Bells on Christmas Day

HENRY WADSWORTH LONGFELLOW

Henry Wadsworth Longfellow, 1807 – 1882

American poet and educator.

This is Longfellow's second appearance in the book. (See, The Three Kings)

A popular carol today, this poem was written in 1863 but not set to music until 1872, and only gained widespread popularity after Bing Crosby recorded it in 1956.

The poem was published as "Christmas Bells" on Christmas Day against the backdrop of the Civil War. The narrator at first despairs upon hearing bells of peace and joy while war and anguish are present, but in the end affirms that, despite present sorrows, "God is not dead, nor doth he sleep." One day, all will be made right.

I HEARD THE BELLS ON CHRISTMAS DAY

I heard the bells on Christmas Day
Their old, familiar carols play,
And mild and sweet
The words repeat,
Of peace on earth, good-will to men!

And thought how, as the day had come,
The belfries of all Christendom,
Had rolled along,
The unbroken song,
Of peace on earth, good-will to men!

The ringing, singing on its way
The world revolved from night to day
A voice, a chime,
A chant sublime
Of peace on earth, good-will to men.

Then from each black, accursed mouth
The cannon thundered in the South,
And with the sound
The carols drowned
Of peace on earth, good-will to men!

It was as if an earthquake rent
The hearth-stones of a continent,
And made forlorn
The households born
Of peace on earth, good-will to men!

And in despair I bowed my head,
"There is no peace on earth," I said;
"For hate is strong,

And mocks the song
Of peace on earth, good-will to men!

Then pealed the bells more loud and deep:
"God is not dead, nor doth He sleep,
The Wrong shall fail,
The Right prevail,
With peace on earth, good-will to men.

Ring Out, Wild Bells

ALFRED, LORD TENNYSON

Alfred, Lord Tennyson, 1809 –1892

English poet.

"Ring Out, Wild Bells," was written in 1850, the year Tennyson was appointed Poet Laureate in Britain. The poem is part of a larger work, "In Memoriam," an elegy to a deceased brother-in-law. Tennyson was Poet Laureate for most of Queen Victoria's reign, and to this day is one of the top ten most frequently quoted writers in The Oxford Dictionary of Quotations. An extremely prolific writer, among his most famous poems are "The Charge of the Light Brigade," and "The Lady of Shalott."

In this poem, Tennyson "rings out" the ending of one year, the old and negative, and "rings in" the new, the hope of better things to come.

RING OUT, WILD BELLS

Ring out, wild bells, to the wild sky,
The flying cloud, the frosty light:
The year is dying in the night;
Ring out, wild bells, and let him die.

Ring out the old, ring in the new,
Ring, happy bells, across the snow:
The year is going, let him go;
Ring out the false, ring in the true.

Ring out the grief that saps the mind
For those that here we see no more;
Ring out the feud of rich and poor,
Ring in redress to all mankind.

Ring out a slowly dying cause,
And ancient forms of party strife;
Ring in the nobler modes of life,
With sweeter manners, purer laws.

Ring out the want, the care, the sin,
The faithless coldness of the times;
Ring out, ring out my mournful rhymes
But ring the fuller minstrel in.

Ring out false pride in place and blood,
The civic slander and the spite;
Ring in the love of truth and right,
Ring in the common love of good.

Ring out old shapes of foul disease;
Ring out the narrowing lust of gold;
Ring out the thousand wars of old,
Ring in the thousand years of peace.

Ring in the valiant man and free,
The larger heart, the kindlier hand;
Ring out the darkness of the land,
Ring in the Christ that is to be.

Merry Christmas!

On behalf of LILLIPUT PRESS,

and Linore Rose Burkard

May Your Christmas Season Be Filled with His Love,

Touched with His Grace,

and Abounding with His Joy!

Thank you for reading!

Did you enjoy this book?

If so, please leave your thoughts for other readers on Amazon, B&N, Goodreads, or any other online book seller. Telling others what you liked about a book goes a long way to helping us and them.

Thank you so much!

Editor Bio

LINORE ROSE BURKARD

Linore Rose Burkard is an award-winning author best known for Inspirational Regency Romance. Her first book with Harvest House Publishers (*Before the Season Ends*) opened the genre for the CBA. A *magna cum laude* English Lit. grad from CUNY, in addition to writing historical romance, she also writes contemporary love stories and, as L. R. Burkard, young adult apocalyptic suspense. Active in her church, Christmas is her favorite time of year. (Decorations fill nearly half a storage room, and an entire bookshelf is dedicated to Christmas literature.) Raised in NY, she now lives in Ohio with her husband where they have five adult children, two cats and a Shorkie.

FREE BOOK OFFER:

Sign up for Linore's newsletter to be the first to hear of book sales and promotions. *Upon sign-up, you'll get a free Regency Inspirational Romance novel!*

Sources

1. "The Reason for Christmas," excerpt, 1 John 1:14, and John 9:5, from The Holy Bible, English Standard Version. ESV ® Text Edition: 2016. Copyright © 2001 by Crossway Bibles, a publishing ministry of Good News Publishers

2. "A Christmas Mistake," and "A Christmas Inspiration," Lucy Maud Montgomery Short Stories, 1896 to 1901

3. "Christmas Carol," Sara Teasdale, public domain

4. "Christmas in the Alley," Olive Thorne Miller, originally published in *Kristy's Queer Christmas*, Houghton, Mifflin & Co., 1904.

5. "A Christmas Carol," Samuel Taylor Coleridge, first published in 1829 in the collection "Sibylline Leaves." Public domain.

6. "Mistletoe" Walter de la Mare, from *Collected Poems*, 1920.

7. "Good Christians Rise, This is the Morn," Anonymous, public domain.

8. "The Christmas Tree" Charles Dickens, 1850, public domain. "Christmas at Fezziwig's Warehouse" and "The Cratchit's Christmas" adapted and excerpted from *A Christmas Carol*, Charles Dickens, 1843, and, *The Children's Book of Christmas Stories*.

9. "The Three Kings," Henry Wadsworth Longfellow, originally published 1878.

10. "In the Bleak Midwinter," and "A Christmas Carol," Christina Rossetti, public domain.

11. "The Unexpected Christmas," published as "The Queerest Christmas," from

The Children's Book of Christmas Stories, public domain.

12. "Not to Jerusalem's Palm-Welcomed King," originally published in "Century Number, Christmas Eve," 1898.

13. "The Burning Babe," Robert Southwell, public domain.

14. "The Set of Poe," George Ade, originally published in 1903.

15. "Ye Simple Men of Heart Sincere," and, "O Mercy Divine," Charles Wesley, public domain. Originally published in *Hymns for the Nativity of Our Lord,* London, 1745.

16. "The Tale of the Little Mummers," originally titled, "The Peace Egg," from, *The Peace Egg and Other Tales,* Juliana Horatia Ewing, published by The Society for Promoting Christian Knowledge, London.

17. "The Burglar's Christmas," Elizabeth L. Seymour/Willa Cather, from, "The Home Monthly," 1896.

18. "The Christmas Babe," Margaret E. Sangster. Originally published 1898, Century Holiday Number, Christmas Eve.

19. "King John's Christmas" originally published in *Now We Are Six,* by A. A. Milne, 1927, by E.P. Dutton & Co.

20. "On Christmas Day in the Morning," Grace S. Richmond. Originally published by Doubleday, Page & Company, 1905, 1908.

21. Washington Irving Christmas Selections from *Bracebridge Hall,* originally published in 1822.

22. "Good King Wenceslas," John Mason Neale, public domain.

23. "The Oxen," or, "Christmas Eve and Twelve of the Clock," Thomas Hardy. Originally published in "The Times," 1915.

24. "The Adventure of the Blue Carbuncle," Arthur Conan Doyle, from, *The Adventures of Sherlock Holmes,* 1892.

25. "The Philanthropist's Christmas," James Webber Linn, from, *The Children's Book of Christmas Stories,* edited by Asa Don Dickinson and Ada M. Skinner.

26. "A Hymn on the Nativity of My Saviour," Ben Jonson, ca. 1600. Public domain.

27. "The Thin Santa Claus," Ellis Parker Butler, published 1809 by Doubleday as, *The Thin Santa Claus, The Chicken Yard that Was a Christmas Stocking,* by Ellis Parker Butler, with original illustrations.

28. "Thoughts on Modern Christmas for Those Who Object to the Feast" is excerpted from the book, *All Things Considered,* by G. K. Chesterton, 1915. (The title of the excerpt is not in the book.) "The House of Christmas" from the public domain.

29. "The Trapper's Christmas Tale," Ruth Sawyer, excerpted from, *This Way to Christmas,* by Ruth Sawyer, 1916

30. "A Christmas Matinee," Mrs. M. A. L. Lane, from the book, *The Children's Book of Christmas Stories,* edited by Asa Don Dickinson and Ada M. Skinner.

31. "Mr. Bluff's Experience of Holidays," from *The Children's Book of Christmas Stories,* edited by Asa Don Dickinson and Ada M. Skinner.

32. "A Christmas Mystery: A Story of Three Wise Men," William J. Locke, published 1910.

33.. "The Gift of the Magi," O. Henry, public domain

34. "Christmas at Cedar Hill" from the book, *Christmas at Cedar Hill,* originally published by New York: Thomas Whittaker, 1869.

35. "The Lone Scout's Christmas" from the book, *A Little Book for Christmas,* Putnam &Sons, 1917.

36. "A Child's Christmas in Wales," Dylan Thomas, public domain.

37. "I Heard the Bells on Christmas Day," Henry Wadsworth Longfellow, public domain.

38. "Ring Out, Wild Bells," Alfred, Lord Tennyson. Originally published in 1850, as part of the larger work, "In Memoriam." Public domain.

39. Painting: "Adoration of the Child" Gerrit Van Honthorn, 1620. Public domain.